The kiss was so unexpected, so hard and desperate, it took Maggie's breath away. Nobody had ever kissed her like Noah.

And he hadn't forgotten how.

His kiss was fierce, demanding, almost like an attack, but she didn't care. She attacked him back, losing herself in his kiss. Her mind started to spin so fast she lost touch with her surroundings, aware only of Noah and the effect he was having on her body.

She forced herself to break the kiss, placing both hands on his chest and pushing with all her might. 'We can't do this.'

His iron grip on her never once wavered. 'Why not?'

'Because it can't lead to anything but trouble.'

'Do you think I'm trouble, Maggie?' he murmured.

She stared into his eyes. Oh, yes, Noah Brant was trouble. Trouble with a capital *T*…

Available in August 2003 from Silhouette Special Edition

The Royal MacAllister
by Joan Elliott Pickart
(The Baby Bet: MacAllister's Gifts)

His Executive Sweetheart
by Christine Rimmer
(The Sons of Caitlin Bravo)

Tall, Dark and Difficult
by Patricia Coughlin

White Dove's Promise
by Stella Bagwell
(The Coltons)

Drive Me Wild
by Elizabeth Harbison

Undercover Honeymoon
by Leigh Greenwood

Undercover Honeymoon

LEIGH GREENWOOD

SILHOUETTE®
SPECIAL EDITION™

First published in Great Britain 2003
Silhouette Books, Eton House, 18-24 Paradise Road,
Richmond, Surrey TW9 1SR

© Harold Lowry 2002

ISBN 0 373 24452 5

23-0803

Printed and bound in Spain
by Litografia Rosés S.A., Barcelona

LEIGH GREENWOOD

has authored twenty historical romances, and three
Silhouette Special Editions. The proud parent of three
grown children, Leigh lives in Charlotte, North
Carolina. You can write to Leigh Greenwood at PO
Box 470761, Charlotte, NC 28226, USA. An SAE with
return postage would be appreciated.

To Anne,
who gave me the germ of the idea for this story.

Chapter One

"**Y**ou've got to be kidding!"

Noah Brant brought his open palms down on the desk of his boss and best friend, Ray Ethridge. Either Ray had had a complete frontal lobotomy and had forgotten everything he ever knew about what happened three years ago, or he had achieved an expert level of mental cruelty. Nothing on the face of this earth could force Noah to work with Maggie Oliver. She was a bleeding-heart liberal who valued emotion over common sense. She let her heart tell her head what to do.

She'd yanked his heart out, ripped it to shreds, then stomped on it.

"She's the perfect person for the job," Ray said. "I couldn't have found anybody better if I'd designed her myself."

"But she quit after only three months."

She had her nerve trying to come back to the special operations branch of the CIA after walking out in the middle of her training course. But then Maggie had always had plenty of nerve. That was one of the things that had attracted him to her. Gumption. And smarts. He had to give it to her. Maggie was smart as a whip. And as dangerous as a loaded hypodermic.

"She'd be a liability in any covert operation," Noah snapped. "She's too goddamned pretty. She'd have every man within a thousand yards following her around with their tongues hanging out."

"That's one reason I picked you to work with her," Ray said. "Nobody will bother her with you around."

Noah was proud of his ability to intimidate people just by looking at them. It was a useful talent to have, but he didn't intend for Ray to use it as an excuse to make him Maggie's watchdog. It would take more than his fierce glare to keep anyone from remembering Maggie. She wasn't just beautiful, she was feminine in a way that made men fall over themselves to take care of her. Not that she was helpless. No, that was another part of her charm. You knew she could take care of herself, but you couldn't help wanting to do it anyway.

That was one of the hooks she'd used to draw him into her snare. He was a sucker for beautiful women who didn't need him.

Then there was her hair. It was difficult to put into words the effect that Titian mass had on him. When she piled it atop her head, she looked as regal as a Renaissance queen. When she unpinned it and a breeze lifted it off her shoulders, she was like a wind sprite just out of reach. When she lay in bed with it haloed around her head—or over one breast—she was a pagan goddess with the power to hypnotize any man. Even after three years, the mere sight of her had the power to unsettle him.

"Get Arnold to work with her," Noah said.

"This job requires your particular talents," Ray said.

"Then let me choose my own partner."

"You'd come to the same conclusion I have, so there's no point in wasting time."

"No matter what this job requires, I wouldn't—"

"Work with her if she were the last person in the world," Ray finished for him.

"Close enough," Noah snapped. "What's she doing coming back? She's a nurse now."

"That's one of the reasons I want her for this job. Besides, she's got connections in Beluxor. She knows the language, the customs and she has relatives there."

"I know, but that could be a complication," Noah said.

"It might also be the way to get in and out with a baby without running into trouble."

"What has my working with Maggie got to do with a baby?"

"The purpose of this mission is to rescue a sick infant."

"There must be thousands of sick kids in Beluxor," Noah said. "What makes this one so special?"

"This child is being held hostage. He's the son of Oleg Grohol, the most popular member of the opposition party and head of a coalition that looks certain to win the next election. The government is hoping they can use the baby to force him to leave the country. Without him, the coalition will fall apart. The police are holding the baby in the hospital, but the underground says they can get him out. The mother is already in this country. As soon as she gets the baby, Grohol will announce that he's standing for election."

"Why do we care?" Noah asked.

"Because the present government has agreed to let one of the rogue nations use its laboratories for the development of a new kind of bio weapon. Grohol has pledged to close down the laboratories."

"Okay, but that's no reason I have to be the one to work with Maggie. Get Arnold, Jerry, Mac, anybody."

"We're stretched thin right now," Ray said. "Not only are we short on operatives, you're the best one for this kind of job. You've got more language skills, have done more work in this part of Europe, have—''

''Since Maggie knows everything there is to know about Beluxor, anybody could work with her. Why don't you do it?''

''Because I'm too old and fat to do anything but sit behind a desk. If I had to run for it, I'd have a heart attack. You're reasonably young, attractive, intelligent—''

''Enough of the soft soap,'' Noah said. ''You're not talking me into this no matter how many compliments you throw at me.''

''Are you certain?'' Ray asked.

''Positive.''

Ray stood and walked to the door to his inner office. ''I guess I'd better tell Maggie.''

''You mean she's in there?''

''Yeah. She probably heard everything you said.''

Noah had already reached that unnerving conclusion. Maggie didn't like being put down. She'd be ready to kill him. But when she walked through the door, he forgot everything. She looked even more beautiful than he remembered.

There never had been anything girlish about Maggie. She'd always been pure woman, but now she seemed the embodiment of everything that stood for. Beautiful, sensual, graceful, confident. Anything any man could want, Maggie had, all packed into a body that caused his blood to pound in his temples. No angular lines here. Maggie had lush curves even Michelangelo would envy.

And that face, wonderful and beautiful though it was now covered with a frown. He'd woken up to it every morning for two years, woken to find it in his thoughts for three more. In some ways it was an ordinary face, yet it was splendidly unique. Nobody looked like Maggie. She had a look of her own, one she'd invented and patented years ago. It wouldn't, *couldn't* fit anyone else. Just Maggie.

"It sounds like your opinion of me hasn't changed," she said.

He started to deny it, make an excuse, but he gave up. She had that look about her—the posture, too—that said she knew what he was doing and wasn't about to let him get away with it. That was something else about Maggie that rubbed him raw. She always thought she knew as much as he did about everything.

"I can't work with you," he said. "It wouldn't work."

"If it makes you feel any better," Maggie said, "I told Ray the same thing when he said I'd be working with you."

Noah didn't like the look she was giving him. He thought he'd memorized her entire lexicon of looks, gestures and postures, but she'd obviously acquired a new one. It appeared to imply she was suffering just as much as he was, and he had no right to complain if she didn't.

To hell with that. He'd been the martyr before. He wasn't doing it again.

"Why don't we forget this, Ray?" Maggie asked. "You can find somebody else to work with him."

"Nobody as good as you," Ray said. "You're perfect, absolutely one hundred percent designed for the job. With relatives already in the country, it's easy to pretend the sick child is your cousin's baby coming to the U.S. for medical treatment."

"But if Noah won't do it—"

"I guess I'll have to put Gregory on the case."

"You've got to be joking." Noah exploded. "He doesn't know his head from his rear end. Besides, he's a desk jockey. He wants your job, not mine."

"You'll take over his job while he's on assignment," Ray said.

There was nothing Noah hated more than desk work. He'd threatened to quit when Ray tried to promote him. Not only would he have been working at a desk, but Gregory would have been his boss. The idea of working behind an anal-retentive pissant like Gregory was enough to give him hives. But the idea of Gregory working with Maggie was even worse.

Gregory was twenty-eight, tall, lanky and convinced he was God's gift to women. Noah thought he looked like a hothouse clone of a beardless matinee idol from the thirties but had to admit grudgingly that he was handsome in a sickeningly suave sort of way. He was exactly the kind of man women fell all over themselves trying to take care of.

And that was the last kind of man Maggie ought to work with. With her soft heart, he'd have her believing every word he said within twenty-four hours.

"You can't put Gregory on that job," Noah said. "You might as well pick a kid off the street."

Ray leaned back in his chair and laughed comfortably. "Why not?" he asked. "Are you afraid Gregory will pull it off?"

The SOB! He knew he had Noah over a barrel and was enjoying it. Noah reminded himself—not for the first time—that it was unwise for his boss and best friend to be one and the same. It gave Ray too much of an advantage at times like this.

"I'm more afraid Maggie will have to drag him out by the seat of his pants," Noah replied.

"He's got an excellent record."

Noah would have liked to knock that smirk off Ray's face. Gregory had built his reputation on cases within the U.S. And he didn't know a thing about babies. He was too busy devoting all his time to *babes*.

"He sounds interesting," Maggie said, casting a speculative glance at both men. "When do I meet him?"

Noah wouldn't put it past her to have already figured out Ray was playing him like a fish on a line.

"How's right now?" Ray asked. "He's just down the hall."

Noah wanted to step forward and knock Ray's hand off

the intercom, but he forced himself to move back a couple of steps. He wouldn't be manipulated into working with Maggie. Ray was bluffing.

With forced calm Noah listened to Ray ask Gregory to come to his office at once. He didn't grind his teeth too hard when he heard Gregory reply that he'd be right there. Noah couldn't understand how Ray could be so blind. Gregory was a pretty boy with all the right connections and a gift for administrative detail, but he wasn't right for this job.

Gregory entered without knocking. "What's up, Ray?" he asked. But in less than a nanosecond his gaze slid from Ray to Maggie, and he perked up like a desert plant after a rain. Noah could practically see the charm beginning to ooze out of every pore. "I do hope it has something to do with this divine creature. Where have you been hiding her?"

Noah felt handicapped competing against Gregory because the younger man had been born into a life of advantages. Gregory's smile showed white, straight teeth, the result of excellent orthodontic care. His grammar was perfect and his knowledge of the societal graces extensive, the result of a private school education and a small private income. His clothes fit his body like they were made for him. Which they most likely were. His hair was still perfectly groomed at the end of the day.

Noah was tall, his body well-muscled and his face generally considered roughly handsome, but his teeth were uneven, he bought his clothes off the rack, his hair looked like a bristle brush and he had to remind himself to use the objective pronoun after a preposition. He'd dropped out of high school at fifteen. After seeing a friend die in a drug-related crime and realizing his life was headed in the same direction, he'd gotten his GED, gone to college and taken a job with the New York City police department. With his background, he was a natural for undercover work. When his superiors discovered his multiethnic neighborhood had forced him to be fluent in six languages, he was recruited for international work.

Noah resented that Gregory could rise so easily to a level he'd had to work like a dog to attain.

"I've got a job for you," Ray said to Gregory.

"I'll do anything as long as I can work with this beautiful creature," Gregory said without taking his eyes off Maggie.

Noah had to clench his fists to keep from jerking Gregory by the collar. He was just as angry at Maggie for smiling at Gregory. Couldn't she tell he was a pretty face and little else?

"It's out of the country," Ray said. "It's impossible to say how long you'll be gone, but you'll be in an eastern European country with a dangerously repressive government. The living conditions won't be what you're used to."

"Will you be going with me?" Gregory asked.

"Yes, I will. I'm Maggie Oliver," Maggie said, introducing herself, "and I'm no *creature* unless you subscribe to Noah's conviction that I'm a nightmare."

"You can't expect Noah to appreciate a treasure like you," Gregory said.

Noah didn't understand how women could tolerate such drivel, but Maggie was grinning like she didn't have a brain in her head. Surely she couldn't be falling for the flattery of a rat like Gregory! Noah had never heard anything so insincere in his life.

"Not all men think I'm a treasure," Maggie said.

"You poor thing. Have you been surrounded by insensitive ignoramuses your whole life?"

"Maybe," Noah said, unable to hold his tongue any longer, "but then she hasn't been plagued by feeling like she had to throw up."

"Ray, do you have your radio on?" Gregory asked. "There's static in this room."

Noah would get Ray back for that belly laugh. Some things couldn't be tolerated, not even from a best friend.

"This job entails rescuing a sick baby and bringing it back to the States for treatment," Ray said.

"I adore babies," Gregory said, his gaze still fixed on Maggie.

"You're not required to adore it," Noah retorted, "just get it safely out of the country."

"Ought to be a snap," Gregory said. "With Maggie at my side, we'll dazzle every border guard in Europe."

The fool probably thought that's all he had to do.

"This is not a friendly country," Noah said. "And they're particularly anxious to hold on to this kid."

"Why is he here?" Gregory asked Ray. "I can't discuss plans if he's going to interrupt all the time."

"Noah is our best man at this kind of operation," Ray said. "Ask him any questions you want."

"I'm sure Maggie and I can come up with all the answers we need."

"We really ought to talk to Noah," Maggie said. "This is his specialty."

"What special talents do I need?"

"Languages, for one."

Gregory broke into perfect schoolboy French. Noah broke in on him in a very different kind of French, the kind he'd learned from a family of cocaine dealers who lived next door when he was growing up.

"Do you know anything about Beluxor?" Maggie asked.

"I'm sure the agency can provide me with all the information I need."

"Do you speak the language?"

"Does Noah?" he asked.

"No," Maggie said.

"Then it doesn't matter."

Noah couldn't take any more. "I'm not fluent," he said, "but I know enough to call for a taxi, book a hotel room and order food."

"Even in out-of-the-way places, you can find someone who speaks English," Gregory said.

"And have everybody know you're a foreigner."

"They would anyway. I don't *look* like someone from eastern Europe."

The ignorant fool said it with pride. Noah wouldn't put it past him to travel with a half dozen handmade suits and dozens of silk ties. He'd not only be known to every government official within twenty-four hours, he'd be marked by every common thief, as well. And he wouldn't realize he was jeopardizing Maggie's safety at the same time.

"You can't go in looking like a rich tourist," Noah said, exasperated that Ray would even consider such an inexperienced agent for this job. "You will be supposedly meeting Maggie's relatives. The whole point is to blend in."

"You do things your way. I do them mine."

"But you can't—"

"Do I interfere with your jobs?" Gregory said, rounding on Noah with unexpected energy. "Do I tell you how to dress, what to do?"

"Of course not." He'd break the little bastard's neck if he tried.

"Then don't tell me how to run my operation." He turned to Maggie, making Noah feel like his presence had already been forgotten. "I'm sure Maggie and I can work out a mutually agreeable plan."

"Are you going to let him endanger Maggie's life?" Noah asked Ray. "What happens if the authorities don't believe that ruse about bringing Maggie's cousin's baby back to the States for medical treatment? They'll have to get out through the mountains."

"I hike the Adirondacks every summer," Gregory said.

"Beluxor isn't the Adirondacks," Noah snapped, "and there's liable to be snow in the passes. Are you strong enough to pack a baby on your back with their special police in pursuit?"

For the first time Gregory seemed to hesitate, but he was just enough of an egotist to insist he could handle the job even when he wasn't sure. Noah didn't want to spend five extra minutes in Maggie's company—much less who knew how many days—but he couldn't let a slicked-up desk jockey like Gregory get her killed. Nor could he let him screw up an important mission.

"You're not cut out for this kind of operation," Noah said.

"I supposed you are?" Gregory retorted.

"Yes, I am."

"But Ray didn't assign it to you."

"He did, but I refused."

"Then your qualifications don't matter."

"Yes, they do. I'm accepting the assignment, after all."

Noah couldn't believe he'd caved in, but he heard his words as clearly as everyone else in the room. He wanted to deny them, blame it on a weird echo, but it was pointless. Being around Maggie would be like having salt poured into his wounds, but she didn't deserve to have her life put in danger.

"You sure?" Ray asked.

"Yeah, I'm sure."

Gregory looked from one man to the other. He got angry as the truth dawned on him. Noah couldn't blame him.

"You never meant for me to have this job," he said, turning on Ray. "You brought me in here to force Noah to take it."

"He was being obstinate," Ray said. "You were the best argument I had to convince him to change his mind."

"You think I'm such a screw-up I couldn't do this job?" Gregory asked, his temper rising fast.

"Noah is better at this kind of job than you are, but that's not the real reason."

"Then what is?"

"Maggie is an old flame. I knew he'd never let her head off on an assignment with a Lothario like you."

As she watched Ray escort an angry Gregory from the room, Maggie had the uneasy feeling she'd waded into deeper water than she'd anticipated. She hadn't expected Noah to like working with her. She hadn't wanted to work with him, but it hadn't taken Ray long to convince her Noah was the best possible choice. Despite their differences, Maggie wasn't one to cut off her nose to spite her face.

But she was ashamed of the way she'd ogled Gregory. She had been trying to make Noah angry for having flatly refused to work with her. She hadn't known until it was too late that Ray was using Gregory to force Noah to change his mind. Now Noah would be even more angry because he'd be certain she'd been part of the conspiracy.

She might as well have been. She'd practically flirted with Gregory because she hoped it would cause Noah to change his mind. She had several reasons for agreeing to take this assignment, and one was to use it as a test to see if she had gotten Noah out of her system. If she could work alone with him for even a few days without succumbing to his charm, she'd truly be over him.

"Don't think you're doing me a favor," she said to Noah. "If it's such a hardship to work with me, get somebody else. My supervisor wasn't thrilled to learn I'd be off the job for an indefinite period of time and she couldn't do anything about it."

The orders had come from the top, and her supervisor was mad as hell. Maggie had to laugh at herself. She'd broken up with Noah in part because he was too controlling. Now she worked for a supervisor who got red in the face every time anything didn't go as she planned.

"I'm doing it because I'm the best person for the job."

"You're doing it because you don't want Gregory to do it," Maggie said.

"That, too," Noah admitted. "As much as I don't want to work with you, I don't want to see this mission botched and you jailed in some retrograde eastern European country while Ray tries to straighten out the mess Gregory made."

"Your nobility overwhelms me."

There was no point in being sarcastic. It wouldn't help if she meant to stay on the job, but his allegiance to his duty had always galled her. It had never mattered what else might be at stake. Duty came first. She could have accepted it if he'd agonized with himself, apologized to her, said he wished things could have been different, but he didn't. Duty was everything. That and his job. She had never been able to come between him and his work.

She'd taken it for two years before she'd cut and run.

"Forget I said that," she said.

"You're letting your emotions control you."

He'd always accused her of letting her feelings dictate her actions.

"Maybe I am, but it's no fun knowing you'd do practically anything to keep from being around me."

Maggie hadn't intended to say that, either. She'd known when she agreed to do this job it wouldn't be easy to see Noah again, much less work with him. She'd promised herself she'd remain detached. She'd already broken that promise. Maybe she ought to back out while she still had a chance.

"We're both professionals," Maggie said. "Ray wouldn't have paired us if he hadn't thought we were capable of putting the past behind us in order to get the job done."

"I'm the professional," Noah argued. "You dropped out, remember?"

"I remember enough to hold my end of the bargain. All I have to do is remember the baby, and I can put up with anything."

"That's just what we don't need," Noah said, "you ignoring procedure because some kid is sick and needs a doctor.''

''There are times, Noah Brant, when I wonder why I ever thought you had a heart. How can you refer to that child as *some sick kid who needs a doctor*?''

''Because if I let my emotions get control of me, I wouldn't be able to get that sick kid to the doctor he needs.'' Noah turned to see Ray reentering the room.

Ray sat behind his desk. ''Now, the mission,'' Ray said. ''Noah's job is to get the two of you out of the country. That takes a cool head and a quick mind. Maggie's job is to make sure the child doesn't get any sicker before we can get him to a hospital. That takes a warm and caring heart. I think you will be perfect foils for each other. I don't see any conflict there.''

Maybe Ray couldn't see the conflict, but those differences had put them at loggerheads three years ago. They had the potential to do the same now.

''I don't see any problem as long as Maggie knows I'm in charge.''

Maggie felt tension hit her in the back of her neck. Noah sounded so much like her father she was ready to walk out of the office without a backward glance. Separating certain aspects of her emotional response to Noah and her response to her father had always been a problem, but Noah wasn't cruel and manipulative. He was just a control freak. Maggie forced herself to relax, to take a couple of deep breaths and to look at Ray a few seconds before turning to Noah.

Even after all that had passed between them, she couldn't really stay mad at him. What red-blooded American woman could stay mad a hunk like Noah? It wasn't fair that he had to be as attractive as he was impossible.

He wasn't as pretty as Gregory, but there was no comparison between the two men. She'd have chosen Noah blindfolded. Just the sound of his voice gave her goose bumps. There was nothing smooth or polished about it. It was rough, gravelly, earthy. It made her think of the essential man, no colognes or unnatural scents allowed. He was tall, big-boned and as strong as an ox. And while he might occasionally stumble grammatically, his mind was razor sharp. She knew she was smart, but she sometimes had trouble keeping up with Noah.

She liked his looks, too. Not just his face, his *whole* look. He always looked rumpled, like he'd just gotten up and had dressed in a hurry. He had a five o'clock shadow at eight in the morning and an in-your-face stare that said he didn't give a damn what you thought about his clothes or the way he lived his life. His ice-blue eyes could cut you like steel. His tongue was just as lethal. He didn't give any quarter and didn't expect any. He was perfect for his job. He only had one flaw.

He didn't know he needed her just as much as she needed him.

It had been the need Noah buried so deep inside him he couldn't see it that had attracted Maggie and held her through two tumultuous years. She knew the agony of going through life without anyone with whom to share the lonely part of her soul. She knew that without the irrigation of another soul, her own soul would eventually dry up and become brittle. If Noah knew that, he denied it. Worse. He denied he had a soul. Noah wanted to be all brain and nothing else.

"I knew we'd come to the issue of control sooner or later," Maggie said.

"I don't see why it should be an issue," Noah said. "This is a covert action, something I do all the time, something you've never done."

"I've had some of the training." -

"But you went back to nursing before you finished," Noah reminded her.

"That doesn't mean I forgot everything I learned."

"Nor does it mean you're equipped to take that knowledge into the field without any practical experience."

Maggie could feel the tension growing between her shoulders. It was the same old battle she'd fought all her life. No matter what she did, no matter how much she knew, some man was determined to show her he knew more than she did about everything.

"Noah, there's a sick baby involved here. You don't know anything about children regardless of their age or the state of their health. You can't expect me to accept whatever you say without having some input."

"I didn't say you couldn't have any input," Noah said, "just that I had to be in charge."

"You mean you'll have the final word on everything."

At least he had the decency to wait a second before he nodded.

"I think we need to do some negotiating here."

"You don't need to do it here," Ray said. "I have work to do. You can do it in your hotel room."

"That won't work," Noah said. "She'll go to her room and refuse to let me in."

"She won't be able to do that," Ray said.

"You don't know Maggie."

But Maggie noticed Ray was looking busy, shuffling papers, fiddling with a pen.

"Okay," she said, "what is it you're not telling us?"

"You'll be sharing the same hotel room."

"I'll be damned if that's so." Noah exploded. "The department isn't that poor."

"Budget has nothing to do with it," Ray said.

Both of them approached the desk, leaned forward, focused their gazes on Ray.

"Out with it," Noah said.

Ray stopped fiddling with the pen and looked at them. "I've reserved a bridal suite for you here in Manhattan. You're supposed to be newlyweds traveling to Beluxor on your honeymoon."

Chapter Two

Maggie turned as Noah closed the door to their hotel suite. "Don't think this means I'm going to sleep in the same bed with you," she said. "I'll take the couch." She still couldn't believe she'd let Ray talk her into pretending to be married to Noah. She must be losing her mind—or letting the fabrications for this rescue operation take over the rational part of her brain. There were times when she wondered how she'd let herself get involved in this operation, anyway. Her parents had been born in Beluxor, but she hadn't. She had never lived in the country. She hardly knew anyone there, except her cousin.

But she hated the militaristic, repressive government there and felt she ought to do anything she could to help bring it down. So here she was, locked up in a fancy hotel suite with Noah Brant, the one man of all men in New York City she least wanted to be locked up with.

She hadn't felt that way five years ago. She'd been gloriously, helplessly, *foolishly* in love.

Fortunately, she got over it.

"I'm no happier about this than you are," Noah said. "If I had known what Ray had in mind, I'd have let Gregory have you."

"I know you don't think much of me, but I hoped you rated me a little higher than that."

She had caught him. Miracle of miracles, he actually seemed embarrassed. Maybe he was human, after all.

"You didn't seem to mind," Noah said, his tone definitely peevish. "You looked just about as besotted as he did."

Jealousy, too. She'd seen that before and could do without it.

"He's very attractive," she said. "I imagine he's a charming companion."

"If you can put up with hackneyed drivel for the whole evening. The man doesn't have an original line in his whole vocabulary."

Noah proceeded to check out the suite. He poked into the cabinets of the wet bar to inspect the collection of liquor, opened the refrigerator to see if it had ice and opened the wardrobe that housed the TV.

"This must be a more important baby than I suspected," Noah said. "The agency spent some money on this place."

"Check the bedroom." She didn't want to draw Noah's attention to the bedroom, but it had to be done sooner or later. Knowing herself—and Noah—sooner was much safer than later. As she expected, there was only one bed, a king-size monster covered by a bedspread with a cupid in the center.

"That's sickening," Noah said.

"Why?"

"Look at it. It's a goddamned cupid, for God's sake."

"Some women like a little romance," Maggie replied. "They don't get much from the men in their lives."

"Let's not go there," Noah said, heading to the bathroom. Maggie followed. They found a whirlpool big enough for two. ''At least somebody had the good sense to include a shower,'' Noah said. ''I never have been able to figure out what people see in those things.''

''I'm sure it's nothing important. There can't be more than twenty or thirty million of them in the whole country.''

''Your sarcasm is wasted on me,'' Noah said. ''I'm immune.''

''You didn't used to be.''

''You inoculated me.''

''Glad I had some lasting effect.''

He turned. He was very close. There wasn't much space.

''That was just one of the effects you had on me,'' he said. ''You're like malaria. You tend to come back when a man's resistance is weak. But don't get your hopes up this time. My resistance is greater than ever.''

She placed her hand in the center of Noah's chest to push him away. That was a mistake. She had never been able to touch him without feeling the effect through her entire body. She practically ran out of the bathroom. ''You don't have to worry about your resistance,'' she said, heading for the sitting room. That huge bed brought forth images she didn't want to remember. ''My resistance is great enough for both of us.''

''Is that why you didn't make any objections when Ray dropped this ridiculous newlywed scenario on us?''

''Yes. I knew there was nothing that could ever again cause me to be attracted to you.''

She turned away from him—intending to do she didn't know what—but Noah came up behind her. He turned her around, put his hand under her chin and lifted it until she had to look him in the eye.

''Nothing?'' he asked.

She should have known it was foolish to throw down a gauntlet to Noah. He couldn't resist a challenge, even when it wasn't one he wanted to win. He stood so close she could feel the energy emanating from his body. He was like an electric force. And every bit of that energy was sexual. Or sensual. She didn't know which, but it didn't matter. The result was that she reacted powerfully in Noah's presence, especially when he turned those megawatt eyes on her.

She was tempted to reach out and touch him. Physically he was everything she'd ever wanted in a man, not lithe and smooth like Gregory, but big, shaggy and powerful like some half-tamed wolf. Canny, intelligent, graceful despite his big bones. And his embrace was so powerful it made her feel that she would be warm and safe and well loved for the rest of her life.

But it was all a mirage. There was nothing inside this beautiful structure but a cold, calculating computerlike brain.

"Let's not start playing power games," she replied, forcing herself to hold his gaze. "We're here to do a job, not rehash our past." She moved away. "What are you going to do with yourself for the evening? I'm going take a leisurely bath in that wonderful tub, order room service and curl up with a nice book. A romance." She couldn't help emphasizing that. He'd always been so patronizing about her books.

"Sorry to rain on your parade, but Ray has already made plans for us."

"What plans?" After what Ray had done to them, she didn't trust him.

"We have dinner reservations at the restaurant upstairs and tickets for a show. I'm sure it's a musical. Ray knows I hate them."

"I love them."

"Then it's probably something I'll really hate like *The Sound of Music*."

"Is *The Phantom of the Opera* more your speed?"

"All you have to do is whisper the word opera, and I get a nervous tic."

"Nothing ever changes, does it, Noah?"

His look was hard to decipher. "Everything changes. It's just some changes are harder than others."

She had no intention of dipping her toes into that pool. She didn't imagine for one minute Noah was nostalgic, but she was. Five minutes of reminiscing about the good times, and she'd convince herself it was possible for him to have changed enough to bring them back. She knew better. That's why she'd concentrated on her nursing career. It had kept her away from Noah.

Or it had until now. She never expected pediatric nursing to bring her into Noah's orbit. It just showed you could never be sure about anything in life.

"What time are our dinner reservations?"

"Seven o'clock."

"Will that give us time to get to the theater?"

"It won't matter if we miss an act or two."

Maggie didn't bother saying it mattered to her. "Do you want to take your shower now?"

"I thought we could spend the time before dinner going over plans for the operation."

"What you mean is you thought you could spend the evening telling me what *you've* decided *I* should do."

"You think you can plan this operation?"

"No, but I have no doubt you have it planned down to the smallest detail. I also have no doubt that over the next few days you'll bore me to death with those very same plans."

"We don't know how long we have before we pick up the kid."

"The *kid* is named Alexi. And we fly to Paris tomorrow. That ought to give you plenty of time to brief me on the important parts."

She didn't wait for him to contradict her. As far as Noah was concerned, there was never enough time to prepare for an operation. His job came before people because people involved emotion, and emotion destroyed a person's objectivity. She had learned through bitter experience that the bottom line was control, and everything Noah did was controlled.

Even making love.

In his case it was having sex. She couldn't believe he could actually love anyone, least of all himself.

"I'm going to take my bath," she said, unwilling to let herself spend any more time thinking about Noah. She'd spent too much time doing that already.

"You look nice," Noah said as he held the chair for Maggie. "Half the men in the restaurant are staring at you."

"All the women are staring at you," she replied. "That means hardly anybody is eating. The chef won't be happy."

Noah hadn't forgotten how beautiful Maggie could be when she got all dolled up. And Maggie did love to dress. She couldn't make much money as a nurse, so she must have spent a disproportionate part of her income on her clothes. Tonight she wore a black dress that clung to every curve on her body. It was strapless, with net covering her shoulders. She had piled her hair into a coronet atop her head. A tall woman, she had looked regal when she walked out of the bedroom.

He hoped his coat had hidden his instantaneous physical reaction to the sight of her. And the memory of nights spent in her arms.

He'd been tempted to go back on his word when Ray said they had to pretend to be newlyweds. But he'd told himself he could handle it, that he'd gotten Maggie out of his system.

Now he wasn't sure. He kept telling himself it wasn't just Maggie—that she was a beautiful woman, and he'd never been able to resist a beautiful woman. No one had to remind him that when temptation and weakness were poured into the same vessel, things were likely to come to a boil pretty soon. He wasn't boiling yet, but he was getting hot under the collar. And elsewhere.

He managed to get himself mostly under control while the waiter handed them menus and took their drink order. By the time they'd looked over what was on the menu, things were back to normal. Or as normal as they could ever be around Maggie.

What had possessed him to think he could handle this assignment with her? Their love affair had ended because they had nothing in common, not because they'd stopped being attracted to each other.

After losing his only real friend in a gang fight when he was fourteen, he'd taken an oath that he'd never let anybody get so close to him he couldn't do without them. He'd forgotten that vow when he met Maggie, and he paid a high price for it. He didn't mean to make the same mistake again. Maybe if he kept his mind on business, discussed the job rather than thought about the softness of her skin, he'd be able to survive.

"About this mission," he began, but Maggie cut him off.

"We'd better not talk about it now."

"Why not?"

"Because we're supposed to be on our honeymoon. We're supposed to be besotted with each other."

"We don't have to act like that until we get to Beluxor."

"That's not what Ray thinks, or he wouldn't have rented this suite. I think we ought to start practicing now. It needs to be such a habit we won't slip up, not even once."

"I'd rather talk about the mission."

"If we do, we'll end up yelling at each other."

"Newlyweds fight."

"Not if they're going to spend the next two weeks in each other's company."

The bottom of his stomach threatened to fall out. "It won't take two weeks. Just a couple of days."

"Ray told my boss she ought to be prepared for me to

be gone for two weeks, maybe three. He told me he couldn't be sure when we could make contact with the underground.''

Noah's palms began to sweat. He didn't think he could survive two weeks near Maggie without touching her. Some men just weren't capable of doing that, and he was one of them. And if he *did* touch her, she would think he meant all kinds of things when he only meant he was so physically attracted to her he couldn't keep his hands to himself.

''I can't see any reason it should take two weeks,'' he said. ''All we have to do is go in, pick up the kid—*Alexi*—and leave.''

''I never said it would take two weeks. Ray did. Talk to him. I'm just along to take care of the baby.''

''I'm glad you realize that. Now we won't have any arguments over who's in charge.''

''I imagine we'll have many arguments over that and everything else,'' Maggie said. ''But my wine is here, and I don't intend to spoil a perfectly lovely evening arguing with you over things that might not even happen.'' Maggie took a sip of her wine the moment the waiter set her glass down. ''Delicious,'' she said. ''You can leave the bottle.''

''You can't drink all of that yourself.''

''You could help.''

''You know I don't like wine.''

''I know the drill. Nothing but the hard stuff for *real* men. Without ice or water. You must be an extra-special *real* man.''

She'd always made fun of any attitude she didn't consider enlightened, but she wanted to try to get along with Noah. This wasn't the tack to take.

''Sorry,'' she said. ''I promised myself I would try to be civil to you. Tell me about yourself. What have you been doing these last years?''

''Working.'' That had been the only way he could cope after they broke up. His mood had been so surly nobody had wanted to be around him. If it hadn't been for Ray, he'd probably have left the department.

"I was sure of that. You never could think of anything else."

She smiled at him across the table. She didn't sound angry or judgmental, just friendly, like they were old chums who hadn't seen each other for a while and were catching up on each other's lives. There never had been anything friendly or chummy about their relationship. They'd been too intense, too hungry, too desperate to reach out and take what they wanted before it disappeared.

It had disappeared anyway, leaving them empty and angry at each other. When he saw Maggie in Ray's office, he was certain he was still angry, but now he wasn't sure.

"Ray tells me you turned into his top agent."

"I didn't have much else to do." He didn't mean to sound like he didn't have a life after she left. "You've been right busy yourself." He wanted to get the spotlight off himself.

"I just got a master's degree. Not anything special about that."

"It is when you're working full time. I don't suppose your father helped?"

When Maggie was a kid he never allowed her to choose her own jobs, dates, courses in school, even how to spend her free time. When he discovered Maggie was practically brilliant, he decided she ought to be a lawyer and pay back all the money he'd spent rearing her. But Maggie had gotten interested in nursing during her mother's long illness. When her father found out she had entered nursing school rather than general college in preparation for law school, he refused to pay her tuition. Maggie had had to work to pay her way through school.

During their worst fight, Maggie had compared Noah to her father.

"Dad doesn't have much to say to me. I check on him

from time to time, but I leave him alone. It's better that way. I don't suppose you ever see your aunt Julia.''

"She doesn't want to see me any more than I want to see her.''

Noah's mother dumped him on her sister's doorstep when Noah was two and ran off to Vegas with a cocaine addict. Even though she'd been alive until two years ago, she'd never made any attempt to contact or see her son.

Aunt Julia hadn't had any children because she didn't want to be bothered with a kid. She never let Noah forget that for a minute. Or that his mother didn't know his father's name. If Noah and her husband didn't do what she wanted, she made their lives miserable. Her husband had escaped by having a massive heart attack. Noah found it easier to run away.

"Looks like we're on our own," she said.

"I heard you got married.''

"Then you also heard I got divorced.''

"At least you didn't make the mistake of marrying me.''

She surprised him by looking straight into his eyes. ''I would have if you'd been willing.''

He didn't really want to know that. It raised too many possibilities, cracked too many doors he'd thought firmly shut. "It's just as well. It saved us the cost of a divorce.''

"Not to mention the emotional strain.''

"Did you love him?'' Why in hell did he ask that question? If she had, he didn't want to know. She poured herself more wine but didn't drink it, just held the glass by the stem, spinning it in the pool of condensation that had collected at the base.

"I was convinced I'd found the perfect man for me. He was sweet, kind, gentle, loving—''

"If he was so perfect, why did you divorce him?'' Did he feel as angry and jealous as he sounded?

She looked up. ''You'll be pleased to know you were right when you said my insistence that nothing counted but feelings, emotion and sensitivity would cause me to make a costly mistake. He was all the things I said, but he was also very emotionally needy. He didn't want to let me out of his sight. At first I thought that was wonderful, but it turned out to be suffocating.''

"I'm sorry it didn't work out."

She took a deep breath, as though shaking off a mood. "It's just as well. It forced me to admit I'm too independent to want to live with a clinging vine. And I can't find a strong man who doesn't make me want to hit him over the head with a bedpan in less than five minutes."

Noah noticed heads turning in his direction before he realized he had laughed too loud. "Does that include Gregory?"

"Probably."

He laughed again, unwilling to admit how relieved he felt.

"I never trust anybody who flatters me that much. I never know what he *really* wants, even after he tells me. At least you were honest enough to tell me up-front."

"Gregory just wants another notch in his belt."

"Thanks for shooting down my pretensions. I was certain he was going to propose on the second date."

"He's had plenty of women who'd have been glad to accept."

"I'm sure he has, but I've learned my lesson. No more men for me."

Sounded like his vow to stay away from women. "Do you make an exception for sex?" he asked.

"Direct as always," she said, but her smile said she didn't mind.

"It saves confusion," he said

"I imagine it does. It's hard not to be confused when you've driven every available female into the arms of the nearest man."

"Is that what I did to you?"

His question seemed to make her draw within herself a little.

"I did that on my own." She started twisting the wine-glass again. "I was determined to find a man who was the total opposite of you." She looked up. "I thought you did everything wrong, so your opposite would be perfect. It was a stupid thing to think. Nobody's completely wrong, not even you."

"That's an improvement on three years ago."

"I don't want to swell your head, but I didn't have to want to marry you to realize you're a very special guy. My marriage made me look at things, I mean *really* look at them. I realized I've been running from my father for so long I couldn't see the good things about you for the bad."

"Couldn't see the forest for the trees?"

"Something like that. Anyway, I doubt I'll ever find anybody I can live with. So I've decided to concentrate on my work and maybe adopt a child in a few years."

That was another point of contention between them. She'd always wanted children. He didn't. He'd been a pain to his aunt, arguing over everything, ignoring her rules, doing stuff just because he knew it made her mad. Any kid of his would be the same. Then there was all that money for clothes and school and college. Hell, he'd never be rich working for the agency. Let other people contribute to the world's overpopulation problem. He wasn't cut out to be a father.

"Don't you need to be married to adopt?"

"They're letting single parents adopt now. Rosie O'Donnell has three, and she's never been married."

He didn't have time to keep up with movie stars, or whatever O'Donnell was. It just didn't seem right for a kid not to have a mother and a father.

Their food arrived.

"Finally," Maggie said. "I thought I was going to have

to sit through the musical and hope my neighbors couldn't hear my stomach growling.''

She had ordered grilled free-range chicken, a green salad, steamed vegetables and no dessert. He'd ordered a thick steak, rare and basting in its own juices, potatoes au gratin, yeast rolls and coconut cream pie. Dinner was a microcosm of their differences.

"I still can't believe Ray bought tickets for *Les Misérables*," Noah groaned as they got into the elevator. "I might as well have gone to an opera."

"Come off it, Noah. You've been griping about the show since the first intermission."

"I don't see how people can stand three hours of that kind of singing."

"It's a great show. I was sure you'd like the couple that rose from gutter rats to become rich."

"I don't happen to like seeing a man pull gold teeth from the bodies of dead soldiers."

"That was pretty ghastly, but they were funny, especially their number in the last act."

"I wouldn't be the least bit surprised to find Gregory bought the tickets. That's just the kind of show he'd like."

"If there were anybody in the elevator with us, they'd take you for the biggest grouch in New York."

"Not if they'd sat through three hours squashed between you and that overweight walrus from Minneapolis."

"You wouldn't have had any trouble if you weren't covered in muscles."

"From the way that yahoo carried on, you'd think he'd never seen a musical."

"He probably hadn't."

"That would account for his liking it."

"That show has been running all over the world for more than ten years. People everywhere love it."

The elevator doors opened, and they got off.

"That just goes to show the human race is overbred."

"This conversation would be funny if I didn't know you were serious."

"I don't really care what people watch as long as they don't make me watch it with them."

"What do you like?"

"I'm not going to tell you."

"You don't have to. I remember. Action. Combat. Dead people everywhere."

He slipped the plastic rectangle into the slot, and the tiny light on the lock glowed green. A faint click told him the door was unlocked. He opened it and let Maggie enter first.

"*Saving Private Ryan* was a great movie."

"So was *Shakespeare in Love,* but I'll bet you didn't see that."

"I saw *The English Patient.*"

"More dead bodies." She shrugged off her coat and tossed it on one of the deep chairs. "What do we have in that little refrigerator?" she asked. "I'm in the mood for more wine."

"We could have gone to the Russian Tea Room after the show."

"I didn't want to."

"Confess. You just wanted to have me all to yourself." He opened the refrigerator before she had a chance to contradict him. "We have wine, liquor and snacks. What do you want?"

"White wine. I have a headache. I loved the show, but I'll never understand why they insist upon making everything so loud. If I didn't have a hearing problem, that would give me one."

"That qualifies you as a member of the older generation," Noah said as he searched and found a bottle of Chardonnay.

"I already knew that." She kicked off her heels and sank

into one of the chairs. Noah noticed she'd given the couch a wide berth all day.

"You'd better rethink your plan to adopt. Kids don't understand the phrase *turn down the volume*. It's a foreign concept to them."

Maggie laughed, accepted the glass of wine he handed her and took a sip. She never used to laugh with him. Not even *at* him. Or look this relaxed. He wondered if three years and a bad marriage really had improved him in her eyes. Probably just made her more tolerant. After all, it wasn't hard to tolerate someone you didn't care about.

It bothered him that she wouldn't care about him. They weren't lovers anymore, but he would never stop caring about her. Despite their stormy two years, she was an important part of his past.

"Okay. Any kid I adopt will have to go through an extensive battery of tests," Maggie joked.

Noah poured himself a straight scotch.

"Maybe you ought to look into a foster program. That way you can take the kid for a weekend, or a summer, and hand him back before you get tired of him."

Maggie sat up, her expression no longer relaxed or tolerant. "You don't think I can handle a child, do you?"

Why couldn't he learn to keep his mouth shut? He probably wouldn't even see Maggie after this job. No point in bringing up issues that would only set them at odds with each other.

"Forget I said anything."

"No. I want to know what you meant."

"I meant people don't come made to order, Maggie. The good comes mixed with the bad. You can throw out a lover or divorce a husband, but a child is another thing. Now before you blow up and start listing my character defects, we ought to discuss the sleeping arrangements. And I'll warn you right now, I don't mean to sleep on the couch."

Chapter Three

Maggie had no intention of sleeping with Noah, but she didn't intend to get upset about it. She'd had a wonderful dinner, seen an excellent show and was enjoying her third—or was it her fourth—glass of wine of the evening. She'd enjoyed the company of a glorious example of the male of the species. Even opening his mouth hadn't completely ruined his attractiveness.

"The couch looks quite comfortable," she said.

She had avoided it all day. She didn't want to give Noah an opportunity, or an excuse, to sit next to her. If the past was any indicator, they'd soon have their hands all over each other.

"I'm sure it is," Noah replied, "but I don't intend to sleep on the couch in Paris or in Beluxor, where I'm sure the couches won't be comfortable."

"Then I'll sleep on the couch," Maggie said. She made a face at Noah and took a sip of her wine. She'd slept on worse when she was working her way through nursing school.

"There's no need for either of us to do that," Noah said. "We have a king-size bed. That's like two double beds pushed together. We won't even touch each other."

"If the bed can be pulled apart, I'll sleep in the bed. Otherwise, I'll take the couch."

"You can't do that."

"Why?"

"We're supposed to be a honeymooning couple. What will the maid think when she comes in and sees one of us has slept on the sofa?"

"It won't make any difference what she thinks. She won't be able to tell anybody in Beluxor."

"Look, it was your idea to act like a married couple from the start. Besides, there are Beluxor sympathizers in New York."

"There probably are sympathizers to every regime in the world in New York," Maggie replied. "It's impossible that any of them would know we're headed to Beluxor."

"They've known since you agreed to be part of this mission and needed to get a visa to get into the country."

She had forgotten that. Despite her family's close ties to Beluxor, she hadn't visited the country since she was a child. Then her father had taken care of all the arrangements. He'd never thought it necessary to share any information about the logistics with his wife, much less his daughter.

But she was too relaxed to get irritated. Well, almost. It irritated her that anyone would spy on her. She was a private citizen obeying the laws of her country. No one had a right to violate her privacy. It irritated her that Noah had come up with a good reason—maybe not *really* good, but one she had to consider—for her to do exactly what she'd made up her mind she wouldn't do. She didn't like being backed into a corner.

"No problem," she said, refusing to let Noah see her

irritation. "I'll put everything away before the maid comes in."

"What about the blankets? There aren't any extra sheets."

"I don't need any."

"The upholstery on the couch will rub your skin raw."

"Then you sleep on the couch."

"No. I'm not afraid of sharing a bed with you. I'm not afraid I'll lose control and—"

She sat up so quickly she spilled some of her wine. "And do what?" she demanded. He looked so pleased with himself she no longer cared that he knew she was irritated.

"I can only assume the reason you don't want to share a bed is that you're afraid you'll succumb to your attraction for me."

She sat her wine down so she could give him her full attention. "Let's get a few things straight right now. You're not so gorgeous I can't resist the desire to throw myself into your arms. I've managed it for the last three years. I can manage it for three weeks."

"But we haven't been sleeping a few feet apart."

"Let me remind you that when we were together *you* were the one who couldn't keep his hands off *me*."

"I never pretended I didn't find you very beautiful. You still are. Maybe even more so."

"Probably because I've stopped being stressed out over you." That wasn't a fair shot, but she was angry.

"You wouldn't have been stressed out if you hadn't tried to change me. Why can't women accept men the way we are?"

"Because you're like unrefined ore, dull and subject to corrosion."

"I thought the usual comparison was to a rough diamond."

"You're as hardheaded as a diamond."

"You're like water dripping on stone—drip, drip, drip until you wear away a man's soul."

"You're—" She stopped in mid-sentence. Their conversation had degenerated into immature squabbling filled with clichés and unnecessary potshots at each other. Their affair was over. They were perfectly happy with their very separate lives. They were both capable of handling their part of the job without raking up the past.

"I'm sorry," she said. "I—"

"I started it," Noah said.

"It doesn't matter who started it. We both jumped in. It sounded like old times."

"Two big babies squabbling over a toy."

"I don't exactly consider myself a baby, but I take your point. Let's make a pact. No matter what happens, the past is over and done with. It won't do us any good to rake it up again."

"I can't forget everything," Noah said. "It wasn't all bad."

There had been many good times, especially that first year. But she couldn't afford to remember them or she'd start questioning her decision to leave when she knew she had absolutely no choice.

"I didn't say forget it," Maggie said. "Just don't talk about it." She picked up her wineglass, stood and walked to the wet bar. "What are we doing tomorrow?"

"Having breakfast in the room, going to a matinee, eating dinner, then boarding a plane for Paris at eleven."

"Then I'd better get to bed. Why, when you fly to Europe, do they put you on a plane when it's bedtime, ply you with so much food and drink you can't get any sleep, then deplane you at your destination with a full day ahead of you? Not all of us are insomniacs."

"I'll sit on the aisle and protect you from any flight attendant heartless enough to attempt to force food or drink on you."

"You're all heart." But she knew he would be as good as his word. Noah was at his best when he was protecting someone, telling people what to do. It was her misfortune that she didn't need or want protection. "Where do they keep the extra pillows and blankets? You may gallivant all over the world, but I'm not used to fancy hotels."

"Look, I swear I won't touch you. I'll even sleep with my back to you."

She was tempted. She'd slept on couches often enough to know she wouldn't get much rest.

"Look, Noah, I'm sure you mean well, but—"

"I'm not a randy teenager anymore."

"You weren't a teenager then."

"But I was still randy."

She couldn't help but laugh. And feel a bit of lingering pleasure at his insatiable need for her. "You said it."

"No, *you* said it, many times, remember?"

"I thought we'd agreed not to bring up the past."

"You already did when you assumed we couldn't sleep in the same bed without me jumping your bones."

"Okay, I apologize, but—"

"I'll make a deal with you. We'll go to sleep in the same bed. If I don't stay on my side, even if I haven't touched you, I'll move to the couch. Fair enough?"

It was more than fair, but it was also dangerous. She wasn't about to admit this to Noah, but she wasn't entirely sure about herself. She found him more attractive than five years ago. She had complained that he never seemed to want to do anything with her except jump into bed, but she had enjoyed their lovemaking. Noah was an accomplished lover.

"Okay, but no arguing. If I say you're over the line, it's the couch for you. Do you want the bathroom first?"

"Go ahead. Maybe if I have another couple of drinks I won't care that I'm forbidden to touch the beautiful woman lying next to me."

"Don't try to make me feel guilty, Noah. It won't work."

The so-and-so actually had the gall to grin.

"It was worth a try."

Just what are you really trying to do? You can't seriously think she's going to sleep with you while you're on this job then go away and act like it never happened. Could you do that?

Noah poured another drink. He didn't want to answer that question. He wasn't acting in a logical manner, something on which he'd always prided himself. He hadn't wanted to work with Maggie because he knew it would be trouble. So what had he done? He not only refused to sleep on the sofa, something even a blockhead would have done, he'd browbeaten Maggie into sleeping in the bed with him. And he'd promised he wouldn't touch her.

You're a fool, Noah Brant. You're too old and too experienced to go out of your way looking for trouble. What made you do it?

He wasn't sure he could answer that question, and another Scotch wouldn't help.

He drank it anyway.

Why couldn't he let go? He'd convinced himself he had, but he knew the moment Maggie walked out of Ray's inner office he'd been fooling himself. The warmth and tenderness were gone, but something remained, and that something was a lot stronger than he was.

He became aware that he was rubbing something unfamiliar on his left hand. *The wedding ring.* He had to wear it, but it made him feel like he was in leg irons. He knew that was a foolish analogy, but that's how he'd thought of his uncle Willis, shackled to Aunt Julia by unbreakable chains. Noah had sworn it would never happen to him. It had been one of the things he and Maggie had fought about. She thought of marriage as a way to support each other, a way to affirm their love. He thought of it as a constraint, a way to keep people together against their wills.

Yet even as he fingered the ring, he wondered what it would have been like if he'd married Maggie.

He'd get to wake up next to her every morning, see her across the table at breakfast, come home to her at the end of the day, make love to her every night. Despite the seemingly endless disagreements, their two years together had been the best of his life. He had someone to share his days, something to go toward, not run away from. And Maggie had always taken an interest in his work, been proud of his successes, commiserated with him over his failures. Maggie was so upbeat, so relentlessly optimistic he couldn't help but feel the same way half the time.

And did they laugh! There'd been times when he thought if he laughed any more it would hurt so much he'd cry. They'd laughed over crazy things, a stupid remark one of them made, bad jokes, silly movies, tall, thin society women in shellacked hair escorted by bald, short, fat husbands. It didn't seem to matter. All they needed was an excuse.

Noah gave himself a mental shake. He wasn't one to waste time on *what might have been,* especially a romanticized version. He prided himself on being coldly logical, in control of every situation at all times. He'd come from a cold, emotionless background. He knew how to be totally pragmatic in his decisions, purely functional in his actions. Yet here he was going against his own principles. He might as well admit that Maggie made him do things he didn't want to do, things that made him angry at himself, and later at her.

He carried his Scotch to the window and looked out. New York had a breathtaking skyline when you looked at it from Staten Island or the Statue of Liberty, but it looked like so many tar roofs on gray buildings when you looked down on it from a suite on the twenty-ninth floor. That sort of described his and Maggie's relationship. When they could lock themselves into their private space and view the world from a distance, he'd found a kind of peace he'd never thought possible. But when they went out among those gray buildings with the tar roofs, everything fell apart.

So, why *had* he talked her out of sleeping on the couch? He had no reason to torture himself when he knew he'd have to sleep on the couch if he failed. He didn't want to attempt to resume a relationship that was most likely doomed to failure. He needed to keep his mind on his job, not on Maggie. He could only come up with one reason for his actions. He couldn't help himself.

And that was the worst possible reason.

He was a man who believed in reason over passion, logic over emotion, sense over sentiment. He had planned his life with the cold precision of a soldier planning a battle strategy. He had executed his plan in the same dispassionate manner. He had no room for irrational actions, certainly not rampant emotion.

Yet he had folded up like a paper house in the wind the moment he came face to face with Maggie.

He didn't know exactly how vulnerable he was—he was afraid he'd have more than enough chance to find out—but he'd better start shoring up his defenses. He didn't intend to come out of this with a broken heart.

Where in the world had that phrase come from? That was the kind of thing a saphead like Gregory would say and not mean a word of it. It was something he'd seen other agents use as an excuse for sloppy or unenthusiastic work. He didn't believe in that kind of emotional devastation. People could get their feelings hurt, could suffer loss, could even feel depressed for a time, but there was no such thing as a broken heart.

At least not for him.

He walked to the bar to pour himself another drink but decided against it. He didn't want Maggie to think he had to drown himself in Scotch to get through the night without touching her.

"Your turn."

He turned to see Maggie standing in the doorway to the bedroom in lounge pajamas. They didn't cover all the delicious curves of her body, but they came unnecessarily close.

She apparently wanted to give him as little excuse as possible to say he couldn't control his attraction to her. It irritated him that she would make such an assumption.

"Did you leave the mirror steamed up?"

"Sure. I didn't want to give you an excuse to spend half the night admiring yourself. I don't want to miss tomorrow's matinee."

"You could always go without me."

She laughed softly, and his gut clenched. He had never forgotten that sound. She used to laugh after they'd made love.

"You're not getting out of it that easily," she said. "We're newlyweds, remember, besotted with each other. A new husband would accompany his bride to the theater, even if it is another musical."

"Don't tell me. I don't want to know."

"*Phantom of the Opera.* I'll have to think of some special way to thank Ray for choosing my two favorite shows. Now if they would just revive *Cats* so I could see it tomorrow night, I could die happy."

"And I would shoot myself," Noah said. He put his empty glass in the sink. "When we get to Paris, we're going to the *Folies-Bergère.* That's more my taste."

Maggie felt her breath coming fast. The man had pinned her against the bed with his body. He was pressing against her, making it hard for her to breathe, making her uncomfortably hot.

And arousing her.

She wanted him and didn't want him at the same time. Even as she pushed him away, her body begged for a stronger, more encompassing embrace. She wanted to kiss him, to feel his lips on hers, but she couldn't see his face, couldn't find his mouth. She felt herself call out to him, but she couldn't hear her words. It was as though she was in an underwater world where sound didn't exist.

She was desperate for more, desperate for less. She turned one way then the other, but the weight remained on her chest. She could feel him moving, she could feel the release of pressure, she could...

Maggie came wide awake with a painful start. She lay pinned to the bed, Noah's arm and leg across her body. His even breathing told her he was asleep, but his right hand wasn't. It gently kneaded her breast. She decided to push him away without waking him. She would have been happier if he'd move to the sofa, but she couldn't hold what he did in his sleep against him.

She pushed his arm away, but it was harder to move his leg. She had to slide out from under him by sliding off the bed. She stood in the darkened room watching him sleep. She had tried to cover herself completely, but Noah wore only Jockey shorts. He used to sleep in the nude. Some things do change.

His body hadn't. He was still as close to physical perfection as a man was likely to get. It didn't make any difference that she knew he worked very hard to keep his body fit. It was worth it, as far as she was concerned.

She muttered a curse. She could feel herself becoming aroused all over again. Noah had always been able to do that to her. Regardless of their differences, he was still the most attractive, sexy man she knew.

She had to get some sleep, but she couldn't do it with Noah rolling over on top of her. If she got too aroused, and he happened to wake up just about that time...well, she didn't want to think about what would happen. She had to get him on his side of the bed and figure out some way to keep him there.

She discovered very quickly that moving a two-hundred-pound man, even when you were only rolling him over in bed, was a lot harder than it looked. By the time she got him fully on his side of the bed, she was panting. She still didn't know how to keep him from rolling on top of her. She knew if she came fully awake again, she wouldn't get back to sleep for the rest of the night. It wouldn't do any good to put the pillows or blankets between them. He'd probably roll right over them without waking. She went into the sitting room, intending to use the cushions on the sofa, but they were sewn to the sofa. She couldn't move them. She looked around the suite, but she didn't see anything that would work

Then she had a brainstorm, the perfect idea. She laughed softly to herself.

Noah came wide awake with a start. He'd been dreaming about falling into the Arctic Ocean, his body battered and bruised by chunks of ice. He couldn't remember a dream anywhere near this realistic. His teeth were chattering. He felt like he was sleeping on blocks of ice. He was grabbing for the covers when he realized he *was* sleeping on blocks of ice.

"What the hell?" he muttered as he sat up in bed. It took only a moment before he remembered where he was. He reached over, and his hand came into contact with a beer can. Or soft drink can. This was crazy. His wandering hands found several more ice-cold drink cans, nine to be precise. And one bottle with a cap that could have given him a nasty scratch if he rolled over on it just right.

He sat up and turned on the bedside light. Three cans of Coke, three of 7UP, three of soda water and a bottle of tropical fruit juice had been lined up in the middle of the bed, forming an ice-cold barrier between him and Maggie. No wonder he thought he'd rolled over on ice cubes. He practically had.

"Maggie, wake up!" he said, shaking her by the shoulders. "What the hell do you think you're doing putting these damned cans in the bed?"

She woke slowly, looking beautiful, dewy-eyed as a child. There was something truly sensual about the way her body seemed to come awake even before she opened her eyes. She never looked disheveled by sleep, never wrinkled, eyes never only half open. She came wide awake like the sun rising out of the ocean at dawn.

"What's wrong?" she asked. "Is it time to get up?"

Her voice was thick with sleep, her features completely relaxed.

"It's three thirty-seven in the morning," he said.

"Too early to get up," she said softly. "Go back to sleep."

"I will as soon as I find out where these drink cans came from."

She rolled her head so she could see him. "What drink cans?"

"The ones in our bed."

"You're dreaming. Who would put drink cans in the bed?"

There was no use talking to her. He took her hand and placed it atop a can of Coke. That woke her up.

"That's cold."

"So I found out. What are they doing here?"

"I don't know. I—" A slow smile spread over her mouth. "I guess I wasn't dreaming, after all."

"What are you talking about?"

"You kept rolling over on my side of the bed," she said. "I pushed you away, but you came right back again."

"You can't hold that against me. I was asleep."

"I know, but I couldn't sleep. So I put these cans between us. I figure if you rolled over on them, you'd wake up."

He couldn't help it. He started to laugh. The more he thought about it, the harder he laughed. "You're clever enough to be dangerous," he said.

"Glad you realize that," she said, a lazy smile on her face.

"All you had to do was wake me up."

"I tried, but you sleep like the dead. You didn't used to sleep so hard. You must have become complacent in your old age."

"I'm only thirty-three."

"Okay, you're not old, but I'm leaving those cans right where they are. And the only one they'll bother is the one who gets off his side of the bed." She rolled away from him. "Sleep tight."

He was awake now, and he wanted to force her to stay awake, too. It was a pretty sneaky trick. It wasn't exactly a cold shower, but it had the same effect. It probably wasn't a bad idea. Being this close to Maggie was difficult. He wondered if they had refrigerators in Paris hotel rooms. He was certain they didn't have them in Beluxor.

He lay down, making sure to keep well away from the cans. Maybe he'd leave them there for the maids to find. That ought to give them something to talk about over the towels and cakes of soap.

He smiled and slowly drifted off to sleep.

"You're not paying attention," Noah said to Maggie.

Noah's appearance filled Maggie with pure, distilled annoyance. She wasn't a morning person, at least not until she'd had breakfast and two cups of coffee. Neither did she consider getting dressed until she'd cleaned up the breakfast dishes and read the paper. Today's breakfast had been delivered by room service and would be taken away the same way, but that was no excuse for Noah to have showered, shaved and be looking positively eager to get on with the day. After having been prevented from making love to her by a barrier of ice-cold aluminum cans, any moderately sensitive male would be slumped across the table from her, his face a mass of bristles, his brow deeply furrowed as he nursed his bruised libido.

Noah charged around the suite with the energy of a man who'd been successful in his quest. Since she knew he hadn't, she could only assume that his lack of success wasn't important to him. That thought increased her annoyance even more.

"It's hard to be fascinated by a lecture on guerrilla tactics when I'm only halfway through my first cup of coffee," she said.

"It's not guerrilla tactics. It's ordinary covert procedure."

"Can't you at least wait until I finish my breakfast?"

"I could have if you hadn't tried to sleep away the morning."

"I worked two extra shifts this week. I was tired."

"Not to mention four glasses of wine."

"That, too." But she didn't have a headache or feel dull. Except for her irritation at Noah, she felt marvelously refreshed.

"We've only got two hours before we have to leave for the matinee. Of course, if you're willing to skip it—"

"Forget it," Maggie said, cutting him off. She picked up a piece of toast and spread grape jelly over it. "I'll never get another chance to see *Phantom of the Opera* from the sixth row in the orchestra. Nothing short of a medical emergency will keep me here."

"How about severe nausea? You wouldn't leave me with my head hanging over the john, would you?"

"You do something underhanded like that, and I'll call Gregory to come look after you."

"How much do you remember about self-defense?" Noah asked.

"I wield a mean can of Mace," she said as she reached for her coffee.

"I mean hand-to-hand."

"I don't need karate or jiujitsu at the hospital. We have security guards."

"You won't have any guards in Beluxor."

"I'll have you. You're not going to tell me you might not be able to defend me, are you?" She couldn't help but needle him. He looked so absurdly serious.

"We have to be ready for anything that might happen."

"I'm sure you'll be ready enough for both of us," she said. She popped the last piece of toast into her mouth and stretched. "I hope our beds in Paris and Beluxor will be as comfortable. If so, I'll be well rested by the time we get back."

"That kind of complacent attitude can get you killed."

"But I don't have to worry. You're vigilant enough for both of us."

"I told Ray you couldn't do this job, but I didn't expect you'd refuse to try."

It was clear that trying to humor Noah wasn't going to work. Maybe if she let him do what he wanted now, he'd leave her alone for the rest of the day. "Okay, what do you want me to do?"

"Show me that you remember how to throw me if I try to attack you."

"I remember," she said, "but I'm out of practice."

"Let's practice now."

"I've just eaten."

"That won't make any difference. I'm the one being thrown."

"Okay, but after I throw you, I'm heading straight for the shower."

She got up from the table, secured her robe and took up her position. But when Noah came toward her and she moved into the well-remembered maneuver, Noah didn't go down. Instead she found herself securely captured in his embrace.

"You knew what I was going to do," she said.

"There's no reason to think all attackers are stupid or inept."

"Okay. Let me try again."

"An attacker won't let you try again," Noah said. "You'll have to break his hold."

"You're stronger than I am, and you know everything I'll try to do."

"Then you're at my mercy. I can do anything I want."

Before she could ask what he wanted to do, he kissed her.

Chapter Four

Noah knew he'd liked kissing Maggie. He'd just forgotten how much, and how much he liked having her kiss him back. No pretense, no holding back. She entered into a kiss like she did into a fight—body and soul. And she pulled him in after her. He'd meant this as a challenge, but in trying to prove he was the one in control, he was in grave danger of losing it.

Noah broke the kiss, struggling to act as though it hadn't rocked him to his foundation.

"Is that what my attacker is likely to do?" Maggie asked, looking at him with assumed innocence.

"Some might," Noah replied more honestly than he wanted, "but I wouldn't depend on it."

"I've found you can't depend on anything when it comes to men." She corrected herself immediately. "That's not exactly true. You can't depend on a man to know what you want. What he wants always gets in the way."

Noah slowly released Maggie and stepped back. "What's that got to do with defending yourself from an attacker?"

"It depends on the kind of attack you're talking about."

As usual Maggie didn't give an inch. "I'm talking about somebody who'll cut your throat or break your neck."

"In that case, I don't think he'd kiss me first. Do you?"

"He would in your case. The rest he'd just kill then go catch a movie."

"Then I don't think I'd better try to throw him. Give me your gun. It'll be easier to blow him away."

Noah admitted that kissing Maggie had short-circuited his brain—all the electrical energy had gone to a different part of his body—but this conversation was ridiculous. "I'm talking about real-life situations here, Maggie. I'm talking life and death."

"Sorry. I guess I thought you were pretending life and death when you really mean seduction."

"Do you think I'm so bowled over by you I can't keep my mind on business?"

"No, but I wouldn't put it past you to use the situation to try to prove I still can't resist you."

"I'm not such an egomaniac."

"*All* men are egomaniacs. Some just control it better than others."

"I suppose you don't think I control it very well."

"You control *everything* very well, even your lovemaking."

"I don't recall you having any complaints three years ago."

"I had them. I just didn't know how to put them into words. By the time I did, I knew you wouldn't understand."

It irritated him that Maggie always seemed able to turn things around so they were his fault. His aunt Julia had been a genius at that. His uncle Willis, poor fool, found himself feeling guilty for things he knew nothing about, but Noah wasn't a poor fool. No one was doing that to him, not ever again.

"I suppose you think you're a modern-day siren, that all you have to do is sing your hypnotic song and I'll be helplessly entranced."

"You've been reading books, Noah. Three years ago you wouldn't have known what a siren was."

"I was ignorant, Maggie, not stupid."

"Ignorant of book learning. I don't know about the rest."

"God, I don't know how you do it, but you always did manage to get me turned around. This is not about us. It's about going into a hostile country with a dictator who doesn't like Americans. He only lets us in and out to keep up his relations with the rest of Europe. One look in the wrong direction and you end up in one of his not-so-comfortable prisons with half-crazy soldiers determined to help you remember that you really are a spy rather than the harmless tourist you thought you were."

"Look, I don't want to be an operative. I'm leaving all that up to you, so you don't have to worry about me trying to flout your authority unless the baby is really sick. In that case, I'll decide what has to be done. You have to agree to that, or I won't go."

He nodded but added, "After consultation. I don't have your medical knowledge, but this is still a hostage situation."

"In a country whose language and customs you know nothing about."

"I've been studying up on Beluxor. I know—"

"Whatever you know, it's not nearly as much as I know. I'll follow your advice, but I'll have some input when I know more about the situation than you do."

"You'll never know more about what to do."

She sighed in obvious resignation. "There's no point in arguing about this now."

Maggie liked to decide every issue as it came up, but he

preferred to get everything out in the open and settled beforehand. It saved him time and wear and tear on his temper.

"I don't want to make a big issue over this," he said, "but it's a matter of safety. There are hundreds of military personnel patrolling the streets who break into any place they want without warning, homes or hotel rooms. And they stop just about every car on the road. They can—"

Maggie cut him off with a wave of her hand. "Noah, I did go through three months of training. I haven't forgotten the basics. You can fill me in on the particulars when we get to Beluxor and know more about the situation. I wonder if they have decaf coffee in this luxury suite. Probably not. I don't imagine they expect anybody to sleep."

Maggie's nonchalance was driving him nuts. "You can't ignore the difficulties of a mission like his," he said, his voice rising in pitch and volume as his frustration level rose. "Doing so can compromise the life of the kid."

"The *baby*," she corrected.

"I realize my life is of no consequence to you, but you will be endangering yourself, too."

The look she gave him was a compromise between *that's a flat-out lie* and *you can't expect me to believe a line like that!*

"Look, Noah, I gave up any desire to be a secret operative years ago. It was probably the result of some unrecognized need to be stronger than my father so I could cause him at least a fraction of the pain he'd caused me over the years, but I got over hating my father. That's when I realized I wanted to help people, not hurt them."

"This is helping."

"What I do is about helping people. What you do is about punishing them."

"You think I'd risk my life just to punish people? What did that husband of yours do to your head?"

"I used to think I could change you. Now I know I can't. That's being smart."

"Every time I try to do anything to bring you up to snuff, it somehow ends up being an object lesson in why our relationship fell apart."

"I suppose this whole situation is a microcosm of why we could never stay together. I want to help a sick baby and enjoy some good food and a few shows while I'm waiting. All you can think about is teaching me to kick butt."

"I'm trying to keep your butt alive."

"One way to do that is to let me eat my breakfast before it becomes stone cold. Or is food not on your list of survival techniques?"

"You can't eat if you're dead!"

He stopped abruptly. He was shouting. He was standing in the middle of a honeymoon suite on the twenty-ninth floor of a swanky hotel and shouting like a stevedore. Noah Brant, a man who was never supposed to feel any emotion—certainly never allow it to overwhelm him—was full of emotion. And Maggie, the soft touch whose heart bled for any cause, was as cold as a fish. He couldn't understand how the roles got reversed.

He blamed it all on her Titian hair, green eyes and soft curves.

When he saw Ray again, he'd strangle him. No, he'd torture him, slowly, painfully, drawing it out as long as possible, because that's exactly what Ray had done by teaming him with Maggie.

He didn't want to remember how he felt after Maggie walked out. He'd been so angry he'd denied he felt anything at all. She'd blamed him for everything then refused to explain. *You wouldn't understand.* He wondered how many women had destroyed a man with those three little words.

Well, she hadn't destroyed him. He was too strong. His mother and Aunt Julia had seen to that. But that didn't stop the hurt. After he stopped being mad, he admitted he missed Maggie for more than the sex. He hadn't realized how much more until she had gone. For a year he'd felt like somebody had pulled his guts out. He'd worked double shifts, weekends, vacations, anything to keep from being by himself, from having time to think about the past. After three years he'd finally put his life back together. Now she was trying to destroy him again.

He remembered the things she used to do to make him knuckle under. He wasn't going to let her get the better of him this time

He forced himself to bite back the words that sprang to his lips. He took a deep breath, counted to three, unclenched his fists.

"You might as well throw out that breakfast," he said, determined to be so civil she wouldn't know how to deal with him. "I'll call room service. Do you want the same thing?"

She looked at him suspiciously. "You planning to put arsenic in it this time?"

"Why would I do something like that?"

"To murder me. Then you could bring in a marine in drag and together you could take the country by storm."

"You always did have a sense of humor," he said, trying so hard not to smile his face felt like it would crack. "A little perverted, but humorous sometimes."

"I don't think I want any more breakfast, and I'll fix my own coffee. I know it's killing you to be nice, so you must have some scheme to send me to Antarctica or some place equally uninviting."

"I'd never do that to you, but I thought of doing it to Reggie. You were too good for him."

Maggie got up and started to make more coffee. "We weren't well matched."

"He was a weak-willed, liberal bleeding heart who thought all the doers of the world had an obligation to support all the slackers."

"I know he wasn't very ambitious, but I think that's a little harsh."

"He was a member of a radical political group, Maggie. What did you expect of him?"

She turned her attention from the coffeepot. "How did you know that?"

Noah realized he'd let his anger cause him to say more than he wanted. "I had occasion to investigate someone who happened to be in the same group."

Maggie's look—he could see the slightest trace of a smile—told him she was wondering if he'd been so upset that he'd checked out her future husband. He had, but he'd be nibbled to death by ducks before he admitted it.

"Not your typical case."

"You'd be surprised what some of your peace-loving fellow Americans get up to."

"After knowing you, nothing would surprise me."

"But according to you, I'm into violence."

"I think the word I used was punishment."

"Same thing."

"No, it isn't. Violence is about destruction. Punishment is about getting even."

"So what are you trying to say?"

"Nothing. Just making an observation. Now before I say something to cause you to lose this marvelously cooperative spirit, I'm going to take a shower. Cut off the coffee when it's done."

She had the audacity to give him a tiny little wave as she vanished into the bedroom. Noah kicked a chair and ended up hobbling around on a hurt toe for his pains. He didn't know what it was about that woman. She'd been out of his life for three years. He ought to have had time to forget a wife he'd been married to for ten years in that length of time. Yet she'd walked back into his life and made a mess of it without even trying. How did she do it?

Why did she do it?

He wondered why she kissed him back. Not because she still liked him. Maybe to find out if he still liked her. Well, he didn't, not the way he used to, but he was still attracted to beautiful women with great bodies, and Maggie scored high on both counts. His mind and heart might be out of danger, but his body wasn't paying attention.

Which meant the next few days—he prayed it didn't turn into weeks—were going to be hell. He wasn't very good at fighting his body when it was in the mood for satisfaction. In fact, he'd been in the habit of satisfying it immediately so he could get his mind back on his work. Now that wasn't possible. It would be hard to explain why a guy on his honeymoon was looking for female companionship.

He was really going to torture Ray when he got back. He would be sadistic and enjoy it.

In the meantime, it looked like he was going to be taking a lot of cold showers. Only they'd never worked before.

"This is nice," Maggie said as the taxi turned off at the exit to the JFK International Airport. "I can't remember when I last rode in a taxi."

"How do you get to the airport?"

"I haven't flown anywhere."

"Not ever?"

"No."

"I can't believe you've never been on a plane."

"I had everything I needed right here in New York. When we went to Beluxor, we went by boat and train. My father wouldn't fly."

"Why?"

"Probably because the FAA wouldn't listen when he tried to tell them what to do." She hadn't meant to mention her father. She and Noah had had a wonderful afternoon and evening, and she had no intention of destroying the mood. "I'm looking forward to it. It'll be a treat."

"Didn't we ever fly anywhere together?"

"No. We planned to a couple of times, but something came up at work." She nearly said *always came up at work.*

It was true, but she didn't need to say it. Work had always been more important to him than their relationship. She had accepted that as she'd accepted so many other things. Then one day she realized all the compromises had ended up compromising her love. Their relationship had degenerated into a way to satisfy their physical need for each other.

When she'd tried to explain that to him, he'd said she was nagging. That she was trying to come between him and his work. Finally came the comparison with his aunt Julia. If the relationship hadn't been dead before then, it would have died an immediate death. Noah despised everything that had to do with Julia Marsden.

Maggie had met the woman only once. She was surprised Noah hadn't grown up to be a mass murderer. He'd survived his mother running off and never wanting to see him again. He'd survived an aunt who tried to make him feel guilty for every breath he took. His background had been so close to her own she was certain they could help each other, that she could help him learn to love, to admit his need, to want to be needed.

She'd been mistaken. The wounds went too deep. He got furious when she tried to get him to face his problems. He said he didn't have any problems. Both women were out of his life, so what they'd done didn't matter. Besides, he was an adult, and adults didn't have the same problems as little boys. She knew better, but he always said she liked to wallow in emotion, to turn herself inside out and examine everything in great detail. He couldn't understand why she had given up her special forces training to specialize in pediatric nursing. But most important of all, he didn't understand why she would follow her heart rather than her brain.

The taxi came to a stop.

"Next stop, Paris," he said with a smile that reminded her of the man she first met five years ago. "Think you can stand it?"

"I've been listening to Maurice Chevalier sing 'I Love

Paris in the Springtime' for years. I can't wait to see if he's telling the truth. *Gigi,*'' she said to the driver who looked mystified. ''It's an old movie.''

She and Noah laughed as they collected their luggage from the curb and headed inside the terminal.

''He didn't know who I was talking about,'' she said.

''Maurice Chevalier was probably dead before he was born.''

''What a shame to have so little past.''

''Is that a good excuse for getting old?''

''No, but it's nice to be able to remember something that happened longer ago than last year.''

''I'm not going to play history games with you. You always win.''

Education was something else that had come between them. He had a GED. She graduated from a very expensive private high school. She'd never been able to convince him that intelligence had nothing to do with diplomas.

''I think they ought to make everyone who comes to this country study our history,'' she said.

''They do, but they teach them about presidents, not actors.''

''Actors are more interesting.''

They managed to joke their way through checking their luggage and changing their seats to an exit row. Noah's legs were too long to fit in a regular seat.

''If I can't get an exit row seat, I have to sit on the aisle, and the flight attendants ram their carts into my knees.''

Maggie imagined there had to be a lot of maimed stewards somewhere on disability. No man hurt Noah. Stewardesses were another thing.

''Want to get a drink?'' Noah asked.

''We just had dinner.''

''We can people watch. The only place better than the airport is Times Square.''

That had been one of their favorite activities. They would

sit for hours commenting about people as they passed by. Their favorite location used to be Rockefeller Plaza.

"You still drinking that dark imported beer?"

"You still drinking white zinfandel?"

She was relieved to find that hadn't changed. It had been part of their comfort zone, knowing what to expect of each other.

She followed him through the airport down one endless corridor after another. She handed him her ticket, let him do all the talking to the agent. She was angry at herself for falling into the old familiar pattern, Noah making all the decisions and she following meekly behind. Not that it was his fault this time. She'd never realized airports were so big. Or so impersonal. Or so crowded. Everybody seemed in a hurry, oblivious to everyone else. Even walking down Broadway during rush hour wasn't this bad. Noah turned in at a small restaurant so dark she could hardly see his face across the table.

"Don't you need more light to see your food?" she asked.

"We're not eating. Besides, it's easier to concentrate on the people passing by."

And ignore ourselves. He'd backed off trying to give her a crash course in being a special operative. It was fair that she put their past aside and think only of the moment. In a few days she'd be at the hospital and Noah would be out of her life again. This time it would be for good.

So they spent the next hour catching up on the last three years while they watched people go by. She had expected it would be hard to work with Noah. She'd refused the assignment when Ray first approached her. But despite the tension between them, she was finding it very easy to be with Noah, to pretend to be in love with him.

Almost without realizing it, they'd both slipped into some of their old, comfortable habits. She'd forgotten how attractive he was, how strongly she was drawn to him. Their relationship had been physical from the first. The chemistry was still there.

They still didn't like the same drinks or food, but they laughed at the same jokes, and he knew who Maurice Chevalier was.

"Look at that," Noah said.

"What?"

"That man and his family. They're just like ducks. He's leading the way, followed by his wife, with the children strung out in a row behind them."

The image in her mind was so vivid she had to cough to keep from laughing aloud. The man looked like a duck, head up, sailing forth without a glance behind to make sure the rest were following, his rear end swinging from side to side in a definite waddle.

"I can just hear him rattling on at the table at night, damned sure nobody but him has done anything worth talking about."

"I imagine she says *Yes, dear* and *Of course, dear* at least a hundred times a day."

They laughed together. "Why didn't you do that?"

"Because I was certain *I* was the only one with anything important to say."

In the beginning they'd listened to each other. They'd been thirsty to absorb every morsel about each other, hungry for the companionship that talking about their day provided. Somewhere along the way they'd lost that.

"I wonder if he treats his parents like that?" Maggie said.

"He probably sent them off to a retirement home when they turned sixty-five. More efficient."

Noah had rarely talked of his family, but he encouraged Maggie to tell him about hers. Her mother had died when she was in high school. Her father practically stopped talking to her after she decided to become a nurse rather than a lawyer. He'd been planning on his brilliant daughter becoming very rich and paying back all the money he'd spent on her expensive education. She didn't know what he'd intended to do with it. He never went anywhere.

In the beginning their isolation from their families had helped draw them together. Their friends would listen and nod in sympathy, but only someone who'd experienced the devastation of being rejected by his family could truly understand. They had a great need to share. Yet in the end it had become a divisive element. It made each of them fear the other had such a bottomless need it could never be filled. Despite her longing for an emotional relationship she had balked at the idea of endless neediness. Which should have been a warning sign when she hooked up with Reggie. But after the wrenching experience of her breakup with Noah, her judgment hadn't been operating very well.

"Do you ever see your aunt?"

"Not since she moved to Arizona. She said she wanted to go where there was nothing to remind her of me. I figured my showing up might do just that."

"No great loss."

"She hated for people to be happy. She especially hated for anybody to smile."

"Then she ought to have been married to that man over there."

A tall man weighing at least three hundred and fifty pounds was talking on the phone and laughing with such obvious enjoyment that people smiled as they passed him. He looked to be an average Joe, but the sheer joie de vivre that shone in his eyes and sounded in his laugh made him exceptional. Noah took one look and grinned.

"He'd drive her crazy. I bet he laughs all the time."

"He looks like the kind of person who could find something funny in a broken dish."

"Or a scratched table."

"A hole in his sock."

"A hole in his wife's sock."

"A puppy's accident in the middle of the kitchen floor."

"Aunt Julia would have killed him and the puppy."

"I bet he'd have died laughing."

"Which would have killed Aunt Julia."

"They could have been buried in the same coffin. The puppy, too."

"That would have caused her to rise from the dead."

"When would she do it?"

"At the wake or at the graveside, whichever would cause the most heart attacks. She would have enjoyed that."

As they both laughed at the ridiculousness of what they were saying, she remembered doing the same thing when one of them had a bad day. Noah was always slow to get started—he took everything so seriously—but once he got in the mood he had a truly wicked sense of the ironic. She wondered if he had anyone to laugh with now.

"I wonder if he's married?" she asked.

"Who?"

"The man on the telephone."

"Single."

"Why do you say that?"

"No married man could be that cheerful."

She kicked him under the table. Not hard. He didn't mean that as a slam against her. "That's just because a married man has so many responsibilities that weigh on his mind."

"I wasn't cut out to be responsible."

He was the most responsible man she knew. Once he took on anything, he wouldn't let go. She imagined he'd only remained interested in her because he considered her a failed task, and Noah never allowed himself to fail.

"I'm not cut out to stay home with babies and pets, either."

"Then why did you become a pediatric nurse?"

"I guess it's a little bit like being a grandparent. I take care of them for a little while. But when I'm done, I send them home with their parents."

"Sorta like my 'children,'" Noah said, referring to the criminals he dealt with.

"Not at all like yours. Mine go home to a loving atmosphere. When you're done with yours, they go to jail."

"Not all the time. Occasionally I get assigned to protect somebody so they can go home to their loving atmosphere instead of a cold cell."

"Is that why Ray put you on this case?"

"Ray put me on this case because I won't take the desk job he's been trying to push off on me for the last two years. He figures by the time I finished working with you I'll be ready to do anything to get out of the field."

Chapter Five

Maggie decided Noah could give Dr. Jekyll and Mr. Hyde a run for their money. After spending two days being obnoxious at worst, extremely tedious and trying at best, he'd been an absolute gentleman on the plane. Charm oozed out of his pores like he had an endless supply. The flight attendants fell over themselves trying to do things for him. They'd ordered only one drink each, but an attendant would materialize every twenty minutes with more wine and Scotch. Maggie had enough meal-size bottles of Chardonnay and drink-size bottles of Scotch in her traveling case to keep them tipsy for several days.

"You could tell them we don't want any more," she said when a fawning male attendant delivered the last round of drinks as the plane was making its approach to Charles de Gaulle Airport.

"Never turn down free gifts," he said. "You never know when they will come in handy as bribes."

"How can I explain all this booze to customs?"

"You won't have to. Put your table up. We'll be landing soon."

Noah didn't have to put his table up. A buxom brunette with bright red lipstick and a figure that strained every seam in her uniform put it up for him. She smiled and chatted and leaned over to give Noah a close look at her bosom. She didn't acknowledge Maggie's presence by so much as a glance.

"Is there anything else I can get you, sir? Another drink? Do you need another pillow for your head?" She placed her hands on his forehead and gently leaned his head back. "I would hate for you to arrive tired or stressed."

"He wouldn't be so tired or stressed if you and the rest of the attendants could remember there are three hundred and ninety-eight *other* people on this plane." Maggie sounded like a jealous wife.

"We'll be at the gate in twenty minutes," the brunette said, acting as though Maggie were invisible. "If you need a taxi or a limousine, I'll be happy to arrange for one to pick you up at the door. If you'll give me your ticket, I'll see that the driver already has your luggage in the car."

"Be sure to pack yourself in alongside the luggage," Maggie snarled. "They don't have personal slaves where we're going."

The woman fussed about Noah a little longer before going away to answer a summons from the first-class section.

"You're shameless," Maggie said, disliking the edge on her voice. "Why didn't you tell her to leave you alone?"

"It would have made her unhappy."

It would have made her unhappy! Like Noah really gave a damn. When it came to people he knew, he had asbestos around his emotional center, yet he got softhearted with flight attendants he'd never met and would never see again.

"You're a charlatan, Noah Brant," she said, laughing despite her ire.

"She obviously has a boyfriend with a taxi. She drums

up a little business and he'll be happy, especially if I give him a big tip. That'll make her happy, too. Getting a little personalized service will make me happy. See, lots of happiness all around, and I just let her do what she wanted.''

''And spend my tax money on an inordinately large tip.''

''Always tip the taxi drivers in Europe. That way they'll be anxious to answer all your questions.''

''But this is Paris. We're not in danger here.''

''You never know. Now sit back and close our eyes. Here comes another attendant.''

She had to suppose the attendants saw a great many attractive men in the course of their work, but there wasn't a man on the plane who came within a mile of Noah in looks. When it came to sex appeal, as far as she was concerned, he didn't have any real competition in New York City. With all that unabashed male attractiveness bottled up on one four-hundred-seat passenger plane, no wonder the attendants were giddy with excitement.

And she was acting like a jealous lover. Or wife.

She didn't understand that, didn't want to accept the most obvious explanation. She had gotten Noah Brant out of her system. It had been hard. She'd even made the mistake of getting married to do it.

Maggie blamed herself for everything that had gone wrong. She should never have married Reggie. If she'd been in her right mind—and she knew she hadn't been for a very long time after the breakup—she'd have known that from the first. She could have been a friend, counselor, maybe even a short-term lover for Reggie, but she should never have married him, because getting married meant something entirely different from being in love.

Odd that she had had to get married to figure that out. Men were supposed to be the ones who thought marriage was an extended date, were supposed to have difficulty making the transition, realizing that commitment meant you had made your choice and would stick with it. Forever. That part had scared her, but not because of the length of the commitment. It was her realization that she'd settled for something so much less than she wanted. Reggie had been willing to settle down for the rest of his life.

She hadn't.

She was appalled to admit how out of touch she had been with her own feelings. Reggie was a sweet guy. He was handsome, kept himself in good shape and was a delightful companion and good lover. But his need for Maggie came from weakness. He needed constant propping up in little ways a person who didn't live with him could never see. The most obvious was his constant need for her presence. As long as she was by his side, he could sparkle. The contrast with Noah was stark.

That first year of her relationship with Noah had been marvelous. Noah came to her from strength. He didn't need her to convince him of his innate worthiness. When Noah was in a black mood, she stayed out of his way. But even then being with him was a bonus because it required nothing of her. And when he came out of his funk—and he always did—he was in a mood to celebrate. They had sometimes spent half the night walking down Broadway, stopping at shops even though they had no intention of buying anything, settling into a corner booth for coffee and doughnuts, watching the people who passed by.

Whenever they saw an interesting face, they would make up stories about that person, embroider an entire life, past, present and future. They could do this for hours. She wished she'd written some of the stories down. She probably could have made enough money to pay off her college loans.

But there wouldn't have been any way to get down on paper the sheer joy of those evenings. They had belonged to each other then. They shared without thinking of who gave the most. They managed to scramble over the rough spots without thinking of blame. They laughed at their terrible childhoods. They told themselves childhood didn't matter. And when they fell into each other's arms at night, that was true.

But one day things changed. It was like walking through a mirror where they saw everything in reverse. Neither of them could pinpoint the time or the incident, though they'd engaged in many acrimonious fights trying to do so.

The plane dropped suddenly, and her stomach ended up in her throat. Instinctively she reached for Noah's hand. She was acutely aware that they were in this comparatively small metal box several thousand feet above the earth. She didn't understand how anything as heavy as a plane could support itself on something as insubstantial as air, but the smoothness of the flight had enabled her to forget her worries. Sudden dips or turbulence didn't.

"We're experiencing some crosswinds," the captain announced. "Everyone make sure your seat belt is fastened securely."

"That's nothing to worry about," Noah assured her. "This kind of stuff happens all the time."

That's what they said about their first fights, those first silent breakfasts, the first evenings when being together caused tension rather than released it. And they'd believed it. The first year had been so wonderful they were certain their warm, easy, wonderful, carefree relationship would soon return.

The buxom brunette came scurrying down the aisle. "Are you all right, sir? You didn't get tossed about in your seat or anything?"

"It was only a slight bit of turbulence," Noah said.

"Occasionally one of our passengers will become unnerved."

"I'm the one who was unnerved," Maggie said. "I grabbed his hand, not the other way around."

She might as well have been talking to a figment of her imagination for all the response she got from the attendant.

"I have to prepare for landing," the attendant said to

Noah, "but if you want anything, don't hesitate to ring for me. Just press the red button, and I'll be here immediately."

You and all the rest of the flight attendants, Maggie thought. "It's a good thing none of the other passengers need any assistance," she said to Noah. "They'd have been out of luck today."

There'd been no one to give them assistance, either. They'd been forced to watch helplessly as they picked at each other until their relationship self-destructed. It probably wouldn't have been any good if there had been anyone to counsel them. They wouldn't have listened. After childhoods during which they both felt betrayed, neither of them would have been able to trust anybody else. They couldn't even trust themselves.

Maggie watched the attendant return to her position, casting glances over her shoulder at Noah. "I hope that taxi driver is her brother."

Noah's laugh told her he'd understand immediately that the woman would have been ready to betray her "lover" if Noah had given her sufficient encouragement. That was one of the things Maggie missed. She never had to explain things to Noah. Well, not little things like this. It was the big, important things where they had a breakdown in communication.

"Does this happen every time you fly?"

"Not as bad as today."

"But we're supposed to be a honeymoon couple."

"It doesn't say that on the ticket."

"It says we're husband and wife. Plus, we *are* wearing wedding rings."

"Maybe I look like I'm in the mood for love."

"If so, they'd expect you to get it from me."

She nearly choked on her own words. The look Noah gave her was hot enough to be felt through her clothes.

"Why else would I have married you? Certainly not to see other women fawn over you. I'm surprised you like it."

''I don't when there's a chance I'll see them again.''

He'd always insisted he didn't need anybody. He avoided friendships because he considered them suffocating. Or they took too much time away from his work. He hated to have anybody do anything for him. He cooked and cleaned up after himself. After living with a father who expected to be waited on hand and foot, it seemed like a minor miracle to see a man carry his own plate or glass into the kitchen, wash and dry it and put it away in the cabinet. It had taken her more than a year to realize that was one more way Noah kept people at a distance.

It hadn't mattered until she realized he was doing it to her, too.

She doubted it had been conscious at first. She had been too much in love and thought it was probably an ingrained habit. He said Aunt Julia had hated having a kid around, had made him painfully aware of every bit of extra work he caused her and had made him do everything for himself. Maybe he'd done that hoping some day his aunt would start to love him. Maggie had never asked. She wondered if he still got angry when he talked about his aunt. She hoped not. He shouldn't have to spend the rest of his life paying because he'd been abandoned by his mother and brought up by a heartless bitch.

Maggie supposed she shouldn't use such words, but if even half of what Noah said was true—and she was certain he'd only told her a small fraction of what happened—Julia was worse than a bitch. How could you calculate the pain and misery to a small boy who was unwanted and had that fact brutally shoved into his face dozens of times every day?

The answer was you couldn't. Nobody could, but Maggie had tried. When things began to fall apart, she'd decided he needed her more than ever and she would become the mother-aunt-lover-friend he'd never had.

But that had made things worse. Above all, Noah despised being pitied. In retrospect, she thought that had been the final blow. They'd spent the last month snarling at each other. They'd only stayed together that long because the sex was still fabulous.

Maggie felt herself getting softhearted about Noah all over again and immediately cautioned herself against it. Noah was strong enough to have endured ten miserable childhoods. He might have been happier if he hadn't been so strong. If he even suspected she was feeling sorry for him, the next few days would be hell.

"We're on the ground. You can release the vise."

The plane had landed with no more impact than that of the wheels taking hold of the tarmac. Maggie hadn't realized she was squeezing Noah's hand so hard her knuckles had turned white.

"Don't tell me a poor, defenseless female can squeeze your hand hard enough to hurt."

"No, but I thought you'd probably like to give the muscles in your back and shoulders a chance to relax before you tried to disembark."

She hadn't realized she was so tense. "It's my first time in a plane."

"I went to sleep on my first flight."

He would. "That's what comes from having no nerves. We nurses have to be sensitive. We react to even the most subtle stress."

Noah made a rude noise, which caused the buxom brunette to come trotting toward him.

"Is anything wrong, sir?"

"He was just making a rude noise at me," Maggie said, at the end of her patience with this woman.

"If I can have your luggage tags, the taxi driver will be waiting for you when you pass through customs. Just look for Armand. Though you won't have to look very hard. He won't be able to miss you."

"I'm going to throw up if she fawns over you one more time," Maggie said through her teeth.

"Jealous?"

"Incensed that a man like you—rude and able to take care of yourself under any circumstances—gets all this attention when people who probably need it are ignored."

"I see you're still struggling against the injustices of the world."

"I gave up trying to tackle the world, but I do what I can for my corner of it."

"You can think what you want but none of what you see for the next several days will be, so relax and don't fight it. You'll have a lot more fun that way."

"I didn't come on this trip to have fun. I came to—"

"I know what you came for, but we're in Paris. You might as well make the most of it. Who knows when you'll be able to come back."

Never. She spent every penny she made paying off her college loans, paying the rent on a tiny apartment she didn't have to share, buying an occasional piece of clothing she didn't have to be ashamed to be seen wearing. Travel had been out of the question. She'd be crazy to let her irritation ruin what would most certainly be her only chance to see Paris. Besides, something—she hoped it *wasn't* the brunette—had put Noah in a surprisingly benign mood. And when he was in a good mood, he could be great company. He might even take her to a show, as long as she agreed to go with him to the *Folies-Bergère.*

She laughed to herself. She didn't know if they still had that kind of burlesque show in Paris. Everything was so liberal these days, burlesque was probably too tame to appeal to the public. She'd have to ask Noah. That ought to get a rise out of him.

As they left the plane, every attendant spoke to Noah personally. She felt like she was traveling with the grand pasha. After the casual incivility of New Yorkers, all this fawning was too much.

"See if you can snow the customs agent like you did all those attendants," Maggie said when they got in line.

"Why?"

"So nobody will see all the wine and Scotch I've got inside my travel bag."

The agent checked their passports and waved them through.

"How did you get him to wave us through without checking our luggage?"

"Special passport."

She should have realized the government would make arrangements for their special agents. She guessed there were a few perks for risking your life in strange countries.

Armand was waiting for them, just as the brunette promised. So was the luggage. That was probably illegal, but who was she to buck the system.

"Le Clos Médicis," Noah told the driver. The driver nodded. "You can sit back and go to sleep," Noah said to Maggie. "It's a long drive into the city, and the hotel is on the other side of the Seine."

"What's it like?"

"I don't know. I always stay at the Hilton, but Ray said he was going to find a hotel that was suitable for a couple on their honeymoon."

"I guess that makes sense."

She guessed she ought to have realized that somebody might be spying on them, but she'd put that thought out of her mind. Noah was here. He would make everything all right. She still felt that way, but it didn't help to be reminded of spies. Supposed they had someone just as fabulous as Noah. No, that was impossible. Noah was one of a kind.

"Put your head on my shoulder," Noah said. "I'll wake you when we get to the hotel."

Ordinarily she wouldn't have done anything that dangerous, but she was tired. They'd left at midnight, she hadn't been able to sleep on the plane, and now she was in Paris with nearly a whole day ahead of her. She'd never last. She shouldn't lean against Noah, but the temptation was too great. Besides, she'd gone to sleep on Noah's shoulder many times before. It seemed a natural thing to do. What could it hurt to do it once more? They were in a cab in a foreign country.

The refrain of some song floated through her head as she drifted off to sleep, something about Paris in the spring being for lovers. That didn't apply to them. They'd never be lovers again.

"Wake up. We're here."

Maggie struggled to pull herself out of a deep sleep. She didn't know what she was doing in a taxi. Even more important, she didn't know what she was doing with Noah. They hadn't seen each other in three years. Despite feeling drugged, she didn't mind waking up. She'd been dreaming about being chased by a faceless villain intent upon unnamed horrors. She woke to find herself in a taxi outside a building that looked like something in a history book.

"What—" Then she remembered she was in Paris on her way to rescue a sick baby from a hostile eastern European government. Apparently reality was just as bizarre as her dream.

She allowed herself to be helped out of the taxi and led inside the hotel. The small lobby was furnished comfortably in a style popular more than a hundred and fifty years ago. She was impressed by the ease with which Noah talked to the concierge in French. She'd forgotten that he could speak four languages by the time he dropped out of high school. By the time he finished college, he'd mastered those and added two more. He absorbed languages like some people absorbed different styles of music.

The small elevator didn't encourage her to look forward to their room. The narrow hallway was even more dispiriting. She hadn't visualized spending her few days in Paris in a poky little room. But when the porter opened the door to their room, she discovered her mistake.

Maggie left Noah to settle with the porter while she inspected the room. Ray had reserved a suite decorated in the Louis XV style, all blue, white and gold. She left the sitting room and entered the bedroom. The bed had a canopy just like the ones she'd seen in pictures of the bedrooms of English kings. She didn't know how she could get to sleep in such a bed. She was an ordinary woman who was used to a tiny apartment in New York. This was like walking into a fairy tale.

The bathroom was less exciting, but that was more than compensated for by the terrace that opened into a lovely little garden in the middle of the hotel. Here she was in the middle of one of the largest cities in the world, and she felt like she had just stepped out into a country garden.

"I hope you aren't allergic to pollen," Noah said. "The concierge said the spate of warm weather has every living plant in Paris breaking into bloom and budding new leaves. It sounds like a perfect recipe for allergies."

"Stop it. This is my first trip to Paris. Any allergies I get here will be special."

Noah laughed. "You never get tired of looking on the bright side of things, do you?"

"I only get tired when everything is depressing, so stop trying to spoil my fun. When can we go sight-seeing? Where are we going to eat? Can we see a show?"

"You're tired. You need to rest."

"I can spend the rest of my life resting. I intend to see every bit of Paris I can before I leave. I don't want to look back and regret that I missed something because I needed a nap."

So they saw as much of Paris as they could on foot. They strolled through the Tuileries garden, walked the length of the Champs-Elysées staring in the windows of the exclusive shops, saw the Arc de Triomphe and climbed the Eiffel

Tower. As the sun set, they headed for Notre-Dame and watched shadows fall over Paris. They had dinner at a quiet little restaurant in the Latin Quarter and watched the students as they strolled arm in arm, some chattering in lively excitement, others moving through a dream world of their own, still others very much aware of their partner and the feel of spring in the air.

"Who said Paris is for lovers?" Maggie asked Noah, then laughed at her own question. "You're the last person who would know the answer to that, right?"

"Maybe not the last, but there can't be more than a couple in line behind me."

He'd been like this all day, making no attempt to pretend he was anything other than what he was, warts and all, but being remarkably charming about it. Apparently he hadn't used it all up on that buxom flight attendant.

"Have you been here a lot?"

"Not a lot, and I never stay long."

"How did you find this restaurant?"

"I talked to the taxi driver while you were asleep."

"How is he related to that brunette?"

"Her brother."

"And he knew about this restaurant?"

"He gets this kind of question all the time. This place is lousy with tourists."

Maggie had noticed very few people who acted like tourists. "I didn't see many."

"Wait until summer. Half the Parisians leave the city to escape them. Now finish your wine. I want to get you to bed before you pass out from exhaustion."

"I feel perfectly fine."

"You look fine, too, but looks can be deceiving."

Boy, was that true. From watching Noah today you'd think he was an inveterate romantic, a woman's dream companion. He'd been charming, witty, going out of his way to please her. You'd never guess he was a cold, hardhearted realist who never did anything without an ulterior motive. But if his motive was to soften her up enough to get her to sleep with him, he'd made a grave mistake. She was tired, mellow and in a very romantic mood, but she wasn't so far gone she didn't know letting down her barriers with Noah was tantamount to committing emotional suicide. She believed love and people were worth taking unexpected risks on, but nothing was worth the risk of falling in love with a man like Noah Brant.

Been there, done that.

Noah paid the bill, once again leaving a generous tip, and they headed to the hotel. She wished the streets hadn't been so well lighted. She'd always dreamed of seeing Paris in the moonlight with the man she loved. Oh, well, she wasn't with the man she loved so she guessed she shouldn't object to artificial light. Still, it was a shame to waste a full moon.

She cautioned herself to be wary. Noah's behavior all day had been atypical. He'd made her feel special, the center of his world. And while he hadn't tried to overwhelm her with his sexuality, she couldn't help but be aware that nearly every woman they passed looked at her with envy. Noah Brant was not a man to be encountered without caution.

And even though she was no longer susceptible to his charm, she couldn't help but feel sympathy for him. He never talked much about his past, but little bits of what he'd said when they were living together had kept coming back all day. She found herself making excuses for the mistakes of the past, admiring him for making something of himself despite his background. She was much too sensible to let sympathy and respect cause her to become infatuated with him again—or to fall under his spell for even one night— but she was very softhearted. Nothing appealed to her more than a mistreated man.

But despite his attractive veneer—and she admitted he was *very* attractive—she knew underneath Noah was a hard, uncompromising man who had virtually no understanding of, patience with or interest in human emotions. He saw everything as a task to be completed. It might require a variety of skills, some of which might appear to be based on emotion, but she knew it was calculated behavior. He used to tell her how he collected information from women too flattered by his attention to realize what he was doing.

Then she'd felt sorry for the women. Now she'd be angry at Noah.

Despite her wariness, she remained in a good mood, happy with Noah, happy with her decision to take this mission. She loved her work, but her life had fallen into a predictable rut. Once they entered their hotel room and Noah locked the door, her alarm system went off, and comfort began to fade. She was locked in a room with Noah, preparing to go to bed, and she didn't have any cold drink cans.

"Let's sit in the garden."

"Why? Are you afraid to get in bed with me?"

Chapter Six

It shocked Maggie that Noah could see through her so easily. It bothered her even more that he was right.

"I need time to think of a barrier to put between us. This bed isn't nearly as wide as the one in New York."

"And you think I'll be all over you."

"Maybe not quite that bad, but I don't expect you to stay on your side of the bed. I think you could sense the presence of a woman in your bed if you were unconscious."

"So it's not just you I can't resist."

She didn't know whether acknowledging his sensitivity to women pleased him or merely kept him from being angry that she thought she was irresistible.

"You could resist me easily enough if you thought going to bed with me meant more than just having sex."

They had remained in the sitting room, which was just as well. She couldn't imagine having this conversation where every hotel guest with a window or a balcony could hear what they said.

"You're afraid of letting emotion enter any of your relationships," she said. "That's why we broke up, remember?"

"I seem to remember a lot of complaints about the amount of time I spent working."

"That was one way of avoiding emotions."

"And being the kind of person more interested in punishment than rehabilitation."

"That's another manifestation of lack of emotion. No empathy with your victim."

"The people I went after were victimizers, not victims. I was protecting other people by putting them out of business."

"But you enjoyed it."

"Why is it so wonderful for a nurse to enjoy her work but so awful if a policeman or a special agent does?"

"It does seem unfair, but you know why."

"Because the world is full of bleeding hearts like you who can't see that some people are so rotten nothing is going to save them."

"You had a tough time but you turned out well."

"I turned my life around because I wanted to. The guys I go after like what they do. They don't want to change."

"Look, Noah, I don't want to talk about your work. That's way off from what we were talking about."

"Not really. I'm incapable of emotion in one area because I'm incapable of it in another. It works for my job but doesn't work for my relationships."

"How many relationships have you had?"

That was a stupid question to ask because she didn't want to know.

"None that count when put alongside what I had with you. The others were just for sex, but I thought I'd found something else with you."

She couldn't believe Noah's pride would have let him make such an admission. He had always been so determined nobody would get close to him. "What did you think you'd found?"

"Somebody who understood me, somebody who could respect me even though I occasionally forgot to use the objective case after a preposition, somebody who could accept me for what I was."

"I did."

"Then what went wrong?"

If he only knew the hours she'd spent trying to find an answer to that question. If she'd found it sooner, it might have saved her a disastrous marriage.

"A lot of things, but I guess the most important was that after about a year, what I wanted out of a relationship changed. You didn't."

"You never told me."

"I tried, but you thought I was nagging."

"You were."

"Maybe, but I was just trying to tell you that I wasn't getting what I needed."

Why were they discussing this at bedtime in a Paris hotel before running off to Beluxor to spirit a sick child out of the country? She'd forgotten that being part of Noah's life was a surreal experience.

"Is there any wine in this place?" she asked.

"I'm sure they'll bring us some if we want to sit in the garden."

"That's a perfect example of what I'm talking about. We're about to discuss details of an intimate relationship, and you suggest we sit in a garden where every person in the hotel can overhear us."

"You suggested it."

"You don't under—" She stopped herself from completing the word. She'd said it so often it was practically a red flag. She walked into the bedroom, found her overnight bag and pulled out one of the small bottles of wine. She had no idea what kind it was, and at this point it didn't matter.

She gathered her thoughts while she opened the wine and poured a glass. She took a sip, moved to the window and looked into the garden. A young couple was seated at a table to the side, their heads together, talking and laughing. She turned to Noah.

"Come here. I want to show you something."

He hadn't poured himself any wine.

"See that couple? That's what we were missing, what I wanted."

"What?" he asked, obviously mystified. "They're just talking."

"But they're talking *together,* laughing *together.*"

"We did that."

"You talked about your world and I laughed, then I talked about my world and you laughed. They're talking and laughing about *their* world."

Noah moved closer to the window, stared at the couple for a moment. "How can you tell?"

"They're constantly touching each other. They hold hands, he caresses her arm, she touches his lips with her fingertips, they lean forward until their foreheads touch. He's looking into her eyes, she's looking into his. They're obviously totally wrapped up in each other."

"They're probably students with nothing to worry about because they have rich parents to pay their bills."

She didn't know why she bothered. He simply could not, *would not,* understand. If he placed any value on emotions— she felt fairly sure he didn't—he was certain they had to be confined to people rich enough to be protected from the pressures of ordinary life.

She emptied her wineglass in a single gulp. "Emotion, love and romance can exist even for the poorest and most disadvantaged. Sometimes that's the only reason they can find to go on living." She put her empty glass down. "But I realize you don't understand that, and it's equally clear I can't explain it to you. I'm ready for bed. Do you still prefer your shower in the morning?"

"Yes."

"Good. I intend to take a long, soaking bath. I'd appreciate it if you'd be in bed and asleep by the time I'm done."

Noah didn't understand why everything always had to be his fault. His mother had left him because he got in the way. His aunt hated him because he meant extra work and responsibility. And Maggie had left him because he didn't bump heads with her and talk nonsense. Look at that young couple in the garden, laughing like they didn't have a worry in the world or the good sense to care if they did. They had to have been protected from the realities around them. They couldn't act like that if they hadn't. Maggie didn't understand. She thought love was the answer to everything.

She didn't understand that love was the most selfish of human emotions. And the least intelligent. Love was concerned only with itself. World peace, prevention of disease, reduction of crime, improvement of the quality of life—all these were unimportant. Nothing mattered but the fulfillment of love. People in love didn't even have the sense to plan ahead so the future wouldn't turn into a rain shower on their sunny parade. No, they forged ahead, certain love would make everything turn out right.

Not that he'd done a lot better. Here he was in a hotel room in Paris with a beautiful woman, but she was taking a bath and had ordered him to be asleep by the time she finished. So what had he done? He'd undressed, fixed himself a drink and was standing in his underwear staring out the window at a lovesick couple making fools of themselves for everyone to see.

He didn't think it was any better to make a fool of yourself in private. When all was said and done, you were still a fool.

He was a fool because he couldn't let go of Maggie, and

he was intelligent enough to know it, honest enough to admit it. He'd investigated Reggie because he was jealous of any man Maggie spent time with. He'd fought this assignment because he knew the difficulty of keeping his hands to himself would only be exceeded by the difficulty of keeping his desire for her out of sight. He could be brutally honest with himself, but he'd be damned if he'd let anybody else inside his head. His aunt had tried because she knew that was the way she could control him. The gang leaders had tried, too, but he kept himself closed in like a tightly held secret. That's how he'd survived. And that's how he'd continue to survive.

He was worried about the increasing warmth of his feelings for Maggie, but the *real* trouble stemmed from the fact that he not only lusted after Maggie's body, he liked and respected her. That sounded like something that kid in the garden would say. He'd never understood why Maggie's father's attitude hadn't made her bitter, but she always seemed to be upbeat despite periodically wading into emotionally deep waters that would have drowned him. If he had any brains, he'd be hoping they'd get the call to fly to Beluxor tonight. Otherwise he might do something he'd regret.

He finished his drink and set the glass on a table. He jerked back the bedcovers and started to lie down. He'd decided to sleep in his underwear because if he didn't Maggie would be certain he was trying to seduce her. He wouldn't turn her away, but he wasn't setting out to seduce her. Still, he'd be asleep when she got out of the bathtub. He slept much better in the nude. It was probably the underclothes that had caused him to be so restless Maggie had to put a barrier of ice-cold soft drink cans between them. A clever trick. He wouldn't have thought of it. But then he wouldn't have wanted to keep Maggie on the other side of the bed.

He stripped and got between the covers. He wondered

what Maggie would say if she discovered he was naked, but a moment's thought relieved his worries. Maggie slept like a log and was always the last one to get out of bed. She'd never know.

Maggie felt one hundred percent better after her bath. She had filled the deep tub with hot water and used the entire container of bubble bath the hotel thoughtfully provided. Then for an hour she'd lain back and let the heat soak out the tension and fatigue of the last few days. After she got out and dried off, she'd rubbed her entire body with a lightly scented body lotion. She felt wonderful, smelled wonderful and was ready to fall into bed and go straight to sleep. She was certain she could sleep for a whole day, but she hoped Noah would wake her. She didn't know how long they would have in Paris, and she wanted to make the most of every minute.

She reached out and grasped the door handle. She hoped Noah had gone to bed like she asked.

She opened the door and sighed with relief when she saw the outline of his body under the covers. He was turned away. He'd thoughtfully left a small lamp burning on her side of the bed. Maggie walked around the bed and came up short. Her breath caught in her throat. The bedclothes had fallen away from Noah's back, exposing his body from his head to the back of his knees.

He was naked.

Maggie's stomach did a wild somersault then balled itself into a tight knot. Noah had slept in the nude when they lived together, but he'd worn his underclothes last night. It hadn't been easy seeing him in Jockey shorts, but it wasn't nearly so upsetting as knowing she was getting into bed with a naked man she still lusted after all these years later.

Okay, she'd admitted it. She wasn't in any danger of falling in love with him, but she couldn't be around him without feeling the intense physical attraction between them.

And seeing him naked in her bed brought memories of nights gone by that made her temperature climb and the sleepiness begin to retreat. How could she go to sleep knowing he might turn over any minute and there'd be nothing between them but her tenuous self-control? He'd made it plain he wouldn't mind taking up where they left off.

She had a simple choice. Either she got into bed and made herself think of anything except Noah, or she slept on the couch. It was a very pretty love seat, but she didn't have to try it to know it would be miserably uncomfortable as a bed. And she hadn't seen any extra bedclothes. It might be spring, but Paris got cold at night, and her nightgown wasn't flannel. She'd been a fool to bring one of pink silk. She hadn't slept in silk since Noah moved out, and half the time before that she hadn't bothered to sleep in anything.

Remembering those years, and nights, wasn't doing her any good. She had to get into bed and go to sleep. And tonight she didn't have any cold soft-drink cans to protect her. She'd always considered herself a mature, responsible woman who couldn't be talked into doing something she didn't want to do, not even by a man as attractive, charming and persuasive as Noah. This was her chance to test her theory.

She eased her way into the bed and lay stiff until she was certain Noah wouldn't wake up or turn over. Yet even after she relaxed, she didn't feel sleepy. If she didn't fall asleep soon, she'd have to try her childhood trick of counting sheep. She hoped French sheep were better at inducing sleep than their American counterparts.

Maggie woke exhausted. Her sleep had been plagued by dreams of endless lovemaking and broken by waking up several times to push Noah back to his side of the bed. Having to make repeated contact with his warm skin didn't make it any easier to recapture sleep. It only made her dreams more erotic. It was almost a relief to wake and find the morning sun flooding the inner courtyard.

And that Noah was no longer in the bed.

She didn't know how long this mission would take, but she had to do better than this or she'd be too tired to think and too hollow-eyed to see. She'd always had a great deal of energy, but she died on her feet when she didn't get her sleep. Those two years with Noah had been difficult. She had often resorted to naps after dinner. He used to tease her that only old men went to sleep on the sofa in front of the TV. She'd responded that his keeping her awake half the night was turning her into an old woman.

But Noah had a way of keeping her from feeling any regret about the lost sleep.

She'd lost even more sleep after she moved out. It had taken her a solid month to learn to sleep without him. It wasn't just the lovemaking. She missed Noah. The warmth of his body when he went to sleep with his arms around her, the comfort of his presence. Noah had never put a price tag on his love. He gave it freely, no strings attached. The irony was their breakup had come because she'd started to want strings.

She should have known better. There was nothing about Noah that said *domesticated animal. No tools required. Attach strings and lead home.* He was generous to a fault, but he wanted no responsibility for anyone else's emotional neediness. To accept such responsibility would have required Noah to acknowledge his own neediness, and he would never do that. Noah Brant had no weaknesses. They had been banished along with his childhood.

All courtesy of Aunt Julia.

Maggie had been tempted to go see his aunt. She might have done so if she hadn't known it would infuriate Noah. And Aunt Julia had moved to Arizona.

The bedroom door opened, and Noah entered bearing a tray.

"Time to get up. I've brought you breakfast in bed. After that, we're going to see everything we didn't get to see yesterday. I've asked the concierge to have a warm footbath ready when we return. You'll need it."

Maggie tried to recover from her shock as she propped herself up in bed. Noah had been a wonderful lover, but he'd never brought her breakfast in bed. His idea of a romantic morning was to make love before getting out of bed. "You didn't have to do this."

"It's your first morning in Paris. I wanted it to be special."

"Where's your breakfast?"

"I've already eaten."

Noah rarely had more than coffee. She had to have a full breakfast or she couldn't function. Another reason they were mismatched. "I hope you brought me something more than croissants and jelly."

"I outraged the chef and asked him to prepare eggs, fried potatoes, ham and biscuits with bits of bacon. I think he rather enjoyed it. It gave him a chance to complain about the gaucheness of Americans."

"There are times I'm truly thankful you have the ability to charm anybody out of their clothes."

"I draw the line at French chefs."

"You know what I mean," she said, too pleased he'd wanted to bring her breakfast to say anything that might cause him to think she didn't appreciate his thoughtfulness. Yet she didn't want to make him think she placed too much importance on it. A difficult balancing act, but then life with Noah had always been a difficult balancing act. No, that wasn't true. In the beginning she'd let him sweep her away. It was only later that the balancing came into play. She hadn't done a very good job. Things had gone from absolutely perfect to unbearable more quickly than she would have ever thought possible.

"How did you manage to find fresh orange juice?"

"The French have orange juice. Haven't you read about the orangeries Louis XIV had at Versailles?"

"You've been reading again," she said, hoping he wouldn't be angered by her teasing. "I warned you that knowledge can be trouble."

"I figured reading about Louis XIV was like reading about myself. He made all the rules, too."

That was one of the things she'd flung at him before she left, that he made all the rules and expected everybody else to play by them.

"I have no doubt that you would have made a fabulous absolute monarch—not to mention being able to seduce all the ladies in the court—but you have to be born of royal blood. I'm sorry, but you'll have to stick to mesmerizing buxom brunette flight attendants."

"She really got in your craw, didn't she?"

Maggie opened her mouth to deny his charge, but when she looked him in the eye she couldn't. "Yes, she did."

"Want to tell me why?"

"And ruin my breakfast?"

Noah laughed. "Eat. I'll stop bothering you."

"Why don't you have a cup of coffee?"

He'd turned to go. She didn't know why she stopped him. Maybe she didn't want to be alone. No, that wasn't right. She didn't want him to leave. Okay, so she wasn't any more immune to his charm than the brunette. That wasn't news. She'd known that the first time she set eyes on him.

He'd been the instructor of one of the beginning classes for new recruits. She would have sworn his job was to scare everyone so badly they'd quit. She would have if she'd been able to pay attention to a word he said. She had been questioning whether she ought to be doing this—it had nothing to do with being a pediatric nurse—but after seeing Noah she wouldn't have quit for any amount of money. It wasn't long before she wanted to meet him. That hadn't been hard. He'd wanted to meet her, too.

They'd talked about her test scores. She'd done exceptionally well, but he didn't think she had the right temperament to be a special agent. She'd been determined to prove to him that she was perfect. Another mistake. She'd convinced him so completely he'd been angry when she dropped out. He'd made it his job to convince her to stay in the program. By the time he knew she wouldn't change her mind, they were in love with each other.

At least that's what she'd thought. It was a whole year before she found out he saw their relationship in an entirely different light.

"I've already had three cups of coffee. The chef took a lot of convincing."

"I've seen you drink that many before you get dressed."

"I don't need the caffeine today. I slept like a log last night."

How could a man spend half the night rolling all over the bed and sleep soundly?

"Okay, but you can't start pacing because I don't gobble everything down in five minutes."

"It always did take you forever to eat breakfast."

"It's the most important meal of the day. I'm not very hungry at dinner."

Another difference. He lived on coffee all day, often skipping lunch, then ate like a king at dinner while she tried to make her salad last. Many times he badgered her into eating a meal she didn't want. Then she'd lie awake half the night. One more reason they should never have lasted together for more than a few weeks. How did they make it through two years? What kept them together despite all the reasons they should have gone their separate ways?

"Okay, you convinced me. I'll go get it."

He returned with a pot.

"Confess, you were planning to drink the whole pot without me knowing," Maggie teased. "I know, you were going to drink it in the garden while you communed with the birds, flowers and nature.''

She nearly burst out laughing at his look of disgust.

''That young couple is out there again. They've been mooning over each other for so long their food must have gone cold.''

''Maybe they're living off the food of love.'' She knew that would get him.

He looked out the window. He was silent for a moment while he took two swallows of coffee. ''I don't know what they're living on, but they haven't touched their breakfast, and the concierge said they hardly touched their dinner last night. I guess they haven't been like this long. They still look healthy.''

He didn't rail against the stupidity of youth or the waste of good food. He actually wondered what was motivating them. To the average person that would have seemed a cynical response, but from Noah it was practically an admission there was something there he didn't see. Even more shocking, he didn't act as though he was certain whatever it was would be something he would scorn.

''They're probably on vacation or maybe a long weekend and have only a few days to spend with each other. They'll go back to their regular habits soon.''

He turned, his look direct and penetrating. ''Did you go back to your regular habits when you left me?''

''No,'' she said, deciding to be brutally honest. ''Nothing has been normal since.''

''It wasn't normal then, was it?''

''No.''

''Is that why it didn't last?''

''Maybe.''

''You haven't thought about it since?''

She was rapidly losing her appetite. ''I've thought about it a lot.''

''And what did you decide?''

"That we were badly mismatched and were lucky to last as long as we did. What was your conclusion?"

"That we didn't have the courage to stick it out, that we gave up too soon."

"Noah, we were screaming at each other. We couldn't be in the same room for more than fifteen minutes without getting into an argument. We were tearing each other apart. It would have killed us to have stayed together."

"It wouldn't have killed me."

"No, because you're bigger and stronger. You'd have killed me. The landlady would have discovered my strangled corpse somewhere between the living room and the bedroom."

"I would never have hurt you."

She knew that. She knew he hid a streak of anger deep inside, a streak that threatened to come out whenever he didn't get what he wanted, but he'd never so much as put a bruise on her, not even during their worst fights.

"You would never intentionally hurt my body, but you were killing my soul. I couldn't let you do that."

"How could I do that?"

She'd answered that question so many times before, but he'd never listened, never understood. She doubted it would be any different now.

"I needed more of you than just your body. And your friendship. I know that was enough for you, but it wasn't for me. When I tried to tell you what I wanted, to show you, you started to pull away. The harder I tried, the more you backed away. The more you backed away, the more desperately I tried. Before long we were like an armed camp. You're complete in yourself—" he thought he was, but he was just as desperately needy as she "—but I'm not. I needed you to need me."

"I did need you."

"No, you *wanted* me. There's a big difference."

He poured himself more coffee and turned to the garden. "Do you suppose they need each other?"

She looked out. The couple was sitting side by side at the same table as last night, his arm around her. They were holding hands. She fed him from her plate, laughing when some of the food fell off the fork.

"I don't know, but right now they don't need anything else."

"It won't last."

"Maybe not, but they'll never regret a moment of it."

"She'll have three children and get fat. He'll take a job he hates and be irritable when he gets home."

"I gained weight eating all those suppers I didn't want, and you were a savage bear, but we didn't notice it until other things went wrong."

"You were perfect. You still are."

How could she not have a soft spot for a man who still thought she was perfect? Reggie had never said that, and he'd sworn on bended knee that he needed her, that he'd go crazy without her.

"You're not so bad yourself. At least the brunette thought so."

"Can't you forget that woman?"

"I bet she hasn't forgotten you."

"I'm sure she has. I'm just another rich American to be steered toward her brother so he can be the one to fleece me instead of a stranger."

"You're an awful cynic. I'm sure she spent the night tossing and turning, wishing she was in your arms instead of your crabby American wife."

"Then she tossed and turned for nothing. Neither one of us got what we wanted."

Before she could feel cornered, he seemed to collect himself, push aside his reflective mood and put on a happy face. "Time to get dressed. Paris is waiting."

Chapter Seven

"I don't think I can move," Maggie said when Noah opened the taxi door for her. "Between the walking and the food, I'm exhausted."

She was reluctant to get out. She knew that would bring to an end one of the most wonderful days of her life.

"I imagine the driver would be happy to take you home with him, but I'm not sure you'd be happy with his agenda."

Maggie heaved a sigh. She liked Paris, but it seemed every man in the city looked at her for the purpose of gauging her suitability for an affair. She'd love to get them all back to New York for just a few days. By the time the resident female population had gotten through with them, they'd be altered for life.

"Give me your hand, unless you want to carry me," Maggie said.

"When did you get to be so fragile?"

"When I've been walked at least a hundred miles and force-fed enough dinner for six people."

He hadn't forced her to eat the delicious dinner. She'd done it all on her own, but she could blame him for choosing the restaurant. He should have known she wouldn't be able to resist eating herself silly after not having lunch. She could blame that on Noah, too, but he'd been absolutely charming. He knew she'd never get back to Paris, so he'd spent his day with her when she was certain he'd rather have spent it coming up with counterplots to foil the Beluxor secret police. And he hadn't once mentioned teaching her how to disable an attacker.

"How far is it to our room?" she asked. "I mean steps. I have to know exactly how many before I can collapse."

"You've gotten soft."

"I was younger then. I—"

Without warning Noah scooped her up in his arms. "I refuse to tell Ray you were so tired you couldn't walk from a taxi to the hotel."

The taxi driver grinned and hurried to open the hotel door. He was the buxom brunette's brother. Maggie didn't know how Noah found him again, but he acted like he was part of the family. She was certain Noah had given him a munificent tip. Probably a few little bottles of Scotch, as well.

"Open the door to the courtyard," Noah said to the concierge.

The young couple was nowhere in sight. There was nobody in the garden.

"Why did you bring me out here?" she asked when Noah settled her in a chair next to a bed of blue pansies.

"So we can finish off the evening by drinking wine in a garden," Noah said. "You'll remember it as the most romantic night of your life, and someday you'll tell your grandchildren all about it."

She would remember many more romantic nights, all of them with Noah, but she would never relate them to her grandchildren. Some things belonged only to her. But this was certainly the most touching thing Noah had ever done. She didn't really want any wine, but she did want to sit in the garden. It had turned chilly, but the moon bathed the garden in its magical light. The concierge had supplemented that with several lanterns placed discreetly among the flowerbeds. It would be a perfect end to a magical day.

Noah had devoted every minute of the day to her enjoyment. He'd taken her to see Montmartre and the Sacré-Coeur, on a boat ride down the Seine, on a trip to Versailles to see the palace and fountains. They'd finished up with a show at La Bal du Moulin Rouge. It had been wonderful, just like a fairy tale. Noah had done more than just read in the three years they'd been apart. He'd studied the culture and art of countries like France and cities like Paris. She'd never underestimated his talent. She had underestimated his determination to give himself the education his background had denied him.

He'd put it all at her disposal today.

And he'd been sweet. That was an adjective she'd never applied to Noah before. Handsome, sexy, masterful, overwhelming, any number of extravagant adjectives, but never sweet. She wasn't sure she liked him this way. It was so different from his usual self she almost felt like she was with a stranger. A fabulous stranger, but still not the Noah she knew.

She laughed softly.

If another woman could know her thoughts, she'd say Maggie was an idiot. Here was a handsome man acting like he couldn't do enough to please her, and she still thought he was an unfeeling brute. Not that Noah had ever been totally unfeeling, but the principle was the same. Something had turned him into the perfect companion, if only for a day, and she was complaining about it.

She didn't know why the change bothered her so much. She ought to be glad. Maybe Noah had learned something from their failed relationship some other woman wouldn't have to teach him. But as she watched him bring the wine from their room, she had a feeling in her gut that the tiger in Noah wasn't tamed, wasn't even sleeping. Noah had caged him, but Noah could also let him out.

The shiver that shook her body had nothing to do with the chilly night air.

She told herself she was a foolish woman. Had one failed relationship and one failed marriage taught her nothing? She was letting her instincts get out of hand, and her instincts not only wanted Noah, they wanted him the way he used to be. Fortunately her brain had learned to counteract her emotions.

Noah handed her a glass of wine. "Are you cold?"

She lied. "No."

"Then why did you shiver?"

"Did I shiver?"

"You know you did."

"Maybe it's a little chilly. I have a jacket in my suitcase. I'll go get it."

Noah's hand on her shoulder held her in her seat. "You can have my coat."

He hadn't been wearing a coat. He must have put it on when he went to pour the wine.

"Now you'll be cold."

He grinned. "Actually it was making me hot."

"You put it on for me, didn't you?"

"I thought you might be chilly."

"I'm surprised you didn't offer to put your arms around me."

"I would have if I thought you'd let me."

She was glad he hadn't asked. She wasn't sure what her answer would have been. She leaned forward in her chair to allow him to drape his coat over her shoulders. It was only a windbreaker, but it provided all the warmth she needed. She put her arms in the sleeves. Noah was bigger than she was. She felt positively lost inside his coat. She pushed the sleeves up until her hands appeared. She probably looked like a fool in a coat at least ten sizes too large for her, but she didn't care. It was Noah's coat. It was supposed to be too big.

"Why would you want to hold me?" she asked. "You didn't want me on this mission. We can't be together without arguing."

He walked around the table and settled into the chair opposite her. Just as he had done all day, he was careful to keep a comfortable distance between them. He wasn't even close enough to reach out and take her hand.

"We haven't argued all day," he said.

"I know, and I want to thank you for sacrificing your day for me. I know you'd rather be doing almost anything else, but it has meant a lot to me."

"It was interesting."

"But you've already seen everything we saw."

"Not all our operations are in places like Beluxor. The more I know about people and their culture, the more effectively I can do my job."

She should have known it had something to do with his job. He probably studied wine, food and art so he could bamboozle female secret agents. Any security chief who sent a woman to deal with Noah was a fool and deserved to have his operations compromised. There should be a special note on his folder in every country.

All female spies become unreliable when dealing with this agent.

She didn't know if there were many female spies. Noah would never talk about his work. He took his oath of confidentiality seriously.

"I'll have to remember to tell Ray what an excellent guide you were."

Noah laughed. "I don't think that's exactly what he wants to hear."

"Your ability to charm women has to be very valuable. If you can charm me after all we've been through, then you can charm anybody."

Her reaching across the table to take his hand was instinctive. If she'd had time to think, she wouldn't have done it. He immediately gripped her hand firmly and sat forward.

"Have I been able to charm you?" he asked.

He looked like he wasn't sure, that the answer was quite important to him.

"You've been extremely charming and thoughtful all day."

His grip on her hand tightened. "That's not what I asked. Did I charm *you?*"

She knew she was getting close to dangerous territory. It always happened when Noah became intense. It was the closest he came to showing any feeling, admitting any need for an emotional relationship with another human, and it always aroused her sympathy. Once that happened, it was nearly impossible for her to control her reaction to him.

She tried to withdraw her hand from his grip, but he held her tight. "You know you charmed me. You always could when you put your mind to it."

His body seemed to tense. His gaze become more intense. "Is that all you thought our relationship was, a kind of mind control game?"

She squeezed his hand. "Not at first."

"But later?"

She didn't want to tell him the truth, but it was best. "I thought you did it to prove I was so weak you could make me do anything you wanted. And you were right. I stayed at least six months too long."

"Are you telling me that for the last six months you didn't feel anything for me, that you just went through the motions because I'd hypnotized you or something like that?"

She almost said yes, but it wasn't the truth. She bore as

much responsibility as he did. "I kept hoping those charming days meant you had changed, or there was a possibility you would change, and if I could find the strength to hang on, everything would work itself out."

He released her hand and sat back. She knew it was nonsensical, but she felt rejected.

"Would you have stayed if I had changed?"

"Probably." She had to be honest. "But it wouldn't have done any good. We'd said too many things that would continue to come between us."

"I remember everything you said."

She leaned back in her chair and took a sip of wine. She pulled the jacket more closely around her. The chill seemed to be deepening. "That's what I mean. The past would keep coming up until it ruined the present."

"But if I had changed, I wouldn't feel the same way about the past, would I?"

She didn't think Noah could change. It wasn't like it was just one part of his personality. He was uniform through and through. Every part fitted perfectly with the others. If he changed any one thing, it would throw him out of sync. Changing bits and pieces, bending them out of shape would leave him worse off than before. It was better that he stayed just like he was, a magnificent creation but not for her.

"I don't know. I couldn't change. I finally realized it was unfair to expect you to do so."

"So you moved out."

"It was the only way we could remain friends."

"But we didn't remain friends."

He'd been unable to accept that the passion they'd shared had finally burned itself out. She'd tried to tell him anything that hot was bound to cool down, but he took it as a personal rejection, the same kind of rejection he'd felt from his mother and aunt. That had made him too angry to be interested in friendship.

"That was my fault, wasn't it?" he asked.

She nodded. "We'd been too intense. People probably shouldn't ever be that intense about each other."

"Why?"

"It skews your judgment. You can't think of anything except as it relates to each other."

"Why is that so bad?"

"It can't go on for long before everything starts to come apart, just like it did with us."

"I never felt like it was coming apart. Those were the best two years of my life."

"Even the last one?"

"Even that. Hand me your glass. I'll get you some more wine."

She didn't really want any more, but after what Noah had just said, maybe she needed it. Had that last year been good for her despite all the tension and the arguments? She had felt she was being pushed farther and farther away, that he was determined she would never get close enough to get a hold on him. She'd tried to tell him she didn't want to hold him, just share him, but he'd been afraid if he lost control, he'd lose everything.

He'd kept his control and lost everything anyway.

She'd lost hers and lost everything, too.

So what had it gotten them? In her case a broken marriage. In his, studying foreign cultures so he could ensnare unwary agents. At least he'd done something to make him better at his job. She'd put her heart through the wringer again. Only the determination that she would prove her father wrong, that she wouldn't fall apart without a man, had enabled her to get through the depression that followed her divorce. But it had been almost like a double divorce. While she was letting go of Reggie, she also had to let go of the idea that their breakup had been Noah's fault. She had failed, too. So while she closed the book on her marriage, she was also closing the book on Noah.

But as she watched him return with her wine and his

Scotch, she knew she'd never been able to close the book on this man. She could never love him again as she had once, but he would always be part of her. And despite their mutual failures, he would be the best part.

"Don't let me have any more, or you'll have to pour me into bed," she said as she took the glass he handed her.

"Is that supposed to encourage me to stop?"

"It's supposed to let you know I don't intend to exceed my limit."

"Aren't you exceeding one now?"

"Do you mean sitting here in the garden with you?"

"Being here in France. When you left me, you said you couldn't understand how I could be an agent, that you couldn't do it if they paid you twice as much."

"I couldn't, but you're supposed to do the hard stuff. I'm just here to take care of the baby."

"Is that the only reason you agreed to come?"

"If you're trying to find out if working with you was an inducement, the answer is no." She smiled at him, not knowing whether that hurt his ego but intending to make it plain she was not, and never had been, chasing him. "I told Ray to find somebody else at least a half dozen times. I only agreed when he said I was the only one who had the knowledge of the language, the culture and the family ties to make the trip credible."

"Did you know about the honeymoon part?"

"No. I wouldn't have agreed if I had."

"Afraid of my fatal charm?"

She didn't laugh. "No, but I wouldn't have wanted to stir up old feelings. I loved you very deeply, Noah, more deeply than I thought I could love any man. That last year I watched that love being torn apart piece by piece. If I hadn't left when I did, it would have destroyed me."

"You weren't so destroyed you didn't run right into Reggie's arms."

"I married him on the rebound because he was exactly

the opposite of you. There, are you satisfied? You always said my emotions would lead me into doing something stupid. Well, marrying Reggie was stupid, but I was looking for the love I didn't get from you.''

"I loved you.''

"No, you didn't. You were too afraid that love would get control of your life. I don't know what you think will happen, but whatever it is, it scares you silly.''

He came out of the chair so quickly he seemed to materialize in front of her. He took her by her shoulders and lifted her to her feet. "I was never afraid of you,'' he growled. "Not then, not now.''

"Not me,'' she said, stunned at her reaction to being held, albeit roughly, by him again. "Of yourself. You never let me get close enough to be a danger to you.''

"Dammit, Maggie, how can you say that? You ripped my heart out when you left.''

"No, I didn't. My love wasn't something you had to have in order to go on living.''

"The hell it wasn't. I nearly came apart after you left. Just ask Ray.''

"I'm sure you were unhappy, but there was never any danger of you coming apart. You're too strong.''

"All I could think about was you. I missed you every minute of the day.''

"You missed my body. Even that wasn't first on your list. You wanted and needed your job more than you ever wanted or needed anything I could give you.''

"That's not true.''

"Then you've done an admirable job of hiding it. You never once called me, tried to see me.''

"You left me, packed up and walked out. What was I supposed to do, come crawling on my knees begging you to come back?''

There was the fear again, the fear of losing control.

"I don't know that you were supposed to do anything.

But if you'd really wanted me back so desperately, you could have told me so."

"I'd already spent a year telling you. What else was I supposed to say?"

She was having difficulty concentrating. He slid his hands down her arms until he gripped her hands. He put her arms around his waist and pulled her to him. It had been more than three years since he'd taken her in his arms like this, yet it still seemed natural for her to be there.

"Nothing. We'd said all there was to say."

"We couldn't have. There must have been something else."

"What?"

"I don't know. You're the expert on feelings. You tell me."

He never seemed to understand. She couldn't be the only one feeling anything in this relationship.

"This isn't something you tell somebody. If you can't feel it yourself, it isn't there, and there's no use talking about it."

"I never stopped feeling it."

"You never started. You only—"

His kiss was so unexpected, so hard and desperate, it took her breath away. If she hadn't been so determined to put Noah out of her life, she'd have known Reggie was a mistake the first time he kissed her. Nobody had ever kissed her like Noah.

And he hadn't forgotten.

Her bones seemed to melt. She always felt weak when he touched her, like her body had turned to rubber. She only remained upright because he held her in his arms. His kiss was fierce, demanding, almost like an attack, but she didn't care. She attacked him back with equal relish. She put her arms around his neck and kissed him back so hard her lips hurt. Their tongues probed each other's mouths, taking part in a wild dance that mirrored their need of each other. She got lost in his kiss. She pressed against him so hard she could feel his ribs rub against her own. Her mind started to spin so fast she lost touch with her surroundings, aware only of Noah and the effect he was having on her body.

Maggie forced herself to break the kiss. She placed both hands on Noah's chest and pushed with all her might. His iron grip never once wavered.

"We can't do this."

"Why not?"

"Because it can't lead to anything but trouble."

"Do you think I'm trouble?"

"Yes, with a capital T in neon lights. A billboard twenty feet high. For me you're more dangerous than an earthquake."

"For me you're worse than a fever."

"Then it's a good thing we don't live together anymore."

"You're also like an addiction. I can't stop wanting you."

"It'll wear off. Give it a little longer."

"How long is it going to take? It's been three years, and it hurts as much as ever."

"See other women. Look up that brunette flight attendant."

"I tried other women, but I couldn't think of anybody but you. Women don't take it too kindly when you call them by another woman's name."

"You didn't do that."

"Yes. I did."

Maggie couldn't help it. She giggled. "Did she hit you?"

"The first one did. The second one threw a radio at me. The third one—"

"You did it three times?"

"Five."

"I'm surprised you're still alive."

"I barely escaped the last time. That's when I decided it was safer to work myself to death."

He still held her close, their bodies touching intimately. She could feel his erection against her abdomen. She had to break his hold. If she didn't, she would soon be too hot to even notice a killing frost.

"I shouldn't have had the last glass of wine," she said, determined to change the subject.

"Why not?"

"It's making it harder for me to remember I don't like you."

"You're lying to yourself. You do like me."

"And that all I want to do is go to bed—alone—and drift off into blissful, unbroken slumber. I plan to spend the whole day in the Louvre tomorrow."

Noah groaned. She knew that would take the starch out of him.

"You don't have to go with me. I won't get lost if I take a taxi there and back."

It would also give her some time away from him, which she desperately needed if she was going to feel less vulnerable.

"Let me go, Noah. I can't go to bed with you holding me like this."

"We did it hundreds of times."

Which is exactly why she wanted him to let her go. Her memory was as good as his.

"We're not going to do it tonight. We're not good for each other. We're only together to do a job. As soon as it's over, we'll go our separate ways and never see each other again."

"We will."

"I doubt there'll ever be another sick baby held hostage in Beluxor."

"When you married Reggie, I made up my mind to forget you. But seeing you again has made me to realize I never stopped thinking about you. I want you back."

Maggie tried to break his embrace, but he wasn't ready

to let her go. "You *want* me, but you don't need me and you don't love me. Those are my terms. I tried it your way, and it didn't work."

"No, you didn't. You ran away."

"I ran away after a *year* of it not working. I couldn't see that things would ever change."

"One thing hasn't changed."

She was almost afraid to ask. "What?"

"We still fit together. Whenever I hold you, I feel like you were made especially for me. Whenever I kiss you and we make love, I know it."

Maggie pushed harder. "We're not going to kiss again. And we're certainly not going to make love."

"You like kissing me. Admit it."

"I like a lot of things about you, Noah, but that doesn't mean I can forget all the rest."

"And you like making love with me."

"If it'll make you feel better, yes, I did like making love to you, but that was because I was in love with you. It wasn't just the sex that made it so wonderful. It was the feelings, too."

"So you admit it was wonderful."

"Yes, it was wonderful. But so was my first date, my first kiss, my first 'A' in nursing school. But all of that is past. It's over between us, Noah, and I've moved on. You, too, even though you don't want to admit it."

"You belong to me, Maggie. No matter where you go or what you do, you'll always belong to me."

He kissed her again, and though she knew she was playing into his fantasy, she kissed him back. There were some battles she couldn't fight.

He broke their kiss, released her and stood back, but his expression wasn't the grin of triumph she'd expected. He looked startled, even a little confused. Good. It would be good for him to be less than absolutely certain he was right. Omniscience had a way of going to one's head.

"You'd better get ready for bed if you expect to have the energy to survive a day in the Louvre," he said. "I think I'll have another Scotch."

"You don't have to hurry. You can sleep in."

"I'll go."

"I know how much you hate museums."

"You can't hide from me, not even in a museum."

She smiled a good-night she didn't feel. She wasn't sure she was strong enough to spend another whole day with Noah, certainly not in the Louvre, which could be thought of as the home of many of the greatest expressions of sensuality ever created. All that paint, all that genius was bound to affect her even if it didn't make any impression on Noah. She'd have to find some way to send him off to the racetrack or some sporting event. She wondered if France had a baseball team.

In the meantime, she had to figure out how she was going to get through this night. She was so keyed up she felt like she was about to jump out of her skin. Just the thought of getting into the bed with Noah had her adrenaline pumping. Being held in his arms and kissed with well-remembered ardor had resurrected the need she'd struggled so hard to put aside, the need only Noah had been able to satisfy, the need she now remembered with such aching clarity.

She shouldn't have let Ray talk her into taking this assignment. She should have known she couldn't be around Noah for even one day and remain indifferent. There had to be a reason she'd avoided seeing him in three years even though she'd picked up the phone dozens of times and put it down again, once after waiting long enough to hear his voice. She was weak where Noah was concerned. She just hoped she could be strong where she was concerned.

She guessed tonight would answer that question.

Chapter Eight

Noah took a swallow of his drink, realized he didn't want it and set it down. He wondered how people got into the habit of eating or drinking when they were stressed. It had never solved anything for him. He just ended up being uncomfortable.

He glanced at their room. Maggie had turned on the light in the bedroom, but she'd pulled the heavy curtains so no one—including him—could see into the room. He didn't need to see her. There was nothing about Maggie's body he couldn't remember in minute detail. He wanted to feel that the tenuous connection he'd established didn't break again.

She had to know their last kiss had established a connection on some level. He could feel it. The sensations had been so strong he'd broken the kiss before he wanted. It was almost like the first time they kissed. The knock-your-socks-off power was there, undiminished after all these years of trying to convince himself he didn't feel anything for her, that she didn't feel anything for him.

But there was something different about it this time. Maggie thought it was the old physical pull that had kept them breathless that first year, but it wasn't that. The physical pull was certainly there, but something about it had changed. Noah couldn't tell what, and that annoyed him. He was used to being able to analyze a situation and come up with an answer. Now he couldn't even analyze it, much less figure out what it meant.

He did know it meant he hadn't gotten over Maggie. He could tell himself anything he wanted, but he was still just as crazy about her as ever. Five years ago he'd have been so hot to climb into bed he wouldn't have been able to think of anything else. He was like one big erogenous zone. He wanted to make love to her now, but the urgency was lacking, the sense that nothing in the universe mattered except making love to Maggie.

He looked at the light at the edges of the drawn curtains. Was this a metaphor for his life, him reaching for the light at the edges while the center remained dark? Where the hell did an idea like that come from? Maybe Maggie was right when she said he'd been reading too many books. He was starting to imagine things. Next thing you know he might actually *like* going to museums. Worse still, he might understand some of that crazy stuff they had there.

He shuddered.

He turned and surveyed the garden. The lanterns had burned low, but they continued to bathe the courtyard in their soft glow. The full moon hung in the sky like a huge Chinese lantern. He couldn't remember seeing it so big before, but he must have. Maggie had probably pointed it out to him several times, but he didn't remember. He couldn't see why she carried on about it so, but it was rather nice, just hanging up there, big and round, like some benevolent god smiling on lovers all over the world.

What possessed him to come up with a phrase like *smiling on lovers all over the world?* It probably wasn't poetic by anyone else's standards, but it was positively sentimental for him. It couldn't be Paris. He'd been here before without turning saccharine. It had to be Maggie. She always did affect him in unexpected ways, but this was a new one. She'd pushed him away, was going to bed alone, and he was standing here staring at the moon and thinking about lovers worldwide. Either he should finish that drink or he shouldn't have had anything at all. He was clearly not himself.

Still, there was a kind of hopeful peace about him that was new. Not that he knew exactly what *hopeful peace* meant. That was something else new, coming up with words to describe his mental state that even he didn't understand. Maggie would say it was the moon and the scent of the flowers in the garden. His aunt would say it was the Scotch. Ray would say it was his Irish blood causing him to believe in leprechauns, fairy folk and other critters.

Noah had no idea what it was, but he was positive it had to do with Maggie and his determination not to let her go again.

He knew that wasn't being reasonable. Or rational. Maggie insisted their differences were impossible to bridge as long as he didn't understand what she was talking about. He wasn't sure he did understand it, but he knew he didn't trust it. Once you let go, you were lost. He would *never* let go. He remembered his desperation before he joined the gang. He hadn't felt in control of anything.

He'd been younger than the other boys, but he was big and strong for his age. He'd kept after them until they let him in. For three years it was everything he wanted, a refuge from Aunt Julia, an identity and something to do with his life. They policed their turf, hocked stolen hubcaps and kept outsiders at bay. He felt important, useful.

Then Milo got killed. It was stupid, a mistake really, but Milo was still dead. That's when he realized that all the time he'd thought he was so cool he was really out of control, that he had to change or it would be his body among the weeds one of these days. It hadn't been easy, but he'd made it. Now he knew who he was, what he wanted and how to get it. He would never be out of control again.

The light in their bedroom went out. Maggie was in bed, waiting for him but *not* waiting for him. How much longer could he deal with this when his desire for her was growing every minute they were together? He knew she wanted him. Her kisses told him that, but Maggie was strong. If she said she wouldn't do something anymore because it wasn't working, she wouldn't change her mind. Did he want her to change her mind? And if not, was it fair to attempt to overcome her resistance just for his momentary pleasure?

He knew the answer to both questions and didn't like either one. Being selfish made him feel bad. Being *selfless* made him feel even worse. He picked up his glass and headed toward their suite. When he reached the door, he turned to give the courtyard one last glance. What was it about the garden in moonlight with lanterns scattered about, and why was he feeling so different? Could there really be something to this romance Maggie was talking about?

He would never have admitted this to anyone, but he was a little bit jealous of the young couple. Not of the way they acted. He could never go around mooning over some woman, not even Maggie. But he wasn't such a fool that he didn't know they had something he didn't have, had never had and never would. While the thought of losing control scared him enough to give him the shakes, a tiny part of him thought it would be absolutely wonderful to be so in love you didn't give a damn about anything.

What a wonderful sense of release that must be.

But that was only a sliver of an impulse, and Noah never let slivers influence him. His course was laid out, and he would follow it to the end.

Noah came awake to find Maggie snuggled up against him, her arm thrown over his chest, her leg thrown across him only inches from his inflamed groin. That accounted for the extremely erotic dream he'd been having. Maggie kept moving against him, making soft mewling noises. He'd never been one to control his physical needs the same way he controlled himself mentally and emotionally. There was no sense putting pressure on himself where he didn't need it. Only now his conscience told him he needed it.

Did he have it?

His right hand had already touched Maggie's back, moving gently from shoulder to waist and back again, enjoying the feel of her soft flesh through her silk nightgown. He loved the feel of the silk as it glided over her skin, shifted easily under his fingertips, rubbed against his bare skin.

His left arm was caught between their bodies, up against her thigh.

He tried to keep that hand still, but his fingers wouldn't obey the signals from his brain. They moved slowly, gently, insistently along the inside of Maggie's thigh. Maggie responded by sighing more deeply and pushing a little harder against him. That forced his rebellious fingers into more intimate contact with her thigh.

His right hand moved up her back, across her shoulder and down her arm. She'd shed the robe that went with the gown. Only two thin spaghetti straps held the gown in place. The silk that moved beneath his touch like liquid skin proved no barrier to the exchange of heat between their bodies. Nor a barrier to the electric charges that flashed back and forth, making it even harder to control his hands, harder to *want* to control them. His hand continued to move over her arm, shoulder and back, its movements becoming more rapid, his fingers becoming more adventurous.

Maggie made a mewling sound and nuzzled his neck, kissing him with lazy abandon.

More heat. More electricity. Noah had never had to control himself in a situation like this, and he wasn't having much success now. Driven by the effect of Maggie's body moving against his, both his hands had taken on a life of their own, not waiting for instructions before claiming rights to Maggie's body. When she threw her arms across him, pulled him to her and kissed his mouth, he gave up the battle he'd already lost.

"Maggie," he whispered.

Her response was to tighten her hold on him, to increase the rapidity of her kisses

"Maggie, wake up." He might not be able to stop himself, but he'd be damned if he'd make love to any women while she was still asleep.

"Noah." She breathed the word like a benediction, as though he were the answer to a prayer.

"Maggie, wake up before we do something you'll never forgive me for."

She opened her eyes and smiled. "Noah," she said before she kissed him again. She pulled him closer until their bodies melded.

He was certain she wasn't fully awake, that she didn't really know what she was doing, but he was lost. There'd be no turning back for him unless she found some more of those ice-cold drink cans and put them where they'd do the most good. But whether she was fully awake or not, Maggie remembered all the things that caused Noah's temperature to spike, caused his libido to soar into the red zone.

"Maggie, do you know what you're doing?"

He didn't know why he asked such a foolish question when she was proceeding to give undisputable proof that she knew exactly what she was doing. She stilled his protest by covering his mouth with kisses so hot he felt he would melt. Maggie had seldom been the aggressor, but she wasn't waiting for him tonight. She knew what she wanted and she apparently meant to get it whether or not he wanted to give it to her.

"Maggie!"

"Shut up and kiss me."

It was a growl rather than a purr, but Noah hadn't heard a more welcome sound in three years. She was awake. He didn't know why she'd changed her mind, but he didn't care. He only cared that Maggie was in his arms again. For the first time since she left him, things felt right again.

"I've missed you," she said.

"You didn't have to go," he said between kisses scattered over her eyes and forehead.

"Yes, I did, but I don't want to talk about that now."

He didn't want to talk at all. That required him to think, and he'd done nothing but think for three years. Right now he didn't want to do anything but luxuriate in the feel of Maggie, in the smell of her, the taste of her. He'd forgotten how much she had done to keep his world on an even keel. Just holding her in his arms caused some of the knots inside him to loosen. She was his touchstone, and he'd forgotten just how much he'd come to depend on her.

Much to his surprise, holding Maggie against his body, his manhood pressed hard against her thigh, soothed him. Rather than being consumed by a hot flame that swept over him with the speed of a prairie fire, he felt a ball of warmth bloom in his abdomen and slowly begin to disperse to the rest of his body. The trembling stopped, and the urgency smoothed out into a deep longing to enjoy every minute, to plumb everything for the last bit of pleasure, to experience every sensation to its fullest.

But being in his arms appeared to have the opposite effect on Maggie. The more she kissed him, the more their bodies touched and rubbed against each other, the harder she kissed him, the harder she rubbed her body against him. Her need seemed to be feeding on itself.

Without warning, she pulled away from him and slid the straps of her nightgown off her shoulders.

"Make love to me," she whispered, "the way you used to."

Without his realizing it, the intervening three years had changed Noah. Just as holding Maggie had a calming effect on him, being invited to make love to Maggie didn't send his body into a mad rage for immediate fulfillment. He wanted something more than physical release. He didn't know what, because he'd never felt this way before, but he knew he was looking for something he'd never sought before. This time the connection between them wouldn't be merely physical. He wanted a union that would bind them together no matter what their futures might be.

He covered her breasts with slow, lingering kisses. Every time she urged him on, he deliberately held back. Every sensation would be heightened by repetition until it became unforgettable in its intensity.

He'd forgotten how much he loved touching her skin. It felt so soft and resilient and smelled of lavender. He used to tease her about her affinity for lavender—lavender candles, lavender sachets among her clothes, lavender room spray after one of his friends had smoked in their apartment—but its familiar fragrance was like coming home to an old and much-loved friend. He cradled himself between her breasts feeling like he'd finally reached a safe haven.

Maggie grabbed him to let him know in a very emphatic manner that she didn't feel quite the same way.

"You're driving me crazy," she said. "I'm going to explode."

"Me, too, if you don't let go."

She had never understood the difference between men and women when it came to touching the most sensitive areas of their bodies. For women it was a stimulus to greater enjoyment. For a man it could very well mean a quick end.

Maggie released him, and he thanked her by taking her nipple between his teeth. Her quick intake of breath told him her sensory level was unusually high tonight. Everything would affect her strongly.

He moved his hands down her back to cup her bottom

and press her against him. She writhed against him, threw her leg over him inviting him to enter her, but he held back, continuing his assault on her breasts with his teeth and tongue, on her body with his hands and the feel of his own body against her. A steady stream of soft moans, her hands plowing furrows through his hair, the restless movement of her body against his provided ample proof he hadn't forgotten how to please Maggie.

But she was no longer willing to allow him to be the one to determine the pace of their lovemaking. The tables had turned. Maggie wanted to rush ahead. He wanted to hold back. But he wouldn't force her to adapt to him. Tonight would be for her pleasure first.

She groaned when his finger entered her.

She took his face in her hands and covered it with kisses. As her excitement level increased, her kisses became mere pecks scattered rapidly and indiscriminately over his forehead, eyes, cheeks, nose and mouth. Her breathing grew heavier, accelerated, blew hot over his face. He struggled to hold his body in check as he drove her toward fulfillment, but her movement against his hand, her kisses, the feel of her hands and leg across his body made it difficult to concentrate on Maggie rather than himself.

When her moans turned to a soft growl he nearly lost control. If she hadn't reached a climax and collapsed on him he would have been ruined.

But while Maggie sagged against the bed, her body spent from its release, his body was taut with the tension that had been ratcheting up in increasingly larger increments. He raised himself above her, and she accepted his body, enfolding him in her arms, wrapping her limbs around him to pull him more deeply inside her. He tried to pace himself, to make the pleasure last as long as possible, but he couldn't control his body. Nature had taken over, and he was along for the ride.

He couldn't count the nights he had lain awake dreaming

of making love to Maggie, holding her in his arms, kissing her until his lips felt too bruised to kiss any longer, losing himself in the lush comfort of her body. Now that the dream had become a reality, his senses, long denied the pleasures his mind had imagined, were in overdrive. He tried to pay as much attention to Maggie as to himself, tried to make sure her body was responding just as much as his, that she was feeling the same sweet agony, the same sense as he was—that if he didn't achieve release soon he would explode.

But the sensations of his body were overwhelming every sense, blocking all perception, focusing his entire being on himself, on the sensations that felt like fiery arcs racing through him with the speed of light. He heard moans but couldn't tell whether they came from him or Maggie. He kissed her with wild desperation but suspected her kisses might be even more wild and desperate than his. He felt heat pouring through his body but couldn't tell whether he was giving or receiving. His taut, straining muscles were a manifestation of his overwhelming need, but he couldn't be certain Maggie's need wasn't just as great.

Then he lost all ability or desire to know anything except that in about three seconds a mind-blowing climax would shake his body from end to end like a rag doll in the teeth of a tiger. He heard himself call out but had no idea what he said. He felt his body tense until his muscles screamed. His breath stilled in his chest. His entire consciousness seemed suspended, wound so tightly he was certain he would shatter.

Then he did.

The entire universe seemed to explode inside his head. Eruptions tore from him with such tremendous force his body shuddered violently. For a brief moment he thought he might lose consciousness. Never in his thirty-three years had he experienced anything like this. He hadn't known it was possible. Every atom of his being seemed focused on the most tremendous, numbing avalanche of sensation imaginable.

He was blown away.

Finally his muscles relaxed and he collapsed next to Maggie. He opened his mouth to tell her what a revelation tonight had been. And he would have told her right then if a terrifying question hadn't popped into his mind.

How was he going to live the rest of his life knowing tonight could never happen again?

Maggie lay awake, unable to move, unwilling to open her eyes.

What have you done?

Okay, she knew what she'd done. The question was why. No, she knew that, too. The real question was, knowing what the consequences of such an action were, why had she done it? She could try to excuse herself by saying she was asleep when she started and unable to stop once she came fully awake. That put her squarely back in the "going with your feeling" syndrome Noah said would get her into trouble someday. She just hadn't expected it would be this particular trouble.

She was a grown woman, capable of making rational, well-thought-out decisions, even decisions that were squarely against what she wanted, physically, mentally and emotionally. Since her failed relationships with Noah and Reggie, she'd concentrated on her career, only went out with men who she knew to be reasonably intelligent and independent and had taught herself not to dwell on the past. Yet in the last few days she'd not only agreed to take part in a covert mission for which she was ill-prepared, she'd agreed to do it with a man who was as dangerous for her as a plague.

It was dangerous enough to go on this mission to try to convince yourself you were over him, but what made you agree to pretend to be his wife?

She couldn't answer that question. At least none of the answers she could think of made any sense. She didn't *want* to pretend to be his wife. She'd never been one to indulge in playacting. She preferred reality to fantasy. She couldn't have done it out of a sense of adventure. Her idea of adventure was going to a new restaurant. She couldn't have done it as a way to punish Noah by holding herself close yet just out of reach. That would have been cruel as well as stupid. Whenever it had been a question of who could hold out the longest, Noah had always been the winner. She couldn't touch him when it came to willpower.

Control was Noah's middle name. You might say it was the only thing about which he was passionate.

Which left her with only one alternative, the least acceptable of all. She was still in love with Noah and always would be.

She knew without looking that she was alone in the bed. There was a certain coldness about the room that told her Noah was gone. When he was near, she could feel the heat of his presence. Everything about Noah was hot. Whenever he was around, she was hot, too.

She turned on her side, reached out and ran her open palm over the depression in the sheets where Noah's body had rested. It brought back memories of the many mornings when she'd done the same, smiling because she knew Noah was in the kitchen drinking coffee and reading the paper. She wasn't a morning person—she didn't care what the sun had to do to come up as along as she wasn't forced to witness it. As for chirping birds and crowing roosters, somebody ought to strangle them—but she needed her breakfast. It was the only way she could get going.

She grabbed his pillow and hugged it to her. The spicy smell of his cologne filled her nostrils. She'd always loved that smell. It was a clean, manly scent, pleasant without being heavy or cloying. Subtle, yet it had stamina. Most probably she liked it because it made her think of Noah. Of snuggling close to him at the end of the day, her head resting on his chest, her anxieties at bay. Of being held in his arms on a cold winter night. Of being cradled when her day had gone badly and she knew nobody could fix it. Of knowing she could walk into a room with one hundred beautiful women and Noah would look at no one but her.

She gave the pillow one last squeeze then put it back, trying to clear visions of the past from her head. Remembering would only make things more difficult. If that was possible after what she'd done.

The door to the sitting room was closed, but she heard someone knock on the door to their suite. She'd let Noah take care of it. She wasn't ready to face him. Maybe she'd spend the entire day in the Louvre. She'd never known him to enter a museum or be interested in a painting. His appreciation was for the practical, the usable. He considered the huge amounts of money spent on art and museums a waste. To give him credit, he did think that rather than spending the money on new sports arenas, it should be spent on providing decent housing, education and recreational facilities and job training that would give the disadvantaged the chance for a future that didn't depend on drugs or gangs. He was very civic-minded, but he didn't have an aesthetic bone in his body.

Her efforts to help him develop one had been a complete failure.

A knock sounded on the bedroom door. Then it opened to allow Noah to enter with a tray.

"Breakfast, milady."

She couldn't interpret his expression. It might be more accurate to say he didn't have one. He was waiting to see how she would react. She wondered if he thought she would burst into tears and blame everything or him, or if she'd declare she'd made a mistake when she left him and that making love to him had shown her the error of her ways.

No, Noah knew she'd never blame him for something

she'd done willingly. Nor would he believe that anything so simple as a night of lovemaking could fix what was wrong between them. He would be expecting her to analyze the situation in depth, try to discern their motives and the shadowy reasons behind them. He'd always hated that, had put up with it only so long before shoving aside all her carefully constructed arguments for some simple phrase. His favorite was *It was the natural thing to do.*

That certainly covered last night.

"I see the chef remembered I'm an uncivilized American and loaded up the tray," Maggie said.

"I reminded him that you were an unrepentant carnivore and that eggs, bacon and sausage were required. There's also fried potatoes, toast, jelly made from a berry I don't recognize, orange juice and a pot of coffee. It looks particularly virulent, so I asked for tea. It should be here in a few minutes. And of course the ubiquitous croissants. I knew you didn't want them, but after he went to all this trouble, I didn't want to hurt his feelings by refusing them."

He remembered everything. But then he always did. Noah was stubborn and domineering, but he had many endearing traits. One was the ability to make a woman feel completely and utterly desirable. Another was the ability to spoil her with numerous little acts of kindness. The fact that he took an almost childlike pleasure in this made it even more appealing. She reached for the orange juice and drank it all without stopping.

"Good thing I asked him to bring another glass," Noah said.

"How did you know I was going to do that?"

"Just a guess."

His expression hadn't changed. He was still waiting. She decided to eat her breakfast. She was never good at making decisions on an empty stomach. She certainly couldn't handle an argument, and it was impossible for them to discuss last night without crossing swords. But eating her way through the entire breakfast, including the extra orange juice and a pot of very strong tea, didn't make her feel any better.

"You must have a lot to say," Noah said. "I've never seen you polish off such a huge breakfast so quickly."

"You mean I gobbled my food."

"You didn't seem to enjoy it."

He'd drunk one pot of coffee and made heavy inroads in a second. She didn't know why the caffeine didn't give him the shakes.

"I'm trying to put last night into perspective."

"And have you?"

"I don't know.

"Can I help?"

"No. You'll say it was all a matter of chemistry, that it was a perfectly normal thing for two people like us to do under the circumstances. You'll probably add that we shouldn't try to read too much into it, just go on with our lives as planned."

Did she sound as cynical to him as she did to herself? She didn't mean to make him sound unfeeling, but she'd lived with him for two years. She knew how his mind worked.

Noah held her gaze for only a moment before he got up from the chair by the window to pour himself another cup of coffee. "Tell me what you think," he said, his back still to her.

She had the uneasy feeling she'd misjudged him this time. It was something about the way he held his body, like he expected some kind of blow.

"I don't blame you for what happened," she began. "I don't have a clear memory of how it started, but I do know I practically seduced you."

"A first," Noah said with a grin.

"Never underestimate a desperate woman."

His grin disappeared. "Is that what you were, desperate? And I was someone handy to take the edge off?"

Surely he couldn't believe that, not after all the arguments they'd had about love and feelings being necessary to make their physical relationship truly meaningful. "You are, and have always been, much more than that. You know there's not another man in the world I'd have done that with, not even Reggie, though I wish I hadn't done it with you."

"You're sorry?"

"What did you expect? We broke up because we couldn't sustain our relationship. Our differences over our physical relationship were at the center of our problem. Knowing how much making love to you meant to me, do you think I'd knowingly put myself back into the same situation?"

"Do you want to know what it meant to me?"

"No."

Maybe it was unfeeling of her to give him such an answer, but she didn't think she could stand to hear it. Noah had a way of making her feel like she was the most wonderful thing that had ever happened to him. He'd say she wasn't responsible for what went wrong, that she shouldn't feel guilty for leaving, but she felt like a Madonna who'd climbed down off her pedestal and slapped him across the face for worshiping her.

"Look, Noah, I know you can handle things like this better than I can. Men always seem to handle sex without a sense of guilt."

"How do you know I'm handling it any better?"

"Maybe I don't, but I know how *I* feel, and at the moment that's more than I can handle. I can't do this."

"I'm not expecting you to make love to me again."

"Why did you say *make love?* Why didn't you say *have sex?*"

"Because even though I'm a man and we handle sex without a sense of guilt, that's never been how it was between us. It was always making love."

"But you don't believe in love."

"Not the way you do, but there was always something

special about everything we did. I won't say every minute was sacred, but the minutes were never profane.''

''Noah, if you could just let go, learn to listen to the poetry in your soul, you'd make some woman a wonderful husband and lover.''

''I notice you didn't say I could make *you* a wonderful husband and lover.''

''It's too late for us. Too many burned bridges, too much scorched earth.''

''So you're giving up?''

''I gave up long ago. But that's not what we need to talk about.''

''What is?''

''This mission, our being together, pretending to be a honeymoon couple. I can't do it any more. You'll have to get someone else.''

Chapter Nine

She hadn't known she was going to say that until the words were out of her mouth.

"I thought you'd say that."

"You're not surprised?"

"No."

"Why?"

"Because you run away from things when you can't handle them."

"I don't run away unless there's no hope of resolution."

"I'm not blaming you. We each have our own way of dealing with difficult issues."

"You seal yourself up in a cocoon that nobody can penetrate. How is that better than running away?"

"It's the same thing."

She hadn't expected him to admit that. He wouldn't have three years ago. "Maybe we both ought to run away, me back to New York and the safety of my hospital ward, you toward some agent who can spend a week pretending to be in love with you without tearing her heart out.''

''Is that what it's doing to you?''

''Why else do I feel like crying? Why do I feel such a desperate need to get out of this room, away from anything that reminds me of you?''

''Because you're in love with me?''

''I don't believe that's true, but if it is, it's all the more reason I should leave.''

The telephone in the sitting room rang.

''Probably the concierge calling to see if you want more coffee. Women always did fall over themselves to take care of you.''

''I never ask them to,'' Noah said, getting to his feet.

''That's part of your allure. We know you don't need us, so we make up our minds to prove you wrong. And when we can't, we only try harder. As soon as you finish with the concierge, you'd better call Ray and tell him to send someone else over.''

The ringing of the phone was getting on her nerves, but Noah was in no hurry to answer it.

''What if he can't find anyone else?''

''He had other candidates. I'll stay until one of them arrives.''

''He must have thought you were the best, to have chosen someone from outside the department.''

''You tried your best to convince him I wasn't qualified, and now you're trying to convince me I *am* qualified. Make up your mind, Noah. For Pete's sake, answer that phone before it drives me nuts.''

The moment Noah left the room, she collapsed against the pillows. She hadn't realized how tense she'd become, how fearful she'd been of what Noah would say. She didn't fool herself. She might not be in love with him, but she wanted to keep his good opinion. It was all she had of their relationship, and she didn't want to give that up.

Of course it would probably be better if they had a huge knock-down-drag-out fight, one that made them so angry they'd never want to see each other again. But she knew that wouldn't solve anything. The good times they'd shared meant too much to her emotionally. They had become a haven, a retreat, a place she could go to remember when things got tough.

She was surprised how depressed she felt about giving up the mission. She didn't know whether it was missing the excitement, missing out on finally getting to do something important or spending more time with Noah. Probably a bit of all three. Okay, a little of the first two and a lot of the last one.

Why had she agreed to this mission in the first place? She'd told herself she'd agreed because she wanted to help free the country of her forefathers from repression, because she was uniquely qualified for this particular operation, because she wanted to do something important with her life while she still could. And to prove to herself she was finally over Noah.

In retrospect it looked as though she'd agreed because she needed to know if *he* was over *her*. If that was the case, she had her answer. To both questions. The attraction was as strong as ever. She was dangerously close to falling in love with him again. He'd already indicated he was willing to pick up where they'd left. And after last night, he had every reason to believe she wanted the same thing.

"Did you thank the concierge for my breakfast?"

"That was Ray. The contact is ready to hand over the baby. We're to leave for the capital of Beluxor in two hours. We don't have time to get anyone to take your place. You have to come with me."

She felt trapped. She'd just proved to herself that she wasn't strong enough to resist Noah's charm—or her need of him. Trying to prove she was over him by spending time with him had been a mistake, maybe even a misreading of her emotions. But whatever the reason for her mistake, she had to leave before things got worse. Before she convinced herself she would love Noah for the rest of her life.

"I can't."

"Then I have no alternative but to go in alone."

"You'll never get out."

"I'll have to try."

"But you don't know anything about sick children."

"I'll have to do the best I can."

"Is Alexi really sick?"

"I only know what I was told."

"And what was that?"

"That if we don't get him out of the country soon, he could die within the next month."

She was trapped. Every day she fought for the lives of a dozen or more children, doing everything she could to keep them alive for one more day. That's what she told herself. Take it a day at a time, an hour at a time. Each hour is a victory.

This was no different. Whatever was wrong with the child, she couldn't abandon him just because she was unable to control her need for an unbearably sexy man. She'd promised Ray she'd do this job. If she quit now, the operation would be in serious jeopardy. She threw back the covers.

"Order the taxi. I'll be ready in fifteen minutes."

"Let me do the talking when we go through customs," Noah said. "If they suspect anything, they'll go through our luggage piece by piece to keep us tied up while they decide what to do with us."

"I told you I'd leave all this gangster stuff to you."

"It's not *gangster* stuff. It doesn't even qualify as espionage."

"Whatever you call it, it's a game people play with guns and jails."

Noah had reverted to type the moment they got on the plane, drilling her on all the things she should and shouldn't do, telling her when she should leave everything to him, which seemed to be all the time. He didn't appear to accept her assurances that she didn't want anything to do with any part of this mission except the baby.

The flight from Paris to Rome had been perfectly comfortable, but everything changed after that. They had flown on a succession of three planes, each smaller and older than the one before it, each airport smaller and less friendly, each set of officials less happy about their visas. She watched anxiously each time Noah handed them over until they were returned. She couldn't recall what it was like when she made this trip as a child, but she didn't remember it being so intimidating.

In Beluxor they deplaned on the tarmac and walked to the terminal though a bone-chilling rain. She doubted the country would attract many western businessmen until they improved their airport.

The inside of the terminal was no better. She could believe the rumors that the rulers were siphoning off money and depositing it in secret Swiss accounts. They certainly hadn't spent any of it on the terminal. It was cold, badly lit and dingy from long neglect. Some of the plasterboard siding had broken away, and she could see rust on the iron beams that formed the frame of the building.

"Stay close," Noah said.

Like she was going to wander off in a place like this.

The customs agent spoke to Noah in short, clipped sentences. She was proud of how well he managed to respond, but his rudimentary knowledge of the language didn't get him beyond the first few questions. The agent seemed determined to be as thorough as possible, and the more Noah stumbled over his responses, the more suspicious the man became. He'd started to look over his shoulder, as though he was thinking about summoning his superior. She'd promised to remain silent, but she could see the situation was beginning to get difficult.

"Maybe you should address your questions to me," she said, breaking in on Noah's stumbling attempts to answer the agent's increasingly specific questions about their vacation plans. "My husband is only just learning the language."

The agent looked from one to the other, apparently reluctant to deal with her.

"Is it all right?" he asked Noah.

Maggie could see Noah hesitate, and she felt sorry for him. Remaining in charge was necessary for his image of himself. As long as he was in control, he didn't need to depend on anyone else. She knew *he* knew she would be able to handle the interrogation more quickly and effectively and that he probably wouldn't understand a lot of what they said. He would not only lose control, he might not know what was happening. He would be completely dependent on Maggie. It wouldn't surprise her if he refused. The swiftness with which he made his decision did.

"She can speak for both of us," Noah said.

Noah expected to feel like someone had reached inside and yanked out part of his insides. To his surprise he felt relieved. He did feel like he'd fallen short of his expectations of himself, but he was relieved Maggie was there to take over when he was clearly out of his depth. She might not want to listen to all of his contingency plans, but she was smart enough to know how to handle this situation. She and the agent had lapsed into a rapid exchange interspersed with what he could only assume were idioms not in the book he'd studied. He was hanging onto the conversation by a thread.

"He wants to know how long we intend to stay," Maggie asked. "He says our plane tickets are open-ended."

Ray always did that when he could, got tickets that could

be used on any flight without having to make a reservation as long as there were seats available.

"I tried to tell him that we were visiting family and our stay would depend on how much I was enjoying seeing my family again, but he wants a definite date."

"They can't, not when they sell plane tickets that don't require it."

"He said he'll have to call his superior if I can't give him a date."

"Tell him we'll be here six days. Why does he need to know?"

"He has to stamp it on our visas. He says the government requires it."

This was a new regulation. He wondered if Ray knew about it. After several more rapid exchanges, Maggie turned to Noah again.

"He wants to know which cities we're visiting and how long we're going to stay in each."

"Can't you tell him we're visiting relatives and can't know for sure?"

"I've tried, but he can't accept that without his superior's approval."

Noah glanced in the direction of the scowling man standing about twenty feet away, where he had a good view of all the booths where agents were questioning visitors. Noah was certain he could get the man to approve a more flexible schedule, but he didn't want to attract any more attention than necessary. Americans rarely traveled to Beluxor. He didn't want to give the secret police any additional reason to interest themselves in what Noah and Maggie were doing.

"Tell him we'll be here three or four days then spend one day each with some of your relatives."

He listened to Maggie and the agent squabbling over exact times and hotel addresses—at least that's what he thought they were discussing—and felt even more helpless than before. He wasn't worried for Maggie and himself.

They could spend their time harmlessly enough sight-seeing and visiting Maggie's relatives, whom she hadn't seen since she was six. But he was worried about the underground's ability to deliver the baby. A change in the schedule, any added police scrutiny would make it more difficult to deliver Alexi and get him out of the country.

Noah cursed under his breath. If he'd been alone, this would be an easy mission. He understood how secret police worked, what they looked for, how they handled surveillance, how to avoid their traps. But Maggie didn't know anything about undercover work or the habits of secret police in repressive regimes. Even worse, he would have a baby to worry about. That was like throwing a cat amongst the pigeons. He didn't know how they could manage to remain inconspicuous.

Especially when he didn't understand what the hell people were saying!

It required a great effort to appear calm, even smiling, while Maggie continued to chatter away with the agent, who had at last begun to unbend a little. Noah knew it was fortunate Maggie had managed to use her charm to allay part of the agent's suspicions, but it was his job, not Maggie's. Intellectually he understood the situation and knew he was doing the right thing. At a gut level, he hated it. It was a struggle not to force this arrogant little man to deal with him.

"We can go," Maggie said, turning to him with a bright smile. "He says we should ask for a taxi from the last stand. He says the first ones cheat their customers by overcharging and driving them around the city rather than going directly to the hotel."

Noah knew that. Taxi drivers everywhere tried that trick.

"I memorized a map of the city. I can tell him exactly how to get to the hotel."

"He also said some of the taxi drivers report everything they overhear to the secret police. He says to ask for his cousin. This is just like your buxom brunette in Paris. I guess things are the same the world over."

"Too much so," Noah said, following the man who had piled their luggage on a rickety cart that threatened to collapse under the weight. "Where are we going?" he asked when the man veered away from the people heading toward the exit.

"He said it's easier to reach the last taxis this way."

Again Noah felt helpless, like he was being carried away on a tide over which he had no control to a destination he knew nothing about. He hadn't felt this way since his childhood, and the experience had been so frightening he'd sworn he'd never let it happen to him again. He only managed now because he knew Maggie could handle the situation. It hurt his pride, but it was nothing compared to the feeling of helplessness that tore at his gut like a sharp-clawed animal.

They emerged from the terminal at the end of a line of six taxis. The last one was well behind the other five.

"They get their positions by paying for them." Maggie explained. "But if you don't have a good position, you can't earn the money to pay for one. A catch-22."

"Let's hope he hasn't used his taxi to haul goats," Noah said.

Probably not goats, but some recent cargo had left a decidedly unpleasant smell. Noah oversaw the luggage being loaded into the car, paid the porter and handed Maggie into the taxi. Glad to be in command, Noah gave the driver the name of the hotel and directions on how to get there. The driver stared at him without comprehension. Noah repeated himself, but when the driver replied, Noah had no idea what he was saying. Maggie intervened. The driver smiled, said something to Noah, and pulled away.

"He's from the same part of the country as my family," she explained. "They speak in a kind of dialect. With your accent, he couldn't understand what you were saying."

"How do you know that?"

"The customs agent told me. He has family in one of the towns."

Noah realized that in such a small country he should have expected people to be connected, but he'd worked alone for so long he hadn't anticipated it.

"The city looks ready to fall apart," Maggie said.

"It's no worse than other poor countries where the rulers siphon off the tax money for themselves."

"I was very young when I visited with my father, but I remember more stores, more color, more people."

Everything seemed to be a uniform shade of gray—the buildings, the merchandise, even the people. Everything showed the deterioration of industrial pollution eating away at the stone or mortar while coating the buildings with a layer of grime. Maggie directed a few brief questions to the driver.

"He says we're passing through one of the poor parts of the town," she told Noah. "A lot of homeless people live here, especially children. He said Beluxor has a plague of homeless children."

"Why?"

A few more questions to the driver.

"Some parents die from overwork or sickness. Others disappear in the night. Still others abandon children they can't support."

"Can't the children go to relatives?"

"Some don't want them."

Noah felt a huge surge of anger. But even as he opened his mouth to tell Maggie what he thought of any parent who would abandon a child to live on the streets, he realized the anger was for his mother who'd abandoned him and his aunt who'd always made it clear she didn't want him. He thought he'd gotten over that years ago. Obviously he needed a situation like this to bring it to the surface again.

He couldn't afford the luxury of raging against the unseen

parents of those children. He had a difficult mission to pull off, and he couldn't let himself get sidetracked. But as he looked into the faces of the children they passed, it was impossible not to feel touched by their plight, not to identify with the hopelessness he saw in their faces, not to feel rage against the adults who'd abandoned them.

"The driver says our hotel is the nicest in Beluxor," Maggie said. "He says most foreigners stay there."

Maggie continued to talk to the driver. She told Noah she was asking about the towns where her relatives still lived, about a couple of people they both knew. Under normal circumstances he'd have been interrogating the driver regardless of the language barrier, asking questions of strategic importance, formulating alternatives for every part of his plan. Yet he sat, regretting the decline of what had once been a prosperous country, feeling sorry for the dispirited citizens, trying to get the image of those children out of his mind.

He fought the tension building inside him. And the irritation at Maggie for being able to converse so easily with everyone around her. It was stupid to feel this way. That's the very reason she'd been chosen for this mission. There were thousands of neonatal nurses in New York, but only one with the connections they needed in Beluxor.

But Noah had always known emotions weren't logical. They clouded your judgment. He had to be careful he didn't fall into the very trap he'd accused Maggie of stumbling into.

"Our hotel should be on the next block," Noah said. At least he knew the layout of the city. He might not be able to talk to anybody, but he wouldn't be lost. He'd brought detailed maps of the countryside.

"I want a bath," Maggie said. "Even the air feels grimy."

"You'll be lucky if there's enough hot water for a shower."

The taxi pulled up to the hotel. It reminded him of some of the grimy, dilapidated hotels in some poor areas of America's inner cities.

"Change that to enough water for a sponge bath," Noah said.

He oversaw the hotel porters as they loaded up the luggage. Maggie paid the taxi driver. From the smiles and extended conversation, Noah figured she'd made a friend for life. Good. They could use a friend in this place.

Noah felt more hopeful about the hot water once they entered the hotel. The grandeur had faded considerably, the carpets were threadbare and the paint dingy, but the wood and brass had been polished to a bright shine. Someone in the place still cared about its appearance.

"Welcome to the Hotel Beluxor. What can I do for you?"

Noah was so relieved to find someone who could speak English he could have kissed the man. It didn't matter his accent was so thick it was difficult to understand. He spoke English.

Moments later he realized that *Welcome to Hotel Beluxor. What can I do for you?* were the only English phrases the man spoke with ease. Everything else came out in halting phrases, grammar a sad casualty. But Noah soon had their room keys and had been invited to join the guests in the lounge while the porter took their luggage to their room. Noah declined. The fewer people who knew anything about them the better.

Their room turned out to be a suite with furniture that appeared to be an amalgam of French styles rather than an example of any one. The ceilings were high and the rooms large and clean.

"This is very nice," Maggie said, inspecting the bathroom, bedroom and closets. "I was expecting much worse."

"So was I."

"Why didn't you want to visit the lounge?" Maggie

asked after Noah had paid the porter and closed the door behind him.

"I imagine at least one of the *guests* relaxing with a brandy is a police plant. Besides, I'm supposed to get a phone call almost immediately after my arrival telling me when to pick up the baby."

"It'll be that quick?"

"I hope so. The plan is really very straightforward. We're supposed to stay in the hotel until we get a call. Then, once we pick up the baby, we leave immediately."

"Does that mean we could leave today?"

"Possibly."

"Then I won't bother to unpack. I wonder if they have a restaurant in the hotel. I'm starved."

Noah wasn't hungry, but he'd never had a big appetite for anything but coffee. You could find good coffee in any country, sometimes even on planes.

"While we're waiting, we ought to go over our contingency plans," Noah said.

Maggie regarded him with what looked like suspicion. "Contingency plans?"

"What we'll do if things go wrong."

"How can you know what to do until something goes wrong?"

"I've worked up several plans. One of them is applicable to almost any possible complication. It goes like this."

"It won't do any good to outline five versions of the same plan because I'll get them confused. Let's go with one. If things don't go the way you expect, we'll improvise."

"But you need to have some idea—"

"I don't want a short course in all there is to know about slinking through back alleys and hiding in cellars. My foremost concern is taking care of Alexi. That's why Ray picked me for this mission. Otherwise, you could have teamed up with Gregory. If the baby's sick, I'll decide what to do."

"You don't know—"

No sooner did Noah start to tell her she didn't know what to do than he remembered she'd known exactly what to do so far. She'd made a friend out of a hostile customs agent and had practically been adopted by the taxi driver. The hotel clerk had taken one look and been smitten. Noah had no reason to think it would be any different for the rest of their stay. This was not the kind of mission Ray usually assigned him. He was obviously going to have to depend on Maggie at various points—he had already—so it behooved him to give in gracefully.

"Okay, we will go over just one contingency plan later."

"Good. Now how long do we have to wait before we can eat? I really am hungry."

"But you had a huge breakfast."

"That was hours ago, and don't tell me you've had even less. I never did understand how a big man like you can eat so little and not waste away."

"Nor I how you can eat so much and stay so slim."

"I'm not slim. I'm positively pudgy. I hope European butter isn't as fattening as American butter."

Noah took her by the hands and pulled her onto an enormous sofa. "You look fine. I don't know when American women are going to get the message, but men don't want a woman to be stick thin. I don't want to feel like I'm holding a skeleton in my arms. I want something substantial, something soft with generous curves."

"I don't know about the soft, but my curves are generous. And in case you want to know, I'd rather you didn't describe me as substantial."

"Why? Substantial was good enough for Michelangelo and da Vinci."

"Those women never had to wear shorts or appear on a beach in a thong bikini."

"You have a thong bikini?"

"No, but if I'd known it would get such a reaction out of you, I'd have bought one just to tease you."

He didn't like to know that having other men gaze at Maggie's body would upset him so badly. He liked even less that Maggie knew.

"I think they're indecent."

"You've got to be the only man to think so."

"Not when it's on his woman."

"But I'm not your woman."

Noah realized the words he'd barely stopped himself from uttering were, *You always were my woman and you still are.* He was in big trouble. To be effective in his work, he had to be in complete control of his emotions. During moments of physical danger he had to be able to act and react with calm, rational judgment. He kept trying to tell himself that his inability to be indifferent to Maggie was temporary and physical. But if he was on the verge of saying things he didn't want to say, his emotions were out of control.

He'd been uptight about this mission from the beginning, and now everything was going wrong. He hated that Maggie had to do simple things for him like talk to taxi drivers. He'd order dinner himself if it took the waiter half an hour to figure out his accent. He refused to be dependent on Maggie. But he couldn't ignore the fact that he could barely think of anybody except her. He could blame it on sex, on being together too much or sleeping in the same bed, but he knew it was more than that.

He found himself thinking—maybe even hoping—they could reestablish the relationship between them, even though he knew Maggie would demand that he learn to open himself to love, something he couldn't do, *wouldn't* do.

He was relieved when the telephone rang. It had to be his contact. Maybe they could pick up the child, fly out tonight and be in New York the next day. He reached for the telephone as though it were a drowning man's lifeline.

Chapter Ten

"I don't understand why they have to postpone the pickup," Maggie said as they walked down a street she remembered as having been lined with graceful, old trees. Now only an occasional stump remained. "What's wrong now?"

"Everything is said in a kind of code. Certain phrases like *Lunch has been postponed again* means something entirely different from what it says. These phrases are agreed on beforehand, but there aren't enough of them for explanations. All he said was I was to wait for another call. Ray said this might happen. In the meantime, we're supposed to act like what we say we are, a newly married couple."

"Won't they ask questions if we don't visit my relatives?"

"Not as long as we're out sight-seeing."

"Wouldn't a newly married couple spend most of their time in the hotel?"

"Are you telling me you want to go to bed with me?"

Maggie gave him a shove. "I spent a good hour on the plane trying to figure out what kind of barrier to put between us tonight. So far, all I've come up with is broken glass."

"A wine bottle, I presume, which you have previously broken over my head."

"Only in self-defense."

"You think you're so devastatingly attractive I can't resist you even when threatened with a wine bottle?"

"I've never been that awful. Now stop teasing me and let's go inside this church. I want to see what it's like."

He'd been really angry when the handover had been postponed. No, he'd been desperate, and he was looking for a way to bail out of a situation he wasn't sure he could handle. Now he'd been plunked down with no option but to handle it himself. He knew that's the way it should be, but he didn't mind admitting to himself he could use a little help. He knew he shouldn't have been, but he was looking forward of having nothing to do but entertain Maggie.

Dinner had been fun. He'd ordered. Maggie had prompted a couple of times when things started to get sticky—like when he wanted cheese on his potato and Maggie said he'd ordered the internal organ of a pig—but the situation was so ridiculous they'd laughed at it. After that, everything became a source of amusement. He was certain everybody in the restaurant was watching them and thinking, *crazy Americans.*

He didn't care. He was feeling too good to worry. And whenever he tried to warn himself that he was relaxing too much, Maggie would say something that would set them off on another series of bad jokes, and he'd forget about controlling his emotions. Now he was going inside a church. A church, for God's sake, not to make a pun. He hadn't been inside a church since he had had to make a drop in a chapel in a cathedral in Budapest.

It was very dark inside. Very little sunlight penetrated the stained glass windows. The few lights suspended from the ceiling did little to illuminate the darkness. Only a couple of chapels, brightly lit from the candles burning before the statues of the saints to which they were dedicated, provided relief from the darkness.

"Maybe we ought to come back on a sunny day," Maggie suggested.

"I don't imagine the worn velvet or dull wood will look better in sunlight."

"I guess you're right," Maggie said. "Better to imagine it looks as I remember it."

Feeling guilty for his cynical attitude, Noah dropped a few coins in the poor box on his way out.

Even though the day was cloudy, the light temporarily blinded him. He halted for a few moments for his eyes to adjust. As he did, he saw a young man on a bicycle swerve to avoid hitting a pedestrian who dashed headlong out of a doorway. The cyclist knocked a little girl into the street. Noah realized the child wasn't getting up, and a truck was headed directly toward her. If she didn't move soon, she could be killed.

The cyclist righted himself and rode off. Pedestrians walked by without noticing the child. The truck driver didn't appear to be diminishing his speed even though he had to see the child was in his path. Noah dashed into the street, grabbed the child and jumped onto the sidewalk only seconds before the truck lumbered past, its driver apparently unaffected about the near tragedy.

"Is she hurt?" Maggie asked.

"I don't know," Noah replied.

"Let me see."

Noah tried to hand the child to Maggie, but the little girl wrapped her arms around his neck and wouldn't let go.

"Don't put her down," Maggie said. "She's too frightened. I can check her while you hold her."

Noah had never held a child before. He didn't like children, but the child was holding him around the neck like he was her shield against the world, and it aroused all his protective instincts. He didn't understand why this should happen with a filthy ragamuffin in a strange country. Maybe it was the callous indifference of the pedestrians who continued to stream by without showing a flicker of interest. They had to know a well-dressed American shouldn't have been holding such a child. He could be stealing her.

"She appears to be okay," Maggie said, "but she's terribly thin. I don't think she's eating enough."

"She hardly weighs anything. How old do you think she is?"

Maggie asked the child something Noah couldn't follow. The child didn't answer.

"I guess she's too frightened to answer," Maggie said. "Let's go inside the church. Maybe the quiet will reassure her."

The church seemed eerily quiet after the noise of the street. Noah seated himself in the last row and set the child in his lap. Maggie sat next to him and started speaking to the child in a muted voice. She kept talking even though the child didn't answer.

Here he was sitting in a church, a child in his lap with her arms wrapped around his neck and Maggie at his side. How the hell did this happen? He felt the first hint of panic. He didn't know anything about children. This wasn't his thing. He was supposed to be on a covert mission to smuggle a baby out of the country, not rescuing homeless children from certain death.

"Sasha."

The word was so soft he wasn't sure he had understood it.

"She says her name is Sasha," Maggie said.

Maggie continued to talk to the child. Occasionally the girl would respond, but most of the time Maggie talked. He hoped she was asking about her family. There must be a family somewhere who were worried about her. Noah and

Maggie would take Sasha home as soon as they discovered where she lived.

Noah wasn't sure how long they sat in the church—the unreality of the situation made it seem forever—but Sasha gradually relaxed her hold on his neck and settled against him, her arms spanning his chest, trying to hold on. The more she tried to bury herself in his protective arms and the more he got used to having her in his lap, the less desperate he felt to find her family and get his life back to normal. The less of a threat she seemed to be.

He didn't understand that. What could this defenseless child do to him?

"She says her parents are dead," Maggie informed him. "She's been living in what seems to be an orphanage for a long time. She doesn't know how old she is, but from some of the things she said I think she's five."

"We have to take her back," Noah said. "Where does she live?"

"She wouldn't say."

"Let's get her something to eat. Maybe after that she'll tell us."

"I want to get something for her cuts and bruises," Maggie said. "She didn't break anything, but she's got two nasty gashes that could get infected."

When Noah started to stand up, Sasha grabbed his neck, locking her arms into place.

"Tell her we're not going to leave her," he said to Maggie.

Noah could tell Maggie was trying to reassure Sasha, but the child didn't loosen her hold. Outside the church, she buried her face in his neck and held on even tighter.

"You've got blood all over your shirt and pants," Maggie said.

Sasha's grip prevented Noah from looking down. Fortunately it wasn't his best suit. He doubted the hotel cleaners would be able to remove all the stains.

"It's a good thing she's not seriously hurt," Maggie said, after she came out of a store that sold medical supplies. "They don't have anything for more than cuts and scratches."

They stopped to buy some fruit, bread, cheese, ham and milk. "I don't know what she'll eat," Maggie said, "but we have to feed her something."

"Where?" Noah asked.

"In the hotel," Maggie replied, looking as though she was surprised he'd ask such a question.

"Won't the people in Beluxor think crazy Americans are stealing their children?"

"We're not stealing her."

"We arrived alone and within a couple of hours we return to the hotel with a child. Wouldn't that arouse your suspicions?"

"I see what you mean, but we can't just feed her in a park then let her go."

"I didn't say I wanted to. I'm just trying to decide if taking her to the hotel is best. I don't want to compromise our mission."

"I hadn't thought of that."

There was no question about taking Sasha to the hotel. The problem was how to get her inside while causing the least comment. He finally decided that the truth would be their best weapon. He went straight to the English-speaking clerk at the desk.

"What do you do with lost children?" he asked.

"Where did you find her?" the clerk asked, eyeing Sasha with obvious disfavor.

Noah explained about the bicycle, the truck and the injuries. He said Maggie was going to take care of her cuts and bruises and then they were going to give her something to eat. He wanted to know where to take her afterward.

The clerk burst into a torrent of language, and Noah didn't need Maggie's translation to know the man was saying they couldn't keep the child in the hotel. It was against hotel rules to allow such urchins in. It would ruin their reputation.

Noah had to restrain the impulse to plant his fist in the man's face.

"Ask him where we can take her," he said to Maggie.

The man responded with another torrent of impassioned speech, which only served to make Sasha hold Noah even tighter.

"He says if she doesn't have any family, we'll have to put her out into the street," Maggie said. "Any orphanage that would take her is closed."

If Sasha hadn't been in the way, Noah *would* have planted his fist in the man's face.

"You tell him we're taking this child up to our suite," he said to Maggie. "We're going to bandage her wounds and see that she has something to eat. After that we're going to put her to bed. And tomorrow, *after we've checked her wounds and given her breakfast,* we'll see about taking her to a decent orphanage. You tell him I want him to get the name of one that will take care of this child so she isn't roaming the streets getting knocked down by uncaring citizens."

"You're getting a little carried away here, aren't you, Noah?" Maggie asked.

But she was grinning. He bet she thought he'd gone all sentimental over a child, but he didn't think it was sentimental to act like a decent human being. How could anybody put this child into the street for the night?

"Do you have a better solution?" he asked Maggie.

"No. I'm just surprised we have the same one."

"I'm not completely without feeling."

"I never said that. It was just a question of which feelings were missing."

"Stop giving me a hard time and tell that clerk if he sets

anybody on me because of this, I'll tell the police he tried to sell me government secrets.''

"Do you think that's wise?"

"Actually I'd like to push him in front of a truck then make him spend the night in the street."

"Take her up to the room. I'll be along as soon as I finish putting the fear of Noah into this man."

With every step Noah took toward their suite, he realized he'd gotten himself into a pickle with Sasha. There was no way this wasn't going to cause trouble. Ray would be furious. Noah didn't know what the Beluxor underground would think, but if that clerk kept his lip zipped, they wouldn't have to know. Noah and Maggie would take Sasha to the orphanage tomorrow, and that would be the end of it.

Sasha continued to cling to him even after they were in their suite. She held on while Maggie cleaned and disinfected her cuts.

"They don't have any antiseptics that don't burn," Maggie said.

"Reminds me of my childhood. I swear Aunt Julia always picked out the ones that would burn the most."

After Maggie finished putting bandages on the worst cuts, they returned to the sitting room, Sasha still clinging to Noah. Her hold relaxed when Maggie put out the food.

"It's all for you," Maggie explained. "You can have anything you want."

Sasha looked from Maggie to the food to Noah and back to the food. Noah took her arms from around his neck, set her on her feet and pointed her toward the food. As much as she wanted the food, she didn't let go of him.

"You'll have to sit next her to while she eats," Maggie said. "Or hold her in your lap."

"I'll sit next to her," Noah said. He had conflicting feelings about taking Sasha to an orphanage, and he hated to be conflicted. *Know what you want to do and do it.* That had been his motto for years. No confusion, no hesitation. No recriminations. *Keep your goal clearly in mind, and you'll always know what to do.* Well, he had a goal clearly in mind, but he didn't like turning a child over to an orphanage that obviously didn't care about her.

Noah sat Sasha in a chair next to the small table where Maggie had set out the food. The child didn't take her eyes off him until he placed his chair next to her and sat down. She reached out to him with one hand and to the food with the other. She was clearly ravenous, but security was obviously more important than hunger.

"It looks like you've got a friend for life," Maggie said.

"She's just scared," Noah replied. "I thought I had it bad, but it was nothing like what her life must be like."

He'd never told Maggie much about his mother or his aunt. It was something he refused to think about. Sasha's presence brought it tumbling out of the closet where he'd kept it closed up for so long.

"You never did tell me much about your childhood," Maggie said.

"I used to think there wasn't anything good to tell, but at least my aunt didn't turn me out into the street."

"Her parents didn't turn her out. They're dead."

"Well, somebody turned her out. A kid doesn't just have parents. Where are her aunts, uncles, cousins, grandparents? Hell, Maggie, could you let any of your relations go around in rags?"

"She does need some clothes."

"And you can bet that *orphanage* won't buy her any."

Sasha knew they were talking about her. She stopped eating, looked fearfully from one to the other.

"Go on," Noah said, gesturing to her food. "We're not going to throw you out." He reached into his hip pocket, withdrew his wallet and handed it to Maggie. "Buy her some decent clothes. I couldn't live with myself if I let her stay in these rags."

"How much do I spend?"

"I don't know. How much do kids' clothes cost in this country?"

"It depends on how much and what you buy."

"Get her three outfits. She can't wear the same clothes every day."

Maggie looked at him with that foolish, sentimental grin she had.

"And stop looking at me like that. Any self-respecting man would buy the kid some clothes. Hell, if we put her story on the news at home, there'd be truckloads at the door within hours."

"It's still sweet of you to spend your money on her."

It was his turn to smile. "I'll charge it to the agency. *Miscellaneous expenditures.*"

"Just see that she doesn't eat too much. I doubt she'd had too many full meals."

Once she'd taken the edge off her hunger, Sasha stopped eating. She seemed more concerned that Noah stay at her side. She kept looking at the door. Noah decided she was worried that Maggie wouldn't return, or that she would return with somebody to take the child away. She looked so small, so frightened and so alone. He wanted to reassure her. He remembered what it felt like to think you were alone in the world.

His uncle Willis hadn't been unkind, but he was too weak to stand up to his wife. They hadn't had any children because Aunt Julia hadn't wanted any. Noah never did know how Uncle Willis felt about that. He figured the poor man was too intimidated to admit even to a nephew that he disagreed with his wife.

Aunt Julia reminded him at least once a day that she didn't want him, that his mother didn't want him, that she was only putting up with him because it was her duty as a Christian not to let any of her family live in the streets. When she was feeling particularly vindictive, she used to keep a running tally of what he cost her on a chalkboard she kept in the kitchen. She tabulated meals, washing his clothes, cleaning his room (which she made him do), time she had to devote to worrying about him, his share of the electricity, hot water—the list went on. Once he heard Uncle Willis mutter that according to Aunt Julia, Noah cost them more than he made.

Noah couldn't count the times when he'd have given anything to crawl into Uncle Willis's lap like Sasha had crawled into his, to sit at the table with his small hand lost in his uncle's big paw, to lean against him when he got tired or sleepy. But Aunt Julia wouldn't allow it. She said it might make Noah think she wanted him in her house, and she never wanted him to forget that she didn't.

Maybe that's why he'd sat in that church, fighting back the panic, struggling to hold off the emotions. He knew how Sasha felt because he'd been there. Maybe that's why he'd insisted that she stay with him in the hotel, that Maggie buy clothes for her. He could never forgive his aunt, never forget what she'd done, but Sasha helped him realize that some children's lives were even worse than his had been.

Sasha crawled into his lap, put her arms around him and leaned her head against his chest. An indescribable feeling swept over him. It was like he was coming down with a fever. Then it vanished, and he realized his eyes were misting. Hell, he was turning into a sentimental old fool. Wouldn't Maggie love that! She'd rib him about it for the rest of their lives.

There was no *rest of their lives* for him and Maggie. His arms closed around Sasha, and she snuggled.

She was so tiny. Surely a five-year-old ought to be bigger. Maybe she was little because she'd never had enough to eat. That angered him. Aunt Julia complained about every morsel he put in his mouth, but she badgered him when he ate less than she thought he ought.

"I won't have people saying I don't feed you," she'd said.

Just once he wished she'd fed him because she wanted to.

He looked at Sasha. She'd gone to sleep. She was probably exhausted. Being afraid could do that. He wondered if he'd ever been that afraid.

Of course he had. He could remember crying himself to sleep because his mother didn't want him. He'd only cried in the dark—the one time he'd teared up in front of Aunt Julia, she'd called him a sissy—but he had been lonely and frightened. He prayed each night his mother could change her mind and come back for him. He wondered what Sasha prayed for. Whatever it might have been, it hadn't made her hard or cynical. She was able to reach out to the first person who was kind to her, able to go to sleep in the lap of a stranger trusting he would protect her.

Things hadn't turned out that way for him, and he realized it had been his own doing. He'd cut off his feelings. He'd never allowed himself to open up to anyone since then, to feel deeply about anything. He'd panicked at the church because he was fighting the natural feelings any normal person would have toward this child.

But even as the door to his heart began to creak open, he slammed it shut. He couldn't afford to feel any emotional attachment to this child. He had to turn her over to a state orphanage tomorrow. Then he had to forget her and complete his mission and return to New York so he could be sent out on another mission. This wasn't the first disadvantaged child he'd ever seen. He'd grown up with plenty of them.

He didn't know what it was, but something about Sasha was different. Or maybe he was different. He knew he wouldn't be able to forget her. He was relieved when Maggie came back. Contemplating his feelings was not something he enjoyed.

"There's not a lot to choose from that's attractive," she said, handing Noah a wad of paper money. "And what there is doesn't cost much."

"Then you should have bought her more clothes."

"I did. She now has enough for a week." Maggie came around where she could see Sasha curled up in his lap. "How long has she been asleep?"

"Half an hour, I guess."

"She didn't eat much."

"Maybe she's not used to big meals or maybe she didn't like it. I don't know what people in Beluxor eat."

"The same things people in other countries eat."

"Well, if she doesn't eat in the morning, we'll have to find something else."

"I expect she's just tired."

"Then we should put her to bed."

"Not until we give her a bath."

"We!"

Maggie chuckled. "Okay, not until *I* give her a bath, but you have to run the bathwater. And make sure it's not too hot."

Noah didn't feel confident doing that. He took showers. He had no idea how hot bathwater should be.

"Don't try to escape," Maggie said. "I'll need help."

He felt the panic again.

"Don't go into a decline. I just need you to hand me things. I don't want to bring her fully awake, so I'll need help giving her a bath."

Maggie seemed to know exactly what to do. With Noah handing her soap, washcloth, shampoo, towel and various items of clothing, they had Sasha bathed and in a nightgown in short order. The bathwater looked far too dirty to have come from one child.

"Throw away her old clothes," Maggie said. "They'll never come clean."

The clothes represented all that was wrong in Sasha's life.

It was easy to stuff them in a wastebasket. It would be much more difficult to change what was wrong with her life.

"Where can she sleep?" Noah asked.

"On the sofa. We can get a pillow from the bed and one of the extra blankets."

"She might roll over and fall."

"Nobody gets hurt falling out of bed in their sleep," Maggie patiently explained.

"Maybe so, but I don't want her sleeping on the sofa."

"Do you think the hotel has cots? We could set up one out here for her."

"What if she wakes up in the middle of the night and is frightened?"

"We'll be in the next room."

"I still don't like it." Noah scowled.

"Okay, we're back to the sofa. We can push a couple of chairs up to the sofa so she can't fall out."

"Maybe we should let her sleep in our bed."

"They haven't discovered queen-size beds in Beluxor. In fact, I don't think that's a full double."

"She can have my side of the bed."

"You'll sleep on the sofa?" Maggie looked at him with her eyebrows raised.

"You said I wouldn't get hurt if I fell off."

"You do have a heart, after all. It's just hidden so deep nobody ever guessed."

"If you've finished making fun of me, go turn back the covers and I'll carry her in. I wonder if the hotel has electric blankets. The bed's cold."

"Why don't you get in and warm it up for her. I can testify that you have a hot body."

"You're enjoying this, aren't you?" he asked as he lowered Sasha to the bed.

"Immensely. I've never seen you in a situation where you weren't completely in control. And I've never seen you act like a worried parent."

"I'm not acting like a parent. I'm just—"

"Acting like every father of a little girl. You're human, Noah, despite your determined efforts not to be. Relax, it's not fatal. At least it usually isn't, but you've been without a trace of humanity for so long you might go into anaphylactic shock."

"I don't like sentimentality, but I'm not allergic to it."

"You couldn't prove it by me. Now give her a kiss."

"Bite me," Noah said and stomped from the room. He went straight to the cabinet, poured himself a large Scotch and took two swallows.

"Trying to drown the little devil, are we?"

He spun around to see Maggie coming toward him with a huge, supercilious grin plastered on her face.

"I'm not trying to drown anything, but I am worried this might complicate our plan."

"How?"

"There are too many possibilities to choose just one."

"Well, pour me a glass of wine, and we can both relax. This has been a most unusual day. It's hard to believe it started in Paris."

Between flying to Beluxor and then finding Sasha, Paris seemed very far away.

"Is it always like this on your missions?" Maggie asked.

"No. I usually work alone."

"That way you don't have to put up with women and children cluttering up your plots."

"That's not what I meant." He took another swallow of his drink. Maggie seemed determined to misunderstand him, yet she was grinning all the time like she was backing him into a verbal corner and would pounce on him in a moment.

"I know exactly what you meant. But I'm beginning to wonder if *you* do."

"Don't be ridiculous. I—"

The knock on the door was unexpected. Maybe the clerk had come to see if they needed anything for Sasha. But when he opened the door, he saw two men who were obviously part of the Beluxor police force.

"We've come to inspect your rooms," one of them announced, and walked in without waiting to be invited.

Chapter Eleven

Maggie felt like a character in one of those old black-and-white movies where the secret police force their way into the hotel room of the hero to drag him off to jail and leave the shy, intimidated heroine to carry out the mission by herself.

"Who are you, and why have you forced your way into our room?" she asked in idiomatic Beluxorian, which caught the policemen by surprise.

"What are you saying?" Noah asked.

"Leave this to me," she said. "They've come expecting to bully foreigners who don't know their language." She blocked their path and asked, "What do you want?"

"You are Americans," the first man began. "We do not like foreigners in our country."

"This is also my country," Maggie said.

"You are American," the man insisted.

"I'm also Beluxorian. How else do you think I know the language?"

The second man mumbled something Maggie couldn't catch.

"You have a baby that does not belong to you."

"Who told you that?" Maggie asked.

"We have our sources."

"Your sources lie."

The second man muttered some curses, the nature of which Maggie didn't want to dwell on.

"Your papers say—"

"Our papers say we plan to take my sister's child back to America for medical attention," Maggie said. "My husband and I are spending a few days sight-seeing before we pick up the child and go back to America."

"Now it is you who lie," the policeman said. "We know you have a baby here."

"Who told you, the clerk downstairs?"

The second man cursed again.

"Your source not only lies," Maggie said, "he's also stupid. Or your friend is stupid," she said, pointing to the second man, "because he does not listen to what he is told."

Maggie had been getting closer and closer to the first policeman, talking louder and louder until her voice was raised almost to a shout. She remembered stories her grandparents had told her about the *old country*. If an accused person didn't become nearly hysterical, the police wouldn't believe anything he or she said. She hadn't had time to explain that to Noah. She hoped he would trust her.

"You lie," the policeman said, grinning in triumph. "We know you buy food. You buy clothes."

"If you know that, you also know we don't have a baby. Would I feed a baby cheese, fruit? If you ever have a baby, I hope your wife never lets you touch it. You are an idiot. Your friend is an ever bigger idiot."

They both shouted at her, but she ignored them. Instead she threw herself in front of Noah, pretending to keep him from attacking the policemen. That was exactly what he wanted to do—she could feel it.

"This is nothing but posturing," she said in an urgent whisper. "They're really hoping to get a bribe."

"Stand aside," the first man said.

Maggie refused to move. "Where is the paper that says you can search my rooms?"

"We have the right," the second man said, finally shedding the dialect Maggie didn't understand.

"You have no paper and you have no right," Maggie said. "But I have nothing to hide, so I will show you what is in the other room. Then you will go away and be stupid somewhere else." With a dramatic gesture, she waved Noah aside and marched toward the bedroom. "You will be quiet, or I will call your superior and complain."

As she had hoped, the policemen were totally unprepared for her capitulation.

"Don't stand there like dolts," she said. "Come look so you can go."

The men followed her into the bedroom.

"See, this is not a baby. It is a little girl my husband found in the street. He kept her from being run over."

"You come to Beluxor to steal children?"

"I asked the clerk downstairs where to take her, but he said the orphanage was closed."

"You cannot keep this child. You must wake her up. She must go."

"I'm so glad you've volunteered to take her home with you," Maggie said to the second man.

The man broke into agitated speech, once again speaking to his fellow policemen in a strange dialect.

"I'll collect her things," Maggie said. She pulled the filthy clothes from the trash basket where she'd thrown them. "You'll have to get your wife to wash her clothes. Tell her to boil them first. I'm certain the child has been around infected people."

Both men backed away from the clothes.

"You won't have to worry that she will eat a lot. You can even have the food we bought for her, but you've got to promise to let her sit in your lap. She's terribly afraid of something. She wouldn't let go of my husband for hours. We were relieved when she finally went to sleep. Of course, if you wake her up now, you'll have to hold her until she goes back to sleep. I imagine she'll throw a fit if you don't."

The two policemen began to back from the room.

"I'm so glad you've offered to take her with you," Maggie said, making an ineffectual attempt to hold one of them back. "I'm not sure she's trained not to wet the bed. My husband is very worried about that. I've tried to explain to him that some abandoned children have never been trained to live indoors. He'll be very relieved to have you take her with you. I don't think she will wet on you before you get her home."

The men continued backing up until they were at the door. "We were looking for a baby boy," the first man said, "not a little girl who is infected and wets herself. Only a stupid American would bother with such."

With that they both turned and left, muttering again in that strange dialect.

"What was that all about?" Noah asked.

She could tell he was very upset, and she could guess why. He'd been helpless to handle a threat to their operation, a threat she'd handled successfully without him knowing what was going on.

"They told me we couldn't keep Sasha here, so I said they could take her." Noah started to interrupt. "I said they had to boil her clothes because they probably contained some infection. I also told them she would cling to them when she was awake and that she would wet the bed."

Noah cracked a smile. "No wonder they backed out of here so fast." His grin disappeared. "You know that means we have to take her back tomorrow."

"Yes."

"It would be too dangerous to our operation to keep her with us."

"I thought that's what you'd planned to do."

"It is."

But he didn't sound happy. He frowned. She was shocked. She'd expected he'd rake her over the coals for taking over the situation without asking his permission. She also expected him to be angry that he couldn't handle a situation as well as she could, that he had failed to come up to his own standards. Instead he was so concerned about Sasha he'd forgotten about himself.

Maggie was certain this was the first time that had ever happened.

It caused her to look at him with new eyes. With the right stimulus, maybe Noah could get past his obsession with always having to be the one who solved every problem, of refusing to become emotionally involved in any situation. She didn't know what it was about Sasha that had enabled her to sneak past his guard, but the child had definitely penetrated farther into the protected area around Noah's heart than anyone else ever had. Including Maggie.

"You said they were looking for a bribe," Noah said. "Is that all they wanted?"

"They said they were looking for a baby boy."

"Dammit to hell! That means the underground already has the baby." Noah's preoccupation vanished. The *real* Noah Brant was back.

"What's wrong with that?"

"They were supposed to wait until the last minute. That way we could be back in Paris before the security forces could be deployed. Now they'll be watching every person who enters or leaves the country."

"They'd have been watching us anyway. Rich Americans don't usually come to Beluxor for their honeymoon."

"I expect they've got someone parked in the lobby right now."

"Maybe, after they've kept us under surveillance long enough to discover we're not doing anything suspicious, they'll stop watching us so closely."

"That's not how these people work. Once they suspect you of anything, they'll watch you for years."

"In that case there's nothing we can do, so stop worrying."

"I've got to come up with some emergency plans just in case."

"In case of what?"

"It's not so much making a specific plan as checking out everything around you, knowing the terrain, so to speak."

She could imagine Noah running one scenario after another through his mind. It was just the kind of thing that would fascinate him. A puzzle. Whenever he got threatened by a human situation, one that might involve some feeling, he could run a few more scenarios through his brain. After all, having to figure out how to capture a criminal or how to keep from getting killed ought to clear your head of mushy emotions.

"The only terrain I want to know anything about is the bed. I'm exhausted. If you come anywhere near me tonight, I'll turn you over to the policemen."

"You were just as much at fault."

"I know. You can threaten to turn me over to the stocky one. That ought to rid me of any romantic inclinations I might have."

"Do you have any?"

"No, so don't ask again. I'm going to get a bath. Why don't you move Sasha to the sofa while I'm in the tub? She'll be fine there."

"Are you sure it won't wake her?"

"No, but she's a kid. She'll go right back to sleep."

* * *

Maggie felt cold. The hotel must have cut the heat off during the night. Still only half awake, she moved closer to Noah's side of the bed. She'd often complained that his body was so hot it made her hot. Tonight she'd been grateful for the extra warmth. But she didn't feel any warmth. She moved closer. She kept moving until she realized the covers had been thrown back and Noah wasn't in the bed. He must be in the bathroom.

But as she lay there waiting for him to return, she remembered that no matter how much Noah drank before he went to bed, he never had to get up in the night. She ran her hand over the mattress on his side of the bed. She could feel the indentation made by the weight of his body, but the sheet wasn't warm. Whatever he was doing, he'd left the bed some time ago.

She sat up and noticed the light coming from under the door to the sitting room. Sasha must have woken up or cried out, and he'd gone to sit with her. Maggie felt guilty that she hadn't heard the child.

She got up and pulled on her robe. It was very cold in the room. She eased the door open, hoping not to disturb Sasha if Noah had just gotten her back to sleep. What she saw at first confused her. But as the true meaning sunk in, she felt stunned.

Noah sat on the edge of one of the chairs he'd pulled up to the sofa to make certain Sasha didn't roll onto the floor during the night. But it was what he was doing that surprised Maggie. He was staring at Sasha. He was just sitting there, as still as a statue, staring at the sleeping child. Maggie opened her mouth to speak, but she didn't know what to say. Would she ask him what he was doing? If Sasha was all right? Tell him it was cold and ask him to come back to bed? She didn't ask any of those questions because she suddenly knew why Noah was sitting there.

He didn't want to take Sasha to the orphanage in the morning. Having to take her back to people who would most certainly continue to neglect her was hurting him. It proved conclusively what she always suspected—the real Noah Brant had been kept well out of sight by Special Agent Brant.

Noah had a heart, and it was bleeding over the plight of this little girl, a stranger who'd clung to him as though he were her only hope.

Maggie didn't need any more proof that the real Noah Brant was a man worthy of love. But she knew Noah didn't believe it. He'd fight to keep from admitting it. He certainly wouldn't accept it from her. He was the kind of man who would have to discover something like that for himself. And even then he'd probably go right on denying it. But Maggie liked what she saw, and she made up her mind to uncover the real Noah Brant—whether he wanted to be uncovered or not.

Maggie was a pushover for a man in need, especially when he was in pain, too. She was certain there was a little boy inside Noah still crying out for all the love he never got. She was just as certain he'd never admit it. His kind of man would rather die than confess a weakness or a need. Maggie didn't see need as weakness. She was emotionally needy and saw no reason a strong man couldn't be needy, as well. The real difficulty would be to get Noah to admit it. She knew he would never be truly happy until he did.

Being careful not to make a sound, Maggie retreated into the bedroom and pulled the door closed behind her. She got into bed, but she didn't attempt to go back to sleep. She piled the pillows up behind her and sat. She had some planning to do. She needed to know the lay of the land just as thoroughly as Noah did, but not for the same purpose.

She was about to plot the downfall of Noah Brant.

"This is not a good part of town," the taxi driver said to Maggie. "Many bad things happen here."

Maggie didn't need the taxi driver to tell her that. He was

the man who'd taken them from the airport. Apparently
Noah believed in keeping up a contact once he'd established
it. He'd insisted that they couldn't take Sasha to the orphanage until this specific driver was free to take them. That
had enabled them to keep Sasha all morning. She had been
amazed at the connection that had grown up between Sasha
and Noah.

It was odd to watch. Big, gruff Noah, not knowing a thing
about children, seeming to understand what Sasha needed
before Maggie did—Maggie, who'd been dealing with children all her life. And Sasha, a neglected child who had no
reason to expect kindness from a stranger, giving Noah her
complete trust. It didn't seem to matter that they could
barely understand each other. The link was there.

Maggie had never seen anything like it.

That made it all the more difficult to take Sasha back.
She was certain Noah had spent half the night *going over
the terrain,* searching for any possible way to give this child
a better future. He'd asked if Maggie's family would consider adopting Sasha. Maggie said she would ask, but they
would still have to take Sasha back. Adoption would have
to come through the orphanage.

"This place looks like a ghetto," Noah said.

"People are poor here," the taxi driver said. "Some even
sell their children when they can."

Maggie didn't bother to translate that for Noah. He was
having enough trouble as it was. Much to her surprise, Sasha
didn't seem to be upset at all.

At least that's what she thought at first. Then she realized
the child had simply cut off all feeling. Sasha knew what
was happening, knew she couldn't do anything to change it,
so she was coping the only way she could, withdrawing
inside where no one could hurt her.

That's what Noah had done, withdrawn so far inside himself that no one could reach him. Only Sasha, a child so
like himself he must have felt he was looking into a mirror,

had been able to reach him, to pull him out of the dark recess where he'd hidden for so long. He must be reliving the pain of all those years. Maggie worried that returning Sasha to the orphanage, knowing he couldn't help her any more than he could have helped himself, would cause Noah to withdraw more, put himself out of Maggie's reach forever.

"Does she have all the clothes you bought for her?" Noah asked Maggie for the tenth time.

"I put everything in a travel bag I bought this morning."

He had carried the bag to the taxi. He knew it was there.

"How about the bandages and medicine? Are you sure she knows to keep using it until there's no risk of infection?"

"I've explained it all to her very carefully."

"I'm worried about that cut on her back. She can't see that one."

"I told her to ask someone to check it for her," Maggie assured him. "It's more of a contusion than a cut."

Maggie knew Noah's insides were in a turmoil, but he appeared calm. Sasha sat close to him, her hands tightly clutched in his, but she didn't look at him constantly as she had done in the hotel. She stared straight ahead out of glazed eyes.

Noah reached inside his coat, took out his wallet and handed it to Maggie. "She'll need some money. I don't want her to go hungry."

"Noah, you can't give her a lot of money. She probably doesn't even know what to do with it."

Noah continued to hold the wallet out to her. "Explain what it's for and how to use it."

Maggie took the wallet and withdrew a small bill.

"That's not enough."

"Too much will be a danger to her."

Noah didn't look happy, but he didn't argue. He knew enough about poor countries to realize how dangerous having money could be. Maggie showed the child the bill, explained what it was for and how to use it, but she couldn't be certain Sasha listened, much less understood. She put the bill in the wallet and handed it to Noah.

"She doesn't understand what this paper stuff is for. Do you have any coins?"

"That won't be enough."

"It's better than nothing."

Sasha's eyes lit up when Maggie gave her the coins. She stared at them for the remainder of the journey. She even released Noah's hand long enough to inspect them one by one. But when the taxi pulled up in front of the orphanage, she lost interest in the money. She showed no reaction when Maggie took the coins from her and put them in the bag with her clothes. She got out of the taxi without being told. Noah reached for her hand, not she for his. She didn't appear aware of Maggie's presence. She'd withdrawn again.

In effect, she'd disappeared.

Despite the run-down look of the building and the unprepossessing appearance of the children, Maggie felt a little bit reassured by the way a motherly-looking matron fussed over Sasha. She'd been worried when the child didn't appear at supper. She even had the police looking for her all night. She was relieved to find her safe but amazed that an American couple would take such an interest in an orphan. Maggie explained that her family came from Beluxor and that they were in the country to take her cousin's baby to the United States for medical treatment. She also explained about the accident and that the matron should check Sasha's cuts and bruises to make sure they didn't become infected.

"He seems very attached to her," the matron said of Noah. Though Sasha hardly seemed aware of her surroundings, Noah still held her hand, still pulled her against him as though protecting her.

"He pulled her out of the path of the truck," Maggie explained. "I think he feels responsible for her now."

The matron's smile was careworn and wistful. "I wish more people felt responsible for these children, but there are so many of them."

Maggie didn't think she could endure a discussion of the plight of the orphans. She was having enough trouble leaving Sasha. She didn't know as much about middle European countries as Noah, but she knew Beluxor, and she was certain the children suffered privation. The orphanage building was evidence of that.

"Tell her Sasha's very young," Noah said. "She needs to give her special attention every day."

Maggie relayed Noah's message, but they both knew it was useless. There were too many children, too few adults, too little money and too much apathy. Finally they'd said all there was to say, and it was time to leave. Noah knelt in front of Sasha.

"I've asked them to take very special care of you," he said to the child. "They're to make sure you get enough to eat, a decent bed and clean clothes. If anything happens to you, *anything,* you come back to the hotel. I'll—"

"Noah, you can't promise that. Even if she could understand what you're saying, it wouldn't be fair."

"You come back to the hotel," he said. "I'll be there."

Then, much to Maggie's surprise, he gave Sasha a quick hug before standing up and leaving the building without another word.

"He's fond of the child," the matron said.

"Yes," Maggie replied, disturbed over the extend of Noah's attachment to Sasha, "I'm afraid he is."

It had been a long time since Maggie had spent a more miserable day. Noah had been about as good company as a bear with a sore nose. He growled at her regardless of what she said or did, or he ignored her. Nothing she did was right, and nothing they did was fine with him. She was certain he had no idea where they had been or what they'd done. She was equally certain he had no idea what he'd eaten. Having exhausted every possible means of taking his mind off Sasha, they had gone back to their hotel room. Noah went straight to the Scotch and poured himself a stiff drink. Then he put it down and ignored it as he stared out the window.

Maggie decided to take a bath.

"Do you think she's all right?" Noah asked when Maggie returned to the sitting room. He hadn't moved from the window. Nor had he touched his drink.

"I don't know," Maggie said, deciding the only way to deal with this was to be perfectly candid. "I don't imagine her situation is any better than it was before."

"I'll go see her tomorrow."

"I don't think that's a good idea."

"I've got to make sure she's all right."

"Noah, we're only going to be here a few days. It's unfair to let her think she can depend on you. There won't be anybody—"

"Did you see the difference in her? She was bright and alive when she was here. When I left her, she looked like a wooden doll."

"I'm sure it's only a defense mechanism, a way to—"

He spun around to face her. "I know what it is because I did it my whole life." He crossed the room in five steps. "She's doing exactly what makes you hate me."

"I don't hate you, Noah."

"You hate what I became, what I did to myself. I'm going back there first thing in the morning, and if anybody's laid one finger on that child I'll..."

He left the sentence unfinished, but Maggie had a much too vivid image of the fury Noah would unleash if he found anyone had harmed Sasha.

"Even if you don't consider the harm it would do to Sasha, getting yourself thrown in jail will seriously jeopardize your mission."

Noah grabbed Maggie by the shoulders so hard it hurt.

"What's wrong with you? How can you think of that child and not have to know what's happening to her?" He released Maggie, drove one balled fist into his palm. "God, I hate leaving her there."

"What could you have done?"

"I don't know, but there must be something."

"I'd like to help Sasha, too, but we can't. Our hands are tied. They won't give her quite enough food or try very hard to see she has a warm bed, but I'm sure she'll be all right. She'll survive."

"Is that all you want for her, to survive? I had a warm bed and all the food I could eat, but I didn't survive. I got left on the cutting room floor of my childhood. That's where you'll find the Noah Brant you're looking for."

Maggie realized that for the first time since she'd known him, Noah had faced his early life and what it had done to him. The real Noah Brant had finally come out of hiding.

"My mother didn't want me, and my aunt hated me. I think she only fed and clothed me for fear of what the neighbors would say, but she made it clear she begrudged every minute, every penny, even the slightest effort I caused her. My mother didn't know which of the men she slept with was my father, or she didn't care enough to try to figure it out. Being a bastard was just about the worst possible sin in my aunt's eyes. When I quit school and went on the street, she had the satisfaction of knowing that even though she'd done her best, I'd turned out to be the stupid, ambitionless, drug-taking delinquent she'd always known I'd be."

"She should be proud of how you turned out."

"She doesn't know. She said she never wanted to hear from me again. After my uncle died, I had no reason not to honor her wish. That's how I know what Sasha's doing. You pull inside yourself, hoping that people don't mean it but telling yourself you wouldn't care if they do. It's hard at first. You keep hoping something will change, that you're wrong, that someone will care for you, but you soon learn nothing's going to change. After that it's easy to stay detached. Then one day you wake up and discover you've forgotten how to do anything else. In my case, there was nothing to forget. I never learned in the first place.''

Maggie didn't know what she could say to comfort him. She couldn't convince him that Sasha would be all right because he knew better. He couldn't ease his pain by promising he'd do something tomorrow because he knew anything he did could disrupt the mission. His boss would tell him they couldn't sacrifice a whole country for a single child. And she knew she couldn't change the past.

The scars of his childhood were permanent and ineradicable.

"There's nothing more you can do about it tonight," Maggie said. "You need to get some rest. Maybe we can think of something tomorrow."

He looked at her, and she saw something in his expression she'd never seen before. Helplessness. Ever since she had known him, he'd always been in control, always confident he could do anything required. She saw no trace of that Noah now.

"You know there's nothing we can do."

"You're tired now, but I've never known a time when you couldn't come up with some solution."

"I never faced a situation like this."

"You'll manage. Now I'm going to bed. Don't wait too long. I might be asleep."

What was she doing? She'd practically issued him an invitation to make love to her. What would she do if he accepted?

Chapter Twelve

Maggie had just gotten into bed when Noah entered the bedroom.

"Did you mean what I think you meant?" he asked.

Leave it to Noah to go straight to the heart of the issue. He never had developed subtlety. She didn't know what she meant. She wasn't sure she could stick to her guns if it meant losing Noah.

"You know I'll always want you. That old song about black magic having me in its spell is probably true in my case, but I wasn't thinking of our physical relationship. When I'm upset or worried, I find it comforting to be with someone, to be able to touch them, hold hands, even be held in their arms. You probably never felt like that, but that's what I was offering."

Noah didn't answer. She couldn't decide whether he was stunned she would think he would want such a relationship or convinced she had lost her mind to offer it to him. Real men didn't cry. They didn't lean on women's shoulders in times of trouble, either. The way they acted you'd think they thought there was some secret chemical in a woman's body that would leap out and kill off their testosterone, leaving them sniveling wimps for the rest of their lives.

But she knew Noah had another problem that went just as deep. He couldn't admit that he needed anyone. Nor could he admit that he loved anyone.

Without speaking, Noah set his drink down—still untouched, as far as she could tell—and began to undress. He didn't stop until he was nude.

"Did you lock the door?"

She sounded like a wife.

He got into the bed. "I always lock the door when I'm in a hostile country."

She'd never thought of it like that. This was her first experience at being a special agent.

"Do you think Ray could increase your expense account enough for you to buy some pajamas?"

"I've always slept nude."

"That was when we were living together."

"And making love every night."

"That, too."

"And you don't want to make love to me tonight."

"Don't put words in my mouth, and don't ask questions like that. You know as well as I do that very often you want to do the very thing we know we can't."

"Like go back and take Sasha out of that prison."

He piled the pillows behind him and sat up in bed. Then he reached out, put his arm around Maggie and pulled her to him. She doubted he was aware of what he'd done. It was a reflex with him to take care of people. It had nothing to do with posturing or ego building. He did it because he couldn't *not* do it. Since he'd never been cared for or protected, she wondered why. That would make most people bitter and angry, wanting to take it out on the world. Instead

Noah took it out on himself by cutting himself off from loving the very people he wanted to protect.

"I guess people wouldn't say she was a pretty child," Noah said, "but I loved to see her eyes when she looked at me. They were huge and gray like a squirrel's fur. Her hair could be a little thicker. Her skin looks so white and thin you can see the blood vessels through it."

Noah's arms tightened around her, but rather than pull her to him, he leaned over until his cheek rested atop her head. That had never happened before. Noah had always insisted that she lean on him.

Noah chuckled without humor. "Aunt Julia would say Sasha must have some blue blood in her. My aunt had thin skin with blue veins. I don't." He slid down in the bed until he was almost lying at her side. "I can't believe no one has adopted her. She'd make some man proud to be her father. Even if he wasn't much of a man, he'd always be a hero in her eyes."

Maggie put her arms around Noah and let him talk. For probably the first time in his life he was allowing himself to talk of the aching need that must always have been inside him. He talked about Sasha, but he talked about himself, as well. She knew he'd only skimmed the surface, but she had finally seen the proof of what she'd suspected all along. Noah Brant wanted to love and be loved as much as she did. She just had to find a way to make him realize it.

"Maybe I could come back after I finish this job," Noah said.

"What for?"

"To get Sasha. There must be some way to adopt her, some government agency I can apply to. Poor countries are always trying to get rid of their orphans."

"Not even backward eastern European countries let single men adopt little girls. Besides, you're gone too much to be a single parent." She couldn't believe he had even considered the possibility of taking Sasha to the United States. Talk about complications.

"I know I couldn't adopt her, but there are thousands of couples who'd be delighted to have a child like Sasha."

He described the kind of life he would want for Sasha. She finally decided that nothing short of being crowned Miss America would be enough. Then he fell silent. She doubted he was aware of it, but the longer he remained silent, the tighter he held her, the closer he moved, until they were nestled in the bed like an old married couple.

Maggie thought she was going to cry. Noah had never been in the bed with her without being ready for action. He'd never wanted to hold her for more than a few minutes—certainly never in silence—and he'd never been content to lie still. Everything about their previous time together had been about their bodies, their lust for each other, the necessity for a physical expression of their need.

For the first time Maggie felt she'd made direct contact with Noah's spirit, that some door inside him had opened up and let her in. Or let him out. Even his kisses were different. He kissed the top of her head. *The top of her head!* The old Noah would never have wasted a kiss like that. He used to start with her mouth then head straight for her breasts, taking just long enough to make sure her temperature was rising as rapidly as his. Since she had a trigger response to his naked body, that was never very long.

Even now she felt so thoroughly aroused it was difficult to keep her hands to herself. She'd never seen this side of Noah. And no matter how strong and insistent her carnal nature, she was determined she wouldn't be the one to break the mood. She knew Noah wanted to make love to her. That would never change. But there was something very different about tonight. It wasn't love, but it wasn't exactly sex, either. If he came to her, he'd come to her for comfort, and

Noah had never done that before. She doubted he knew what he was doing, but it was enough that she did. He couldn't have done anything more guaranteed to make her fall in love with him. The beauty of it was he didn't even know it.

He kissed her on the lips. Then, rather than kiss her again, he settled back, still holding her tight.

"You always wanted kids, didn't you?" he asked.

"Yes."

He kissed her gently again.

"I never did. I couldn't understand how anyone would want to put up with the hassle."

"Not all kids are a hassle."

"I was. Were you?"

"Not at first."

"What changed?"

"I finally realized my father would never give me the love I wanted, that he would use my love for him to force me to do what he wanted."

"Did I ever do that to you?"

He pulled her close, kissed her on each eyelid. "You never tried to change me. I used to think you did, but I know better now. You were the best friend I ever had."

Maggie wasn't certain how she felt about that. She had always wanted to be Noah's friend, had tried hard to make him feel she was his friend when they were together, but any relationship with him would have a very strong physical side. She could be close to every other attractive man she knew without developing any physical awareness of him. Let her get within ten feet of Noah, and her sensual antennae went on full alert.

She smiled when she felt his body begin to swell. She wanted to change some things, but other things were perfect just the way they were. And everything about making love to Noah was perfect. Now that she felt he wanted to make love to her, not just her body, it was better than perfect.

* * *

Maggie woke to the sound of a ringing phone. She didn't consider getting up to answer it. Noah would be up. He would answer it.

The ringing stopped.

She rolled over, unwilling to get out of bed, unwilling to shed the last of the magic of their night of love. She expected Noah would argue with her, but that's how she felt about it. That's how she thought *he* felt about it, despite anything he might say. He'd been so gentle. Even when she'd become impatient, his touch never lost its gentleness. Nor had he rolled over and gone to sleep afterward. He'd continued to hold her, to caress her body, to tease and tantalize her until she had practically assaulted him. He'd laughed, called her his sex maniac, swore he was only trying to show her how much he liked being with her.

He'd laughed when she said he could damned well show her in more ways than one.

She blushed, remembering her own aggressiveness. At the same time she felt a chill of apprehension. She was very close to falling in love with Noah again. She didn't think she could stop herself now that she knew he had the ability to love if he'd just let himself. She knew people did atypical things during times of stress. In a way it was like a summer romance. For a short time, all rules were suspended.

Then the summer ended and you reverted to your old self.

She didn't know if she could stand that. She'd always known she'd taken this assignment in part to see if she was truly over Noah. Well, she had her answer. She was not over Noah and never would be. And he wasn't over her. The question about his ability to love remained, but she'd seen a crack in the hard shell he'd built around his heart, and she wanted to see if she could crack it completely.

And not just for herself. She wanted a different future for Noah. He deserved more out of life than good sex and a dangerous job. He was a fine, honorable man who could make a wonderful husband and father. More important, he would have a chance to grow into the wonderful human being he truly was rather than turn into a shriveled piece of lemon peel, like his aunt.

She wondered if he'd ever be able to forget what his aunt did to him. Psychologists said you needed closure for something like that, but how did you get closure when the person you needed to close with didn't want to see you? Who was she to talk? Her father was still alive, and she hadn't come to closure with him. She'd have to—

The bedroom door opened. "They've called. We're to pick up the baby in three hours at a public park."

Maggie hadn't needed the words to know Noah had reverted to the automaton who lived for his job. He looked different. There was none of the softness, the uncertainty, the openness of last night. He was Noah Brant, secret agent, and nothing else mattered.

She didn't know whether to cry or heave a sigh of relief. She wouldn't have her heart torn out again, but neither would she know the sweetness of Noah's love. Even as she was ready to give up, something inside wouldn't let her. Noah had cracked. It would be her fault if she didn't find a way to keep that crack from closing again.

"We need to pack," Noah said. "We'll leave as soon as we get the child."

"Won't they be looking at airports for a couple with a child who doesn't belong to them?"

"Yes, but we'll have papers to prove the child is who we say he is."

"Where will you get them?"

"The underground will provide them."

He pulled their suitcases from the top shelf of the narrow closet. "Even if we can't leave the country immediately, we have to change hotels. We're being watched. I went down about four o'clock. The same man is sitting in the lobby. He was asleep, but that doesn't mean everyone watching us is."

Maggie threw back the covers and got out of bed. She

would have to pick up the pieces of her life some other time.

Noah went into the bathroom and began tossing things into his overnight bag. Maggie wondered if all men packed by throwing their stuff together the same way they tossed junk into a trash can. She heard a knock at the door. It was so soft Noah wouldn't have heard it in the bathroom. She probably wouldn't have heard it, either, if she hadn't gone into the sitting room to look for her shoes.

"I'll get it," she said, figuring Noah had ordered breakfast for her and a pot of coffee for himself.

She opened the door and was shocked to see Sasha standing there in old, worn, dirty clothes. "What happened?" Maggie asked. "What are you doing here?"

In a halting voice Sasha told her that the other kids had taken her money and clothes and told her to go back to the rich Americans for more.

"If that's the concierge," Noah called from the bathroom, "tell her we need breakfast in a hurry."

"It's not the concierge," Maggie said. "It's Sasha."

Noah was at her side almost before she could take a breath. He knelt in front of Sasha and held out his arms. "What did they do to you? Tell me who did it, and I'll…"

He didn't finished the sentence. Sasha's face crumpled from its stoic mask, and she threw her arms around his neck and started to cry. Noah held her close, alternating between murmuring soothing sounds and threatening every person inside the orphanage. Not once did he loosen his grip on Sasha.

"You'd better bring her inside," Maggie said.

Noah picked up the child, walked to the sofa, sat down and cradled Sasha in his lap. She hugged him close, still crying. "What happened?" he asked Maggie.

"The other kids took everything and sent her back to the *rich Americans* for more."

"Didn't the matron try to stop them?"

"I didn't have a chance to ask her."

"Ask her now."

Maggie did. "The woman we met only works there part-time. It seems the other people in charge of the children thought Sasha should share."

Noah's expletives made it clear he hadn't intended Sasha to have to give up anything he'd given her, not even to children who might have a greater need.

The fierceness with which Noah cradled Sasha caused Maggie to tumble the rest of the way to being helplessly in love. She knew he couldn't see that he had a great need for love as well as a great capacity for giving it. He'd always been afraid if he opened up to love he would be hurt again, the way he was by his mother and aunt. But Sasha had brought his need out into the open. Maggie was certain he would never again be able to deny it so completely.

At the same time she felt a terrible sadness. Against all odds, Noah loved this child. No matter what happened to Sasha, even if she were adopted by a wealthy family who loved her as much as he did, he would always be haunted by her memory. He would always hurt for her, want to know what was happening to her, want to be part of her life. Maggie wondered if knowing he couldn't keep her would make any difference. She didn't think so. For the first time in his life, Noah had bumped up against something that was stronger than he was. Losing this child would break his heart almost as painfully as his mother and aunt had done.

"We need to get her some more medicine and new clothes," Noah said to Maggie. "Take the money out of my wallet."

"What's the point? The kids at the orphanage will just take everything again."

"She's not going back to the orphanage," Noah said in a voice she'd learned long ago meant his mind was made up and couldn't be changed. "She's coming with us."

* * *

Noah refused to think of the consequences of what he'd done. He knew he was asking for trouble, that he was breaking his own rule of not changing plans after they were set, but he couldn't take Sasha back to the orphanage. He didn't know what he could do for her, but anything was better than the orphanage.

"Where is this park?" Maggie asked their usual driver.

"On the edge of town," he replied. "It is not a safe place."

Noah didn't seem surprised. "I expected it would be some out-of-the-way place."

"Won't we be even more conspicuous?" Maggie asked.

"I would have chosen the busiest part of the most public park, sidewalk or train station in the city, but I don't think this underground network has much experience."

"I would prefer to think they were experts who could slip a tank through a mail slot."

Noah laughed. She didn't know why. She didn't find anything funny about the situation.

"Underground agents are amateurs, just like you. They're only doing this because of their strong beliefs."

"But why are you doing this?"

Noah shifted Sasha in his lap. She was clean again—Maggie had given her a bath and dressed her in some new clothes.

"The government has been trying to shut up the leader of the opposition for years, but not even prison has broken Grohol's spirit or diminished his popularity. When his wife had a baby, the government kidnapped the baby and said they wouldn't return it until Grohol left the country. Fortunately for us, one of the government agents was a sympathizer who turned the baby over to the underground. Grohol's wife has already left the country. Once his baby is safe, he'll feel free to oppose the government again."

"So Alexi's not really ill. You didn't need me after all."

"We did need you. The message we got said he was sick

and they wanted someone who could make sure he got well. Our government decided to help.''

''You don't know what's wrong with Alexi?''

Noah shook his head. ''It's probably some ordinary childhood disease.''

Maggie doubted that. Children got childhood diseases—infants didn't. ''How are we supposed to make contact?'' she asked.

''We're to park the car by the statue of a some local saint then take a path that skirts a small lake. They will contact us.''

Maggie knew she wasn't used to undercover work, but this seemed rather slipshod to her. She had never taken seriously the movie and TV ploys of wearing a pink rose or carrying a week-old edition of the *New York Times*. And this was the twenty-first century. It was dead simple to send pictures by the Internet. Even she could do it. She was surprised Noah didn't object to such amateurish methods.

The taxi stopped by the statue of a thoroughly depressed-looking saint, and they got out. Maggie imagined they looked a lot like a typical family, mother and father walking in the park with their daughter. Only the daughter had eyes for no one but Noah. Maggie could see nothing wrong in that.

The park was deserted, but that was to be expected on the morning of a workday. Everything around her showed signs of neglect, the flower beds overgrown with weeds, the walkways cracked, with grass growing through the broken and uneven pavement, large pieces of lawn allowed to revert to meadows of tall grass and weeds. Yet there was a kind of wild beauty, a lush greenness and a quiet solitude that Maggie found appealing. If she had to live in Beluxor, she would come here often.

But the picture that appealed most to her was Noah walking beside the lake, holding hands with a smiling Sasha, looking very much like a doting father. She'd never suspected his need for love was so profound, his capacity so great. This orphaned child, an average-looking waif, had slipped past his defenses and gone straight to his heart. And whether Noah knew it or not, all his resistance had promptly collapsed.

And she had fallen in love with him all over again.

Which was a stupid thing to do. Just because Sasha had been able to penetrate Noah's shell didn't mean Maggie could. Nor did it mean the new Noah would survive the return to New York, to his old job, and the loss of Sasha. He was likely to become even more cynical. She nearly smiled when she realized she'd already confronted that possibility and made up her mind she was going to save Noah from himself.

The classic mistake of a woman in love.

Well, she didn't want to change him—merely liberate him. Nor was she certain she wanted to marry him. For one thing, he'd never shown any interest in marriage. For another, her one attempt at matrimony had been a disaster. Maybe neither of them was suited for the house with a white picket fence and two-point-four kids.

She saw the man long before he approached them. He was sitting on a bench reading a newspaper. Not exactly imaginative. He didn't appear to notice them until they were directly between him and the lake.

"Noah Brant?" he asked with a heavy accent.

"Where's the baby?" Noah asked.

The man held up the newspaper as though showing Noah something of interest. "This is just a trial run," the man said, shaking the newspaper like he was arguing a point. "We had to see if the police are following you."

"I haven't seen anyone," Noah replied.

"The taxi driver?"

"He's a friend."

"What about this child?"

"She's an orphan."

"Good cover for today, but get rid of her by tomorrow. The pickup is at the airport. We'll have the tickets along with the baby."

"She goes with us."

"She can't. She has no papers."

"Then get her some."

"I can't."

"Then find someone who can."

"This could jeopardize the whole operation."

"She goes or nobody goes."

Maggie couldn't believe her ears. Noah putting a human being ahead of his work! This wasn't the man she'd lived with for two years. It was hard to believe that Noah could change so quickly, but she had the proof right in front of her.

Maybe he'd wanted to change all along. Maybe he'd just needed the proper stimulus. She wondered if he realized his life would never be the same after this.

"Your government said nothing about a kid," the man said.

"They didn't know," Noah replied.

"We should have accepted Germany's help."

"You still can."

The agent was growing more agitated. Anyone watching would have had no doubt he was arguing with Noah. If the argument lasted much longer, the newspaper would be in shreds.

"We can't, you imbecile. We've already turned them down. You've ruined everything."

"Get some papers for her and everything will be fine. Her name's Sasha and she's five years old. You can say anything you think will get her through customs."

The man launched into a loud and pungent denunciation of arrogant Americans and Noah Brant in particular, but since he'd momentarily forgotten his English, Noah had no idea what he was saying. Maggie didn't intend to tell him.

"I'd better be going," Noah said. "With all this shouting, you're bound to attract attention. What time at the airport?"

"How do I know? You can't take that child."

"What time?"

"Twelve-thirty."

"And you'll have papers for Sasha?"

The man shouted and gesticulated some more. "I will do what I can," he said before turning and stomping off into a thick growth of trees.

"What are you going to do with Sasha when you get her to New York?" Maggie asked as they resumed their walk.

"I don't know," Noah said, "but I can't leave her here."

Maggie decided she wasn't cut out to be a secret agent. She'd hardly slept a wink all night. She thought the secret-agent business was the cause of her insomnia, but she couldn't be sure. They had gone back to the hotel. Noah had explained they'd taken their luggage with them because they feared it might be stolen. The clerk didn't seem surprised. Maggie assumed theft from hotel rooms wasn't unusual in Beluxor. It was to her. She didn't like knowing people could enter her room at will.

Then there was the triangle she'd become an integral part of—Noah, herself and Sasha. She'd served as translator when Noah told Sasha all about what her life would be like in America. Sasha appeared short on enthusiasm, but Noah had enough for both of them. Maggie had refrained from questioning him. She knew there'd be time for that later. And people anxious to do it. Ray would be at the top of the list.

Sasha had gone to bed on the couch, and Noah had gotten up at least three times to check on her. Even though Maggie welcomed the change in Noah, loved every minute of it, she kept waiting for him to give a start like he was coming out of a trance and go back to being his old self.

But he hadn't. He didn't act like he was on a serious

mission. Not once did he suggest that they go over emergency plans or that she had to practice some violent form of self-defense. They could very well have been a family on vacation.

Only they were in a foreign country, they were planning to spirit an orphan out of the country, and they were going to do the same with the infant son of the leading political dissident. Her entire life had turned into an otherworld experience. And nothing was more out of this world than the wedding ring she wore on her left hand. It had felt strange from the first, and she kept telling herself it didn't mean anything. It was just part of her disguise. But that didn't work any more. It had come to stand for everything she didn't have.

And everything she feared she would *never* have.

She might fear she was too independent to live with a strong man, but that didn't mean she didn't want exactly that. She might be certain her relationship with Noah would never evolve enough to allow her to consider marrying him, but that didn't mean she didn't want that, too. She had no place in her life for an orphan child who adored the one man Maggie couldn't live with, but that didn't mean she didn't want Sasha. She couldn't imagine being happily married to a man who would regularly take off on covert operations in hostile countries—his destination unknown and his safety impossible to predict—but she couldn't imagine being married to anyone else.

She fingered the ring, turning it around her finger before pulling it off. Was her life, her chance for happiness an equally easy choice—put the ring on if she wanted Noah and Sasha, take it off if she didn't? Sometimes she felt it was. Noah had offered himself and Sasha. All she had to do was accept him, to slide the ring on her finger. Three years ago she wouldn't have thought it was possible. Even after her divorce and her realization she was equally responsible for the break up with Noah, she still wouldn't have thought it was possible. But now she did.

Noah had changed. She had changed. She knew her only chance for happiness lay with Noah. She intended to reach for it. It wouldn't be easy. Noah was a stubborn man. It wouldn't be easy for him, either. She had very high expectations and a low tolerance for compromise. But if Noah could change, so could she. He needed her even though he didn't know it yet. She was the only woman who could make him whole.

She slipped the ring back on her finger.

"Are you nervous?" Noah asked. They were on their way to the airport to pick up Alexi Grohol, the baby whom greed had turned into a political pawn.

"I have butterflies in my stomach, if that's what you're asking."

"There's no need. Everything's under control."

"We're kidnapping an orphan and stealing a political hostage, and you say everything's under control."

"You can't play this game by ordinary rules."

Maybe that's what was wrong. They were playing a game, and she didn't like any of the rules.

"If I ever wondered why I gave up wanting to be a special agent, I don't any longer. I can't wait to get back to New York and my own apartment."

Noah's surprise was unmistakable.

"What did you expect me to do?"

"I thought—"

He didn't finish his sentence. "What did you think?"

He didn't answer.

"Let me guess. You thought that since we'd made love the last few nights, we would go on doing it once we got back to New York."

He didn't answer, but he didn't deny it.

"You know we've never been able to keep our hands off

each other. You also know I was in love with you, but we couldn't make it work. What has changed now that makes you think it would be any different?''

She knew what had changed. She didn't know if he did.

Chapter Thirteen

"Everything has changed," Noah said.

He had assumed Maggie knew what he was feeling because she'd always been so attuned to what was going on with him, sometimes far more than he wanted. It was like she had X-ray vision and could see inside him. He'd never liked that. Now he wished she still did it. Maybe being apart for so long had dulled her perception.

"Given our present circumstances, I think you need to be a little more specific."

"I wasn't talking about now."

"I think you have to. Start with Sasha. What do you intend to do about her when you get to New York?"

"I don't know." He knew what he *wanted* to do, but it was impossible.

"Do you plan to put her up for adoption?"

"No."

"Then what?"

"I want to raise her myself."

There, he'd said it, and it sounded just as crazy as it had in his thoughts. He had no business even thinking about keeping a child. He couldn't leave her at home while he went off on one of his missions. She was practically a baby. Even worse, he couldn't talk to her without Maggie's help.

"How do you propose to do that?" Maggie asked.

"I don't know, but there has to be a way. People adopt kids from foreign countries all the time."

"Adopt, yes. Kidnap, no."

"I'll find a way." And he would. He wasn't about to let Sasha end up in an American orphanage or be handed over to strangers. "I was hoping you would help."

"How?"

He'd assumed she'd jump at the chance to help with Sasha, but she didn't sound enthusiastic. She looked about as happy as Ray when Noah turned down the desk job.

"I was hoping you could move in with us," he said, hurrying ahead before she could flatly refuse. "I don't know anything about children. And I'm gone all the time. Besides, I can't understand half of what she says unless you translate for me."

"You haven't forgotten that I work, have you?"

"I'll hire a baby-sitter."

"You realize what you're talking about is only a temporary solution."

"Yes." He hoped somehow to talk Maggie into staying. He'd realized over the last couple of days that she was more important to him than he cared to admit. It wasn't just making love to Maggie. She was different. Softer, more understanding, more accepting. He didn't know if she appeared more understanding because she wasn't listening, more accepting because she didn't care. That was possible. She'd been the one who walked out. She'd also been the one who insisted she didn't feel anything for him except lust.

Lust. Such an unattractive word for something that was really quite wonderful. Lust was beautiful. Lust felt mar-

velous. Lust put spice and vigor into life. People were fools
to talk about it like it was something to be ashamed of. He
couldn't imagine life without lust. He'd rather be dead. He
would be dead.

But lust wasn't everything anymore. He'd once thought
it was, hadn't believed there was anything else in life worth
feeling, but he had been wrong. There was more. He wasn't
sure what it was because he'd only begun to sense its presence, admit his need. It was virgin ground for him, and he
felt very unsure of himself.

Hell, admit it! He was scared.

"I can understand how you feel about Sasha," Maggie
said. "I don't understand why you of all people are feeling
it, but I do understand."

"You sound like you think I don't like children."

"You told me that more than once, but it's not the point.
There probably isn't a single person in Beluxor who cares
what happens to Sasha, but you just can't take a child in
like you could a stray kitten. There are laws in both countries that won't let you."

"You can adopt her. You're a woman. They'll let you."

"Noah, I have a life of my own. I—"

"It won't be forever, just until I figure something out."

"It won't even last that long. They won't let her through
customs."

"I'll cable Ray as soon as we get to Paris."

"She'll need a visa to get into France."

He knew that. But he'd never tried to adopt a child before.
He wasn't certain what he could do, but he refused to take
Sasha to the orphanage. They were coming to the airport.
He would worry about Sasha after they picked up the baby.

He told the cab driver to wait. The man smiled, lit a
cigarette and settled back.

It didn't take Noah long to decide the airport wasn't a
good place to hide. It was impossible to get lost in the
crowd—there wasn't one. He didn't know when the airport

was busiest, but he'd assumed the underground had chosen the busiest time as the best time to hand over the baby. Either nobody flew into or out of Beluxor, or the underground was operating on the same theory that had caused them to use a deserted park for a rendezvous. If there was nobody around, nobody could see them.

"We'd have been less conspicuous in the hotel," Maggie said.

"I told you the underground wasn't very experienced."

"You'd at least think they would have some common sense. Talk about making it easy for the police to find you."

"I don't see any police. Maybe that's why they chose the airport."

But he didn't believe it. His gut had tied itself into a tight knot, and that was a bad sign. His instincts were never wrong. This handover wasn't going to go down as planned. They would have to abort and start all over again. He cursed under his breath.

Sasha clung to him. He didn't know what instinct prompted it, but he leaned down and picked her up. She immediately wrapped her arms around his neck. When she pressed her cheek hard against his, he felt his insides turn to mush. He had no feelings for the baby they were supposed to pick up—Alexi was no more than an object to him—but his feelings for Sasha had been real and intense from the first. He didn't intend to waste time rummaging through his past trying to decide if he saw himself in her or if he was trying to protect her from what happened to him. Some way, somehow, he was going to keep her.

He involuntarily gave her a squeeze. She hugged him back, and he thought he was going to embarrass himself by crying. He had to get a grip or he'd screw up this whole operation.

"How are they supposed to contact us this time?" Maggie asked.

"There was supposed to be a skycap to help us with our

luggage,'' Noah said. They had loaded their luggage on a cart, which Maggie pushed along the corridor.

"What do we do if they don't show up on time?"

"We wait. Our flight doesn't leave for more than an hour."

They found an inconspicuous corner. The chairs were few, made of wood and looked very uncomfortable, but there was no one else in their corner of the airport.

For the next several minutes, nothing happened. No one showed any interest in them, not even two policemen who hurried toward the door that led to the planes. The Beluxor airport didn't have those metal tunnels that rolled out to meet the plane and allow the passengers to disembark in comfort regardless of rain or cold.

Then, quite unexpectedly, passengers began to gather. In moments the airport was filled with milling masses of people who were ominously quiet. It made Noah think of a silent movie, all action and emotion but no sound.

"What's happening?" Maggie asked.

"I would guess that the only planes of the day are coming in and going out at the same time."

"Maybe this wasn't such a bad idea after all."

But the sudden activity didn't unravel the knot in Noah's stomach. Something was wrong. Seeing nearly a half dozen policemen hurry toward the exits didn't reassure him.

The seats all around them had been taken as soon as the crowd began to gather. Most were men who appeared to be traveling alone. They buried themselves in newspapers or occupied their time with laptops and cell phones. Even in Beluxor, technology had invaded the airports. Sasha stood on the chair next to Noah, her arms still around his neck.

The man on the other side of Noah got up, and his seat was immediately taken by a man with a newspaper. It must have been local. It was printed in a script Noah found nearly impossible to read.

"Have your wife take the little girl to the bathroom," the man behind the newspaper whispered in a heavy accent.

"Where is the baby?" Noah asked.

"Your wife must take the little girl to the bathroom," the man repeated in the same urgent whisper.

"Do you have the papers for the child?"

"They're wrapped up in the baby's clothes," the man said. "Your wife will get them when she takes the baby."

More policemen hurried by and disappeared through the exit doors.

"What is going on?" Noah asked. "Why all the policemen?"

"They're detaining all passengers with babies," the man said. "You can't leave by plane. You must go through the mountains."

Noah had brought several maps, which he'd studied carefully before leaving New York, but that had been merely a precaution, part of his being prepared for every contingency. He had never expected to have to use them. "How do I know which mountain passes are safe?"

"There are names of contacts with the papers. They will see you safely out of the country. Tell your wife to hurry. When the police don't find anybody trying to get a baby on one of the planes, they'll start checking everybody in the airport. After that they'll set up roadblocks around the city. You must be gone before then."

Noah turned to Maggie. "You're to take Sasha to the bathroom. Someone will meet you there and give you the baby."

"How will I know her?"

"You won't. She'll have to know you."

"What am I supposed to do after I get the baby?"

"Head back to the taxi. We can't leave today. All those police we saw are checking every passenger."

"Are they looking for you?"

"No. They're stopping anybody with a baby."

Noah didn't know how Maggie was going to take the change in plans and the extra danger, but she didn't appear ready to panic. She spoke softly to Sasha. The child's grip on Noah tightened, but Maggie gently removed her arms from around his neck. Noah couldn't understand all she was saying, but he did get the part about having to go to the bathroom before getting on the plane. Sasha shook her head, but Maggie insisted.

"What are you going to do?" Maggie asked as she lifted Sasha down and prepared to stand.

"I'll follow in a few minutes with the luggage. With luck there won't be any policemen to ask why I'm going in the wrong direction."

Maggie took a reluctant Sasha to the bathroom, and Noah turned to the man behind the newspaper.

He was gone.

Noah didn't allow himself the luxury of looking around the airport. No one must even suspect they had talked. He was on the verge of getting to his feet when more policemen hurried by. The moment they disappeared, Noah left as unhurriedly as he dared. At the rate policemen were arriving, they'd soon outnumber the passengers. If that happened, Noah's escape would be cut off.

He worried that some of the venders would see him leaving with the same two suitcases he'd arrived with, but they appeared to be too interested in what was going on to take any notice of a nameless passenger, even if that passenger happened to be a rich American. Usually their faces only came alive when a potential customer approached one of their kiosks.

On exiting the airport, Noah was relieved to see Maggie and Sasha getting into the taxi. Maggie held an infant in her arms. At least the transfer part of the operation had been successful. Now it was up to him to get them out of the country.

"Alexi is sick,' Maggie said the moment Noah got inside the taxi.

"I know."

"I mean he's really sick. He's burning up with fever. He's covered with a rash. I can't be positive, but I think it's scarlet fever. We've got to find a doctor. It's usually easy to cure with antibiotics, but if he doesn't get the proper medication, he could die."

"We can't afford the time. The contact said the police would set up roadblocks soon. I don't know how much time we have, but we've got to get out of town immediately. We can see about a doctor after that." He turned to the driver. "What's the most direct route to the mountains?"

But Maggie broke in before he could answer.

"We've got to find a doctor for Alexi."

"Can't you do what has to be done?"

"No. I don't have any medicine."

"You don't need prescriptions over here. You can buy anything you need over the counter or on the black market."

"I can't treat him myself."

"But you're a—"

"A nurse, Noah. Not a doctor. We're trained to do different things."

"You'll have to do the best you can. We run the risk of being caught if we go back."

He turned to the driver.

"We made an agreement when I accepted this assignment," Maggie said, forcing him to face her again. "I would leave everything about this operation up to you except for the baby. But when it came to anything having to do with him, I'd be the one to make the decision."

"But this isn't a decision that affects just the baby. It affects all of us."

"You're not going to find a doctor, are you?"

"We can't afford the time now. I promise I'll stop at the

first town we come to. It shouldn't take long. I'll ask the driver—what are you doing?''

Maggie had opened the door and was clearly preparing to get out of the taxi.

''I'll get another cab to take me to a doctor.''

Noah reached across Maggie and pulled the door closed. ''You really think he has to see a doctor right away?''

''Yes, I do.''

He couldn't doubt the look in her eyes. She faced him squarely, not in the least intimidated by his size, strength, personality or the knowledge that he knew more about the dangers of their situation than she did. It was the look he'd seen the day she announced she was leaving him. It was a look that said she'd weighed her options and decided this was the only one that made sense. It was a look that said she could do this on her own.

Noah knew he ought to trust Maggie. It was part of their bargain. Not to mention the fact that he didn't know anything at all about sick babies. But he had to weigh the baby's need for a doctor against the danger that they would be caught. He was certain if they were captured the police would consult a doctor immediately—the child was only useful to them if it was alive—but he would have failed, and an entire country would continue under the domination of a despot.

But that wasn't the real reason he hesitated. He had to trust Maggie, and he'd never been able to truly trust anyone in his entire life.

It wasn't that he didn't believe her or that he didn't trust her knowledge. The problem was with him. He couldn't let go.

It didn't seem like much. It was nothing more than accepting a medical opinion from an expert. He'd gone to a doctor a couple of times in his life. He'd listened to what they said even if he hadn't exactly done what they wanted. He'd even taken orders from Ray. Okay, so he hadn't exactly done what Ray wanted, either, but things had turned out all right, hadn't they?

That wasn't the point. He'd never really let go. In every part of his life, he'd been in control, filtering everything through his own sensors, deciding what to accept and what to reject. At this moment everything he'd ever come to depend on to help him do his job—experience, training, intuition, his gut—told him they had to get out or they'd be caught. The contact had said the same thing. The large number of police was unnecessary proof that the government was determined to stop anyone from taking Alexi out of the country.

Yet Maggie was asking him to set aside all this and trust her judgment.

"Okay. Take us back to the hotel," he said to the driver. "We'll ask the concierge for the name of the closest doctor."

Maggie rewarded him with a worried smile before she turned her attention to Alexi, but Noah didn't feel any of that adrenaline rush a man was supposed to get when gaining the unqualified approval of the special woman in his life.

The special woman in his life.

Was that who Maggie was? She was *a* special woman. She always had been. But was she *the* special woman? That was a stupid question. There never had been any woman in his life except Maggie. He'd tried very hard a couple of times after she left him, but it hadn't worked. There was no one like Maggie. There never would be.

"Can Sasha get what he has?"

"Yes. We could all get it."

He'd never been sick a day in his life, but he worried about Sasha. Poor nutrition could make her susceptible to any sort of infection.

"We ought to let him look at Sasha, as well."

"Even if she is infected, she won't show any symptoms in such a short time."

"You can ask him to give her something just in case."

"Don't put yourself in a sweat until we're sure what it is," Maggie said with a smile that made him feel thoroughly foolish. "I'm just as concerned about Sasha as I am about Alexi."

She made him feel rotten because he'd thought only of Sasha. He hadn't worried about Maggie because she seemed indestructible. But common sense told him that no one was invulnerable.

He pushed away the vague feeling of desperation, of being unable to control a situation that posed a danger to the two most important people in his life. He'd never felt this type of fear before and knew immediately it could be dangerous at a time like this. It was essential that he remain objective, detached.

But that was impossible. After she walked out on him, he'd tried to convince himself Maggie didn't mean anything to him. He'd repeated it to himself like a mantra, but he knew he was lying. He had been trying to do what he'd done with his mother and aunt, only it hadn't worked with Maggie, either. Certain things never left him. His mother and aunt wouldn't.

Neither would Maggie.

He'd have to tell her. Somehow he had to convince her they had to get back together. He knew they had a lot to work out but—

The taxi had come to an abrupt halt. They were still three blocks from the hotel "What's wrong?" he asked the driver.

The driver pointed to two cars parked in front of their hotel. "Police."

Chapter Fourteen

Maggie didn't need to be told the reason for their abrupt stop. The black, boxy cars bore the prominent insignia of the Beluxor police. You only had to see it once and you'd never forget it.

"What are we going to do?" she asked Noah.

"Find another hotel."

"How can you be sure it'll be safe?"

"I can't. Ask the driver if he knows of any place where we will be safe."

Maggie turned to the driver, but he made it plain that while he was happy to help them, he couldn't afford to get in trouble with the police. They could take his license and then he wouldn't have any way to support his family.

"He says there are no safe hotels. He says Americans will be noticed anywhere they go."

"Then ask him which one he thinks will be the safest. We have to start somewhere."

But before Maggie could translate Noah's question, Sasha

pulled at her sleeve. She spoke so softly Maggie could barely hear her, but she said she knew where they would be safe. "Are you sure?" Maggie asked.

Sasha nodded, and Maggie told Noah what she'd said. "Do you think she knows what she's talking about?" she asked.

Noah's glance slid to the child. "I think she probably understands safety much better than either of us. See what the driver thinks."

The driver didn't appear to know much about the address Sasha gave him, but he was clearly anxious to get rid of his dangerous passengers.

They hadn't gone far before the neighborhood deteriorated markedly. Buildings were run-down. Many appeared to be empty, some with windows broken out. Maggie began to question Sasha's judgment. They might be safe from the police, but what about the criminals who hid in the dark and out-of-the-way corners in every city? Even the taxi driver had begun to mumble about the danger.

He turned and said something to Noah.

"What did he say?" Noah asked Maggie.

"He said he wouldn't come here at night. He said we should be very careful to hide our money."

Maggie wasn't reassured when the taxi stopped before the gray, featureless exterior of a narrow-fronted building between two larger buildings. A very small brass plaque announced the name of a hotel. There was no awning from the street, no revolving door, no doorman. It looked like a rooming house. Sasha scrambled out of the taxi and hurried to a group of old men seated on a stone wall where it curved around the base of a very old tree.

Noah helped Maggie out of the taxi. She waited while he paid the driver, curious about what Sasha was doing. The child was talking very rapidly and pointing at them.

"What is she saying?" Noah asked.

"I can't be sure, but I think she's asking for their help."

"What can they do?"

Maggie had no idea, but when one of the men stood up and started in their direction, she figured she was about to find out.

"This child tells me you have a sick baby," the man said when he reached them.

"Yes," Noah said.

"Let me see him. I'm a doctor."

Maggie was surprised by the man's excellent though heavily accented English, but she wasn't sure she could believe he was a doctor or that she could trust his skills. Her doubts must have been reflected in her face.

"You needn't worry that I'm too old to know what I'm doing," he said. "Come inside. It will only take a moment to get my bag. Don't worry," he said when Maggie still hesitated, "no one will harm you. You're among friends."

"Do you believe him?" she whispered to Noah as they followed the man into the hotel.

"I don't think we have much choice. The taxi driver cleared out the moment he got his money."

The hotel lobby was small, dark and shabby, but it appeared to be clean. The young woman who appeared through a door behind the desk eyed them with distrust which didn't entirely disappear after Sasha told her they were her friends.

"It looks like we've wandered into a corner of Sasha's world," Maggie said when they entered their suite. It was composed of two small, sparsely furnished but clean rooms.

"I don't know why one of these people didn't take her in," Noah said. "Anybody can tell she hasn't been treated well."

Noah still couldn't think of anybody but Sasha, but Maggie had gradually grown more worried about Alexi. The child was hot, the rash was more pronounced, and Alexi was unnaturally quiet. A baby feeling bad should have been fretful at the least, whimpering or crying.

They didn't have to wait long for the doctor to make his examination.

"He has scarlet fever," he said. "I'll give you an antibiotic for him, but you'll have to sit up with him until the temperature breaks. You can give him some Tylenol, and I want you to give him cool sponge baths. It's the fever that's so dangerous in an infant."

"Just tell me what kind of antibiotic to buy," Noah said.

"I'll get it for you," the doctor said. "It will cause less comment among people whose interest you don't want to attract."

"And just who would that be?" Noah asked.

Maggie laughed to herself. Noah looked like he was about to assume his Ninja warrior stance. She could appreciate his determination to protect them, but surely extreme measures weren't needed against this frail old man.

"I'm opposed to the government," the doctor said. "There are quite a few of us, but we have no power. We look to that baby's father to lead us to democracy."

"How do you know about this baby?" Noah asked. "Are you part of the underground or just the political opposition?"

"I guess you could say I'm both. I wanted to take care of the baby when I heard he was sick, but the underground decided I was too much of a risk."

"Well, my job is to get the baby to the States. I can't be involved in local politics."

"I don't want you involved. It would be unnecessarily dangerous. You're doing more than you know by getting this baby to America."

"I haven't gotten him there yet."

The doctor smiled. "You will. Young men like you have confidence enough to do anything. I used to be like that. Now I know better. Wait here while I get the medicine."

Noah took out his wallet.

"I don't need your money," the doctor said.

"I'm sure you don't, but you may need your own money to help other children like Sasha." Noah handed him what Maggie was certain was many times the cost of the medicine.

"You're generous," the doctor said.

"It's not my money."

But Maggie knew it was. Noah didn't want to be seen as softhearted.

"Does he know what he's talking about?" Noah asked Maggie as soon as the door closed.

"As far as I can tell. His examination was quick and thorough, and his diagnosis is the same as mine."

"So you trust him?"

"Don't you?"

"I'm talking about medical. As far as this mission is concerned, I don't trust anybody."

"Well, I'm glad he appears to live near the hotel. It's a relief to know I'll be able to call him if Alexi gets worse."

"He's not going to die, is he?"

"No, he won't die, but the fever could cause permanent damage if it lasts too long or gets too high."

"I'll leave that to you. I don't know anything about sick babies."

Maggie tried not to smile. Noah had the nearly universal male horror of being responsible for a sick child. She wondered what made men think women were any better equipped by nature to deal with it.

She was relieved when the doctor returned. He told her how to administer the medicine and insisted she was to call him at any time if Alexi should get worse. Someone would have to sit up with him until the fever broke, but there was little else anyone could do for him.

"Is this hotel safe?" Noah asked.

"It's as safe as any place in Beluxor for opponents of the government."

"I have a bad feeling about it. That girl downstairs doesn't speak English."

"Very few people in Beluxor speak English. I only know it because I went to medical school in England then practiced there for more than thirty years."

"Why would you come back to a place like this?"

"I made a lot of money in England. I lived very well, but this is my country. Even though I despise the government, it did my heart good just to get off the plane knowing I would never leave it again. I can't do much, but my little bit combined with the little bits of thousands of others will make a difference."

"Or you could be crushed like so many ants."

"Ants work together very well. Maybe we will, too. Now, my friends have been at work to help you."

"I don't want anybody to get involved."

"Let me tell you what we've done. Then if you don't wish our help, let me know."

Maggie wondered what it was about Noah's past that made it so hard for him to admit he couldn't do everything alone. It must be a terrible burden to feel you alone held the world together.

"Tomorrow we'll move you to a different hotel. It's not good to stay in one place too long. If the police don't notice you, thieves will. Keep your doors locked at all times."

"I plan to leave the city as soon as Alexi is well enough to travel," Noah said. "The police are watching airports and train stations, so we have to get out through the mountains."

"Then you'll need a car," the doctor said as he took a key from his pocket and handed it to Noah. "This car is parked in the street behind the hotel. If we have to move you to a new hotel tomorrow, we'll give you a new car." He handed Noah a piece of paper. "This is the license plate number. If you need any help, the girl at the desk downstairs can be trusted. Do not speak to her parents. They're too afraid to be of any use."

"Anything else?" Noah asked.

Maggie couldn't tell if Noah was grateful for the doctor's help or resentful. He was all business, and business for Noah meant a total lack of emotion.

"Don't go outside the hotel."

"What about food?"

"I'll have a restaurant send dinner."

"Won't that make them suspicious?"

"I'll tell them you have a sick child who's infectious and must be watched at all times."

"You've done a lot for us," Noah said. "Will it put you at risk?"

The doctor smiled. "I've been at risk ever since I returned. The government dogged my footsteps at first, but I behaved so whimsically they finally gave up following me."

Noah extended his hand. "Thanks for all your help. England lost an outstanding citizen when you left."

"Beluxor needs me. England doesn't. Now I must go."

"So what do we do next?" Maggie asked Noah after the doctor had gone.

"You watch Alexi. I'm going to check out this hotel. The good doctor's efforts to protect us have made me feel very uneasy about this place. I need to know where the back door is in case we have to use it. You've got to stay here," he said to Sasha when she started to follow him.

Sasha wasn't happy to remain with Maggie, but Maggie tried to calm her fears while she changed Alexi and gave him a cool water bath in an attempt to bring down his temperature. Even though her hands and voice were busy dealing with matters of immediate concern, her mind was focused on Noah and the changes she'd seen in him. There were the old and the new, both existing side by side, both claiming to be a valid part of a man she very much wanted to know and understand better.

Experience told her people didn't change, especially men. Her father hadn't. Whenever any crisis reared its head, he would become even more inflexible. If challenged by undeniable proof, he would ignore it. Despite his considerable intelligence, she'd seen some of that in Noah. She'd attributed it to his determination that he had to be in control at all times. Now she wasn't so certain.

She supposed he held on so stubbornly because he was afraid if he let go, he would lose everything that had protected him from hurt, lose the energy that had supported him as he struggled to make something of himself despite his aunt's repeated assertions that he was no good and would come to a bad end.

He'd started off this trip pretty much as the Noah she used to know, arrogant, inflexible, insistent and so sexy she couldn't think straight when she was around him. And she had acted pretty much as she used to, fighting against the attraction because she knew it wouldn't work but giving in because the physical need for him was too strong for her to resist.

Then Sasha appeared, and he had become a different man. And Maggie had tumbled into love with him all over again.

Did she have it right this time, or was she making the biggest mistake of her life?

"Are you sure you want to sit up with him?" Maggie asked Noah. "You said you didn't know anything about sick babies."

Maggie looked at her watch. It was past two in the morning, but her body was so confused by changing from one time zone to another that it hardly mattered.

"You can't do everything by yourself."

The old Noah would have figured sitting up with a sick child was women's work regardless of the circumstances.

"I'm not doing anything difficult. I just check on him every few minutes. It's very boring work."

"I should have told you to bring lots of books. This kind of work is always more waiting than anything else."

"I brought some books," she said, reaching for her bag, "but I've had a lot of thinking to do lately." She held a book out to him. "Would you like something to read?"

Maggie laughed when Noah practically recoiled.

"It won't bite you."

"It's a romance."

"So what's your point?"

"Men don't read romances."

"Maybe they should. Then they might possibly have a vague idea of what women want."

Noah grinned. "We know."

"We want more than sex." She tossed the book aside. "But I guess that's hard for a man to understand, since he doesn't want anything else."

"Sure we do."

"Food and probably a warm bed and a TV remote. What more could a red-blooded male want?"

"Lots of beer and buddies to watch sports with."

"Ah, yes. We sink deeper and deeper into the mire of the male psyche. I don't know how the Bible can hold that woman was created from man, or vice versa. I believe we're two distinctly separate species."

Noah's grin turned into a frown. He pulled up a chair and sat next to Maggie. "I hope your romances aren't responsible for this less than cheerful mood. I thought they were supposed to have happy endings."

"They do. It's just my life that doesn't have a happy ending."

"You're only thirty. Your life has hardly begun."

"You're talking biology. I'm talking relationships."

He reached out and took her hand. She tried to pull away, but he wouldn't let her. "Tell me what's wrong?"

Three, four, even five years ago she wouldn't have told him. She'd have recognized his question as the male's automatic reaction, one he'd learned by rote and said because he was told he had to say it. But most men didn't mean it.

The last thing they wanted was to have some female dump on them.

But Noah made the mistake of sounding sincere. He compounded that by looking sincere, as well. The gates opened, and her feelings came pouring out.

"I've fallen in love with you again."

Did he look shocked? Did he withdraw slightly? Maybe she thought so because that's what she expected him to do.

"No, you haven't," Noah said.

She jerked her hand away. "Don't you dare tell me what I do and don't feel, Noah Brant. I *am* in love with you. I recognize that sick feeling in the pit of my stomach."

"Maybe it's something you ate. The food over here—"

"God! Sometimes I want to hit you so hard your head will split wide open and I can pour in a little intelligence. *I'm thirty years old. I'm an intelligent woman. I know when I'm in love.*"

If she hadn't been so upset, she might have been able to judge his reaction, but he seemed unmoved, like he was patiently waiting for her to get a grip so he could show her why she was wrong.

Of course there was the possibility he was stunned and didn't know what to say, but she wasn't depending much on that.

"Why would you fall in love with me again?" Noah asked. "You said I was worse than ever."

"I thought you were. You certainly acted that way in the beginning, but you've changed."

"How?"

"Look at Sasha. You've never shown the slightest interest in a child in your life, yet you've risked jeopardizing this mission to make sure she doesn't have to go back to that orphanage."

"That's nothing but common decency."

"Well, it wasn't *common* with you before. And now you want to sit up with Alexi. I'd have said you'd rather be chased through ice and snow by six gun-wielding hired assassins.''

"You don't think much of me, do you?''

"You've changed. You're not like that anymore.''

She had calmed down enough to tell it was surprise rather than know-it-all confidence Noah was feeling. Maybe even fear. But it was hard to see inside a man who faced real danger all the time. Regardless of what he might be feeling inside, on the outside Noah didn't show panic.

"You've let your bleeding heart take over your brain.''

"I didn't.''

"Sure, you did. You see me do something nice, and everything bad about me simply vanishes. You *want* me to be good so you're willing to believe one good deed has reformed my character.''

"I *am* going to hit you.''

"I never said—''

"I don't want to be in love with you. I'm angry as hell as myself for even considering it, but it's something I can't help, especially when you're turning into a decent human being right before my eyes.''

"I'm not—''

"It started before Sasha. I guess I didn't see it because I didn't want to. You were still angry, still blaming me, but you were willing to listen. You'd learned to think of somebody besides yourself.''

"You're wrong. I never—''

"Shut up and let me finish. I'm not asking what you think. I'm telling you what I saw. I don't care if it frightens you. It's about time something did.''

"I'm not frightened.''

"You're scared to death, but unfortunately not about being in love with me.''

"My feeling for you—''

"I don't want to hear about your feelings. This is my time. It's about me. And don't say it always has been.''

"My lips are sealed."

"Another smart remark, and I'll turn violent."

"What did I say?"

"Men! Why can't we do without them!" She strode across the room, but it was much too small to allow for more than four steps, far too few to release the tension building inside her. She turned to Noah, and immediately her mood swung. For a moment she was surprised to see a look of naked fear on his face. Then it was gone, but she'd seen it, she knew it was there.

She had her man.

"You love Sasha. It caught you as much by surprise as it did me, but you couldn't rationalize this one away. There was nothing to distract you, no competing careers, no emotional scenes. She loved you like a puppy, adoring, silent, willing to lick your feet or be tossed back into the void. No matter what you did, she'd still worship you. You didn't know what to do with that kind of love, and all your defenses fell apart."

"You're talking nonsense," Noah said. "I don't love anybody. I can't love anybody, remember? I'm too bound up in myself to be able to think of anyone else long enough to fall in love."

"You didn't have control over this."

"I feel sorry for the kid. I'd never have noticed her if that truck hadn't nearly hit her."

"You saved her life, and now you feel responsible for her."

Noah ignored her interruption. "I just wanted to find a good home for her. That doesn't make me a saint or a love-sick fool."

"You certainly aren't either of those."

Maggie stopped long enough to feel the baby's body to see if the temperature had gone down. It remained about the same.

"But you're no longer the unfeeling, self-centered man I

knew who was so afraid of feeling any emotion he would strike out at it rather than let it touch him.''

''I never—''

''Somewhere something undermined your defensive walls. When you rescued Sasha, they were so weak they came tumbling down, and you haven't been the same since.''

''Nonsense. I—''

''That child loves you.'' She glanced over to where Sasha was sleeping on the sofa. ''You can leave her here where she belongs, and she'll understand. But if you take her back to the States and then leave her, she'll never understand. She might never trust any man ever again.''

''You're not going to force a guilt trip on me,'' Noah said, angrily. ''I'm only trying to do something for a kid who's gotten a rotten deal. It's nothing any other man wouldn't do.''

''Wrong. Most men wouldn't bother. They certainly wouldn't when it could jeopardize their job.''

''It would be stupid for her to stay with me. Can you see me playing with dolls?''

A crack of laughter escaped Maggie. ''No, but I'd love it.''

''Well, you're never going to.''

''I never thought I would see you sit for hours, a child in your lap, her arms around your neck and her cheek pressed against your shoulder.''

''Give me a break. She's a kid. I'm not a monster.''

''No. That's what I find so amazing.''

''*Will you stop it!* I wouldn't make a good father. I'm away all the time. I like my job. I like coming down on people occasionally.''

''Gives you a chance to work out some of your repressed childhood aggressions?''

''I don't know. I just know I like what I do. I like my life the way it is, and I don't intend to change it.''

Maggie knew Noah was making excuses. He'd thought he was in love with her when they moved in together five years ago. He'd been certain he loved her because he always wanted her. But he hadn't *needed* her. Now he was facing the possibility of *really* being in love with her, and it was forcing him to reevaluate decisions, feelings, convictions, attitudes, habits—in short, his whole life—which he'd thought were absolute and unchanging. And that scared him.

Yet despite his struggles to break loose, to run far away to safety, love drew him like a magnet. Maggie just hoped the magnet was stronger than the fears that had ruled his life up until now. After so long, habits would be hard to break.

"Are you sure you want to watch Alexi?" she asked him.

"Yeah. Just tell me what to do."

She explained about his temperature, how to tell if it went up or down, when the next dose of medicine was due. "You can wake me up if you don't want to give it to him yourself."

"I can handle it," he said with what she thought was a clear lack of conviction. Silly man. What better proof could she want that he had changed? The old Noah would have taken on the KGB single-handed rather than attempt to give a baby liquid Tylenol.

"He didn't tell me which was the best route," Noah said to Maggie. "He just said I had to leave through the mountains then disappeared."

"But the country is ringed by mountains on three sides."

"I know. I've studied the maps."

Alexi's temperature had broken during the night, and the doctor had said it was safe for them to leave town. As soon as they had packed, Noah would bring the car around to the front of the hotel. He moved it last night. He said it was to give him a chance to get used to it in case he had to drive it. Maggie thought it was more of his obsessive planning, more looking ahead to every possible contingency.

The doctor had been as good as his word about arranging for food to be sent to them in their rooms. Last night's dinner had been excellent. Breakfast this morning had been big enough to last them the whole day. She and Sasha had demolished their food and eaten what Noah hadn't wanted. Sasha had wanted to take the empty dishes to the girl in the lobby. They had struck up a friendship. Maggie had encouraged her to make the several trips necessary to carry so many plates. Sasha's adoration of Noah caused her to follow him around even when he remained in the same room. That made it impossible not to stumble over her.

"I'll take a look at the maps," Maggie said. "Maybe I can remember something from when I was here as a child."

She could see that didn't set particularly well with Noah, but she had to give him points for not refusing her help outright. He would have five days ago.

"It shouldn't be too difficult," he said. "All we have to do is find a border patrol that's never heard of us."

"Won't they wonder why two Americans are wandering about the countryside?"

"Maybe, but they won't have any reason to stop us."

The door burst open, and Sasha tumbled into the room, words pouring out of her mouth so rapidly Maggie couldn't understand what she was saying. But once she held up the newspaper, showed them the front page, words were unnecessary.

A ten-inch picture of a man was centered on the front page beneath a single word in huge block print, in one of the few Beluxorian words Noah knew—"Spy."

The picture was of Noah.

Chapter Fifteen

"She says the police are on their way to the hotel," Maggie told Noah. "The girl downstairs said she heard a taxi driver tell the police where to find us."

"Get Alexi and Sasha and go to the end of the hall." Noah snapped the last bag shut. "You'll find a stairway. Keep climbing until you reach the roof."

Maggie didn't stop to ask Noah why she should be climbing stairs when they ought to get out of the building before the police arrived. She didn't ask why he was staying behind. Noah had a plan. He *always* had a plan, and it would work a lot better if she followed his orders without question. He might be staying behind to make sure they'd left nothing in the hotel room, but she was certain he was staying behind to head off the police.

"Where are we going?" she asked. Noah had caught up with them before they reached the top floor.

"There's a door at the top that opens out on the roof. We

can reach the car by going from roof to roof until we reach the end of the block.''

"How are we going to get down?''

"I'll figure that out when we get to the end of the block.''

Maggie had seen movies where people escaped across the roofs of a city, but she'd never imagined doing it. She felt like she was in a movie, that none of this was real, that she'd wake up to find herself in her own bed and due at the hospital in half an hour.

But this had to be real. She could hear the sounds of traffic below—buses, cars, the distant rumble of a train. Her feet slipped on roof tiles made slippery by dew. It would have been a lot easier if she could have strapped Alexi to her body, but she'd never planned on a rooftop escape. Noah took her by the arm and practically lifted her along the sloped roof to a flat place.

"We'll never cross all those buildings,'' she said, looking at the nearly dozen buildings stretching ahead. "They're not the same height.''

That didn't slow Noah. Sometimes there was a ladder leading from one roof to the next. At other times he would lower himself, then have her hand him the baby then Sasha. Once the drop was so far he had to catch her. Only an act of faith enabled Maggie to throw herself into space and believe Noah would be strong enough to catch her.

Of course he was. She could believe that Noah had been preparing his whole life for just such an emergency as this.

But Noah didn't appear to be having fun. There was a grimness about his expression, a tightness around his mouth, that said he wasn't enjoying this at all. For a man who thought of every person he met as a potential enemy he had to be prepared to overcome, this should be a lark. It was rather like the championship game he'd worked toward for years but had never reached because something always went wrong before he got there. This was it, the showdown, the payoff for all those years of hard work and preparation.

She wasn't having fun. She was a nurse trained to save lives, not to risk them. Nor had she spent years in a gym preparing her muscles to haul herself over a series of roofs while carrying a baby and holding Sasha. After watching Noah effortlessly handle their two heavy suitcases, she didn't dare complain. He had brought a couple of backpacks to use in case of emergency, but there hadn't been time to repack.

There was a fire escape on the last building, but it only reached the windows of the apartments on the top floor, not the roof.

"I'll have to drop down," Noah said.

"It doesn't look safe."

"We'll have to risk it."

"Why can't we go down through the building?"

She didn't need an answer to her question. There was no opening on the roof.

"I'll go first," Noah said.

He climbed over the edge, supported himself on a narrow marble ledge, then dropped to the fire escape. It shook ominously but held.

"Drop Alexi," he called.

Maggie wanted to close her eyes, but she kept them wide as she lifted the baby over the short parapet and dropped him. Noah caught him effortlessly, as he did Sasha, who climbed over the edge and jumped willingly into space. At least one of them was enjoying this adventure.

"Your turn," Noah called to Maggie.

She felt her heart in her throat. Jumping onto a solid roof was one thing. Jumping onto a wobbly fire escape was quite another.

"Take Sasha and Alexi to the bottom."

"It'll take too much time."

"I'm afraid all of us will be too much weight."

Noah didn't argue. He took both children and both suitcases to street level, then clambered up. "Quick. I can't leave them for long."

Maggie understood the urgency of the situation, but she couldn't move. She didn't understand why her nerve should fail now. She wasn't a coward. She had faced every challenge squarely.

"Put one leg over the wall and rest your weight firmly on the ledge," Noah said.

She was afraid he knew what was happening to her and despised her for it. Noah never pulled back from danger. He wouldn't think much of anyone who did.

She put her leg over the low retaining wall and tentatively reached out until she found the ledge and could rest her weight firmly on both feet.

"Don't look down," Noah said. "Now bring your other leg over and sit on the wall just as you would a low stone wall in a cemetery."

She did as Noah directed, but it wasn't easy when she found herself facing directly into the upper branches of a very tall tree. It might have been easier to look at the ground.

"Stand up slowly," Noah urged. "Hold on."

Not for one moment had she considered *not* holding on. Standing up didn't seem so bad, though it did give her an odd sensation to be looking down into a bird nest that contained five speckled eggs. She shouldn't be anywhere where she could look *down* on birds. She didn't have wings.

"Now let go and jump," Noah said. "I'll catch you."

Noah always did what he said, but she couldn't let go. She willed her fingers to release their grip on the rough stone, but nothing happened.

Then Alexi cried.

Suddenly the gravity of their situation hit her so hard it overshadowed her fear. With a quick prayer to whatever deity might be watching over this benighted country, she leaped into space.

Nothing had ever felt so nice as Noah's arms under her, supporting her, preventing her from breaking every bone in her body on the iron fire escape.

"Good job. Now we have to get to Alexi before his cries attract attention."

Maggie wasn't at all sure how she made it down the fire escape. She was certain her legs were too weak and shaky to support her, but she did reach the ground and she did discover a soiled diaper was the cause of Alexi's unhappiness. Apparently he enjoyed clambering over rooftops and dropping off the edge of buildings as much as Sasha as long as he was comfortably dry. He wasn't, and he wanted the game to stop until his comfort was restored.

"Go," Maggie said to Noah. "I'll attract less attention if I'm not seen with a man holding two suitcases."

Noah and Sasha disappeared around the corner while Maggie took advantage of a stoop to lay Alexi down so she could change his diaper.

"They never can wait until you get home, can they?" a woman asked. Maggie looked up to see what appeared to be a middle-aged woman hanging out the window nearest the steps. Her face was creased and tired, but she smiled.

"Not this one," Maggie said. "He demands instant attention."

"You're not from around here, are you?" the woman asked.

"No. I came to visit my sister," Maggie lied.

Maggie hurried to change the diaper as quickly as possible. People seemed to think they had a right to ask strangers all the questions they wanted.

"She has too many children to leave home," Maggie continued.

"Is this your last one?"

Maggie almost answered that it was her first before she remembered that many women her age in Beluxor were already grandmothers.

"He's my youngest sister's baby. Now I'd better catch up with her husband and daughter before they leave me."

She didn't know if the woman had seen Noah and Sasha, but if she had, this would explain the suitcases.

"I used to live in the country," the woman said. "When I got married, my husband said there was nothing for us there, that we had to come to the city."

Maggie finished changing the diaper and bundled Alexi, who cooed as if in thanks. "The country can be awfully quiet sometimes, but I like it."

She waved then hurried down the street. She turned the corner to see Noah talking to a stranger. Her stomach clenched then relaxed as she realized this had to be one of the members of the underground the doctor had spoken about. It was probably his car that had been put at their disposal. The suitcases were already in the trunk.

"This man is going to show us how to get out of the country," Noah said. "You and the children get in the back. He's going to drive because he knows the way better than I do."

Maggie felt some of the tension leave her. It would be a relief to have someone help them. She was tired of doing this alone. She got into the cramped back of the small car with Sasha and Alexi. Noah folded his large frame into the front seat, and they pulled out into traffic.

They'd hardly gotten underway before Sasha pulled at Maggie's sleeve. Maggie wanted to listen to the conversation Noah was having with the driver, Noah trying to speak in halting Beluxorian and the man speaking in equally halting English. It would have been funny if their situation hadn't been so serious.

"What is it?" she asked Sasha.

The child stood on the seat until she could put her mouth directly against Maggie's ear and whispered. Maggie's stomach clenched in a tighter knot than before.

"Tell me again," Maggie said.

"He's a bad man," Sasha said, her words unmistakable this time.

Maggie had no way of knowing if Sasha could know who in the underground might be a spy, but it was obvious the child was frightened. Maggie decided that any chance this man was a government spy was too great a chance to take, but how could she alert Noah without alerting the man at the same time?

She tried to think of ways to work the names of well-known spies into a conversation, but that seemed too dangerous.

"Pull into that small park," she said to the driver.

"Why?" Noah asked.

"I forgot to take the baby's medicine out of the suitcase." Noah started to disagree with her.

"Something terrible will happen if we don't stop," she said before he could say anything. "It'll be very bad for all of us if he doesn't get his medicine immediately."

She kept her expression as calm as possible because the driver was watching her in the rearview mirror. Noah's eyes had grown hard.

"Pull over to a secluded spot," she said to the driver. "I'm embarrassed to have people see me go through my suitcase."

The driver offered to take her to his house, to the house of a friend so she could go through her suitcase in private, but she insisted he stop immediately.

"Turn into the park," Noah said. "I can't risk the baby getting sick again."

The driver grumbled but turned as asked. Noah kept him moving until they came to a place where the maintenance people dumped compost. Maggie put her hand on Noah's shoulder to stop him from getting out of the car at the same time as the driver.

"Sasha says this man is bad. He may be a spy," Maggie whispered as soon as the driver went to open the trunk.

"He's not heading toward the country. I think he's trying to take us to police headquarters."

Noah nodded and got out of the car. Maggie couldn't see what happened because the trunk lid was up, but she heard a grunt and felt the car lurch.

"I need your panty hose," Noah said.

"They're in a compartment on the divider in my suitcase," she said. She handed Alexi to Sasha and got out of the car. The driver was lying half in and half out of the trunk. Noah was rifling through her suitcase.

"Here they are," she said, reaching into the compartment. She handed him all the panty hose she had. "I don't think they'll fit."

"They'll keep him tied up, which is what I want."

Noah tied the man's arms and legs then gagged him. When Noah was sure the man couldn't get loose, he picked him up and dumped him behind one of the compost piles.

"What if nobody finds him?" Maggie asked. "The signs say keep out." She didn't like the man, but she didn't want to feel responsible for his death.

"Somebody will. A kid's favorite place to play is where it says keep out."

"Are you speaking from experience?"

"Definitely. Now let's get back in the car and get as far away from here as possible."

She got in the front seat. Noah handed her a map.

"You have to navigate."

"Where are we going?"

"You're the one who visited this country. Do you have any good ideas?"

"How was I to know I'd be an undercover agent some day and would need to map out escape routes?"

"I'm appalled at your lack of foresight."

"I'm amazed you can make light of our situation. We don't know where we're going, we've assaulted a policeman and it's possible we're in a stolen car."

"You only live once."

"I'd like that once to last as long as possible, thank you."

"So would I."

The look Noah gave Maggie was so hot she could practically feel it on her skin. It caused the temperature in the car to change so quickly that it left her breathless. She didn't know how at a time like this Noah could be thinking of anything remotely connected to romance—more likely sex in his case—but she discovered it was quite easy. She was thinking of the same things…romance *and* sex. And Noah. She knew she'd never really thought of anyone else. When she married Reggie, she'd been running away from something she didn't want to admit…couldn't admit. She loved Noah. She always had, and she'd never be able to love anyone else.

That was a stupid mistake for a grown woman who considered herself intelligent. She had been so determined to prove she had gotten over Noah, she had allowed her emotions to overrule her brain.

Noah had never allowed his emotions to overcome his mind, but his relationship with Sasha gave her hope he could learn to trust other people to love him and let himself love them in return. She had to convince Noah he wanted to be loved. But she hadn't been able to do that when she talked to him about Sasha. How could she hope to do it for herself?

"We'd better decide where we're going or neither of us will have a good chance to collect social security," she said.

"I know how to get out of the city. You study the map and come up with some choices."

But looking at the map didn't help. Every mountain looked alike on the map. There was no way to tell which exit would be safe.

"I think we ought to go to my cousin's house," she said.

"Why? That's where the police would expect us to go."

"We need somewhere to stay for the night and advice on

which mountain pass to take. Do you know anybody else we can trust?''

She knew he didn't. The underground was a shadowy group who jealously guarded their identities. The New York office had no idea who they were dealing with. Everything had worked very well until the taxi driver turned on them and they nearly got caught. They needed someone whose loyalty they knew.

''Are you sure your cousin is trustworthy?'' Noah asked.

''Yes.''

''Our visiting her now might endanger her.''

''I know, but she'll never be really safe until the present government is out of power.''

''Okay, we'll go.''

Maggie's cousin gave them food, some clothing suitable for travel in the mountains and directions to a town near one of the border passes, but she was afraid to let them stay more than an hour. She said she'd already been questioned by the police. She directed them to a small inn in a neighboring town.

Next morning, Sasha found a boy with a horse who was willing to take them into the mountains. Maggie said she'd rather get blisters on her feet than on her bottom, so they used the horse to carry their backpacks. Noah had abandoned the suitcases at the inn. Sasha started out riding but ended in Noah's arms. He thought she was jealous that Maggie carried Alexi.

''This would be a beautiful day under other circumstances,'' Maggie said.

Noah thought it wasn't too bad as it was. He'd gotten the baby he'd come to get and was practically out of the country without having run into any major difficulty. He had rescued a little girl and managed to get papers that would allow her into the United States. He knew what he was doing was against the law—he planned to initiate proper adoption procedures once he got home—but his conscience was clear. Sasha deserved a chance for a better life. She would probably have died if he'd left her in Beluxor.

But being around Maggie was trouble. It meant being pulled in directions that were dangerous to him. It meant being on his guard against the lure of the flesh. He wanted Maggie. He always had, and knew he always would, but she was involvement, commitment, a promise of something he didn't have.

He was safe as long as he didn't lose control.

"This is so beautiful," Maggie said. "Fields of flowers with mountains in the distance."

"And government police hiding behind every rock."

"I hope not," Maggie said.

"Me, too. We still have a long way to go."

"How far?"

"I can't be sure because of the terrain, but we'll never reach the border today. I hope this kid knows of a place we can stay."

The place turned out to be a stone hut, one Noah imagined probably housed some goatherd of a previous generation. The boy stayed to eat supper with them. He would head back in the morning.

Noah had never spent the night in such a small place with so many people. It forced an intimacy he found uncomfortable at first. Yet before long the feeling changed to one of sharing, belonging, depending on each other. It was a new feeling for Noah. He'd always made certain he didn't have to depend on anyone. And while he continued to fight the feeling, he found it wasn't as bad as he'd expected.

He liked being responsible for Maggie, Sasha and Alexi. He'd been responsible for the safety of numerous people, the success of many operations, and after the operations the people had all disappeared leaving no trace. It felt different to have a real stake in the mission. He couldn't decide if it made him feel bigger than life or dangerously overmatched.

"I don't know if I will be able to fall asleep on the cold ground," Maggie said.

"It can't be so bad," Noah said, pointing to their guide who'd rolled up in a ball and gone to sleep in the corner.

"He's probably used to it," Maggie said. "I'm used to a heated apartment and a soft mattress." She laughed.

"It's only for one night."

"As long as the police don't find us. I can't help wondering if that man we left tied up in the park escaped."

"I'm more concerned about us escaping."

"You haven't spread out your blanket. Aren't you going to sleep?"

"I want to take a last look at the map."

"What for?"

"You know me. I always like to have a plan in reserve. You go on to sleep. Put the baby on one side of you and Sasha on the other. Sharing body heat will help."

"You've got more body heat than any of us. Come on. You can look at the map tomorrow."

It was probably just as well. It was nearly impossible to see by the light of the tiny flashlight.

"We'll put the children between us," Maggie said.

He would have liked a different arrangement, but this was the only one that was sensible. Maggie cradled Alexi in her arms. Sasha pushed up against Noah until he put his arms around her. After that she settled down and was soon fast asleep.

"I have to keep pinching myself to make sure I'm not dreaming all this," Maggie said.

"You're not dreaming."

"That's what frightens me. How am I supposed to make sense of the rest of my life after this?"

"What do you mean?"

"I mean you, me and Sasha. Something has happened here, Noah, something I can't forget just by going back to

New York, sleeping in my own bed and going to work at the hospital on Monday morning.''

He didn't like hearing her say that. He'd had the same feeling, but he had hoped he was wrong, that it would go away if he refused to think about it. Knowing Maggie felt the same unnerved him.

"You're tired. Things may seem different tomorrow."

He heard her release a long sigh. "You can't hold out forever, Noah. One of these days you're going to have to admit you're human. And you can be damned sure I'm going to be there when it happens so I can say *I told you so.*"

Why did the idea of her refusing to push him out of her life excite him? He knew what Maggie wanted and he knew he wasn't the man to give it to her. But as soon as he admitted that, he knew he hated the idea that she might find another man who could give her what she wanted. He knew he was being selfish to want to hold on to something he didn't want just so no one else could have it.

But he did want Maggie. He'd always wanted Maggie. It was just that she wanted different things, things he couldn't give her. Things he didn't *want* to give her.

But as he settled into a comfortable position with Sasha, while he listened for Maggie's soft breathing, the realization gradually settled in that he did want nearly everything Maggie wanted. If he allowed himself to be truthful, they'd always wanted the same things. He'd just told himself he didn't want them because he didn't trust them, knew they could hurt him, could betray him. If you knew something wasn't good for you, was going to hurt or betray you, the only sensible thing to do was stay out of its way. And it was easier to do that if you could convince yourself you didn't want it in the first place.

Noah didn't know when he'd started to cut himself off from people, to deny that he wanted anything people could give him. It seemed he'd always done that. His mother, his aunt, the kids at school, even those in the gang he'd belonged to for a short while. He wasn't sure he knew how to do anything else.

Sasha moved, and his arms involuntarily tightened around her. He reached out until he found Maggie's hand, holding the sleeping baby against the warmth of her body. He touched her hand, felt the softness and the warmth.

He felt a sense of peace, not quite contentment but something more akin to it than he'd ever felt before. It was like the people in this hut were his family and he had to protect them. He *wanted* to protect them. But it didn't stop there. He didn't want their dependence on him to stop there. He wanted…he wasn't sure what he wanted, but he knew he would want it for a long time to come. Not just a night, a week or even a year. He wanted it forever. Now if he could figure out what it was he wanted….

Then he knew.

He supposed that deep inside he'd always known. The truth had probably always resided in those places he never let himself go, waiting for him to throw open the doors and let it out. He wanted to be loved. But even more than that, he wanted to love.

Something inside him shattered. It was like a wall around him had come tumbling down, a protective coating had cracked and fallen away, a chain had broken. He'd spent so many years denying himself, it may have been all those things. He felt a great weight lift from him, a pressure inside him deflate and leave him feeling weak. He was defenseless.

That's when he knew he loved Maggie, that he'd always loved her. He didn't think he could go on living if he lost her again. The whole idea of being vulnerable, of exposing his heart, frightened him so badly he started to shake. But he knew this was his one chance to have the kind of love he'd never admitted to himself he wanted. Maggie was a strong, self-reliant woman, able to follow or lead. She could give him support, not merely expect it from him. He realized he was bone tired of being impregnable, a man untouched and untouchable.

He rolled onto his elbow. He could barely make out her features in the light coming through the small window. He'd watched her sleep before, but this time was different. He was in love, had admitted it to himself, had quit resisting, had yielded to it without reservation. It was like some tiny leprechaun had sprinkled magic dust over him, and everything in his life looked different, new, untouched.

He felt new.

He leaned across Sasha to brush Maggie's lips with a gentle kiss. She smiled and cradled Alexi closer to her. Noah smiled and settled under the blanket. He knew what he wanted now. He was sure of it. He didn't know why it had taken him so long to figure it out. He didn't know why Sasha had been able to open him to love when no one else had. She wasn't afraid to put her entire dependence on him. Her courage made him feel like a coward. Maggie's generosity made him feel like a heel. He'd taken without realizing he'd never given.

But he would give now. He *wanted* to give. He'd stored it up for so many years he didn't know if he could live long enough to give away all of himself that he wanted to share with Maggie.

A terrible thought struck him. Maybe she didn't want anything he had to give. Maybe he'd turned his back on her so many times she had given up.

No. She'd spent the last night in the hotel telling him she loved him, trying to convince him he wanted and needed love. He'd tried to keep up the old pretense. Did she know? Could she see through him? He wanted to wake her immediately, to tell her that he was the world's biggest fool, that she'd been right all the time, that he wanted to love her more than anything else in the world. But if he woke her she'd probably think she was dreaming—and not believe a word he said. He would have to wait, but he couldn't wait long.

He would tell Maggie as soon as she woke.

Someone was shaking him. Noah came awake with a start, reached for his gun before he realized it was the boy who'd guided them to the pass.

The boy pointed in the direction of the mountain pass that would take them to freedom and uttered the one word Noah didn't want to hear.

"Police."

Chapter Sixteen

"What do we do now?" Maggie asked. "We're trapped."

The boy had taken his horse and galloped away as soon as he woke Noah. They were on their own.

"We're not going back," Noah said. "That would bring certain arrest." He pointed to a distant mountain. "According to my map, there's a pass over there."

Maggie looked toward the mountain, and her heart sank. "We'll never make it. It's too far away."

"We'll make it," Noah said. "We'll leave everything behind except the food. We have to make it to the border by nightfall."

"How far do you think we have to walk?"

"I don't know. I'd guess at least twenty-five miles."

Maggie felt panic begin to close in. She'd never walked as much as twenty-five blocks. New Yorkers didn't. They took a cab, a bus or the subway. Nobody walked twenty-five miles. That was practically a marathon. She didn't know if she could manage it even if she had all the time she wanted.

"Pick your most comfortable pair of shoes and put on double socks," Noah said. "It'll help prevent blisters."

Maggie wondered why she'd ever thought there was anything glamorous about being an undercover agent. Sure, she had gotten to stay in a nice hotel in Paris and eat at classy restaurants, but days like this more than canceled that out. "There's snow on that mountain."

"We aren't going to the top. Besides, walking will keep you warm."

She wasn't sure. She could see her breath in the cold morning air. She hadn't thought much about the fact that they'd been climbing since they left the capital of Beluxor. They were probably over seven thousand feet. Maybe higher. If she remembered correctly, the tree line in the United States stopped somewhere around nine thousand feet. It if was too cold for trees, it was definitely too cold for people.

"I don't have extra diapers for Alexi," she told Noah.

"We'll have plenty after we cross the border."

"Sasha doesn't have a warm coat."

"I'll wrap her in a blanket."

"The rocks will tear up her shoes."

"I'll carry her. She won't be able to keep up the pace."

Maggie wanted to ask if he intended to carry *her* if she couldn't keep up the pace, but she decided to suck it up and not be a wimp. This was the last time she volunteered to do anything like this—future revolutionary leaders would have to look to somebody else to rescue their babies—but she refused to embarrass herself in front of Noah. From the beginning she'd insisted she could handle this mission. Except for climbing over rooftops, she'd had it easy so far. Now was the time to prove she had what it took to be an undercover agent.

She never intended to be one again, but if she ever wanted

to marry Noah, she had to prove she was his equal. They both knew she wasn't, but if she kept up with him today, she'd have a good argument.

"Give me a minute to make sure I have everything I'll need for Alexi."

"Is he still okay?"

"Seems to be thriving. Apparently being on the run agrees with him."

"I think it's your excellent care that he likes so much."

Okay, a compliment here and there wasn't too over the top. "We'll see what a doctor says when we cross the border."

If we cross the border.

She wondered how the police knew where they had gone or if they were closing all the borders as a precaution. "Do you think they'll have police where we're going?" she asked Noah.

"I won't know until we get there."

A typical male response. She wanted comfort, not a pragmatic response.

"I'm ready," she said as she hooked a bag over her shoulder. She hoped she had everything she'd need for the baby. "Now if we only had an orchestra in the background."

"What are you talking about?"

"The Sound of Music."

Noah looked at her like she had lost her mind.

"The movie, remember? With Julie Andrews? Forget it." She refused to explain. He'd undoubtedly call it a chick flick. "Lead the way."

The trek began almost as an adventure. The air was crisp and cold, the sky crystal clear and the views spectacular. The upward slope was gentle, and the path was cleared of stones. They passed numerous cattle, and she waved to the men and boys guarding them. Spring was late this high in the mountains, and the meadows were covered with tiny white wildflowers and new grass so vividly green it was impossible to describe. The air was so pure it tasted like water from a cold mountain stream. And she got to taste plenty of it. Noah set out at a pace that virtually required her to run.

"If I've got to keep this up all day, you're going to have to slow down," she said before they'd been walking fifteen minutes.

He walked ahead of her because the path was too narrow to allow them to walk beside each other. She didn't mind. It gave her an opportunity to study Noah's body. No woman could tire of looking at Noah's body. He wouldn't have been out of place in a physical fitness ad.

Noah turned. "Do you want to set the pace?"

"No. I just don't want you to have to abandon my exhausted remains somewhere in these mountains."

"I'll never leave you again."

There was a great deal in his words that had nothing to do with their present situation, but Maggie decided she'd rather explore that later. As tempting as it was to ask him to explain, she knew their future depended on getting to the border before the police discovered where they were.

"Good. Now lead on. I have the uncomfortable feeling that the police are digging through our abandoned luggage right now."

"They won't find that until later, if they find it at all. I shoved everything up the chimney."

She had wondered what he'd been doing when he told her to get started while he finished up. She'd figured he gave her a head start because she was so weak and slow he'd have no problem catching up. It made her feel better to know he was covering their tracks.

As the morning wore on and her muscles began to complain despite Noah's slower pace, she tried to distract herself by gazing at his bottom. She thought a well-formed derriere was just about the most attractive part of the male anatomy.

There was something about the narrow hips and the swell of muscle that started all her juices flowing. The ancient Greeks and Romans must have agreed. You never saw a statue or a design on a pot of a man with a flat bottom. That would be the same as depicting women with small breasts.

But as the morning passed into midday and midday turned into afternoon, not even the allure of Noah's backside could make her forget the burning sensation of exhausted and strained muscles, the bruised and tender bottoms of her feet, the muscles cramped from holding Alexi for hours. At times all that kept her going was Noah striding along before her, carrying Sasha and talking nonstop to relieve the boredom. She might have given up and insisted they stop and rest if Noah hadn't started looking over his shoulder about an hour ago.

"Do you see anybody?" she asked. Wearing contacts gave her reasonably good vision, but Noah had eyes like an eagle.

"No."

"Do you expect to?"

"I hope not."

"That's not what I asked." She was too tired and irritable to endure evasive answers.

"If they know we're here, then they've got to know we've left the main pathway. They'll start looking on both sides. With no cover, we're very exposed."

Settlers had cut down the forests long ago to provide pasture for their grazing animals. Except for small pockets of trees along creeks, the mountains were covered in grass and snow. They could seen for miles.

"But it works both ways," Noah said. "We can see them coming."

Fear of looking around to see the police pursuing them enabled Maggie to walk faster, but after an hour she was exhausted.

"How much farther?" she asked.

Noah pointed to a narrow valley. "According to my map, the border's down there."

"How far is that?"

"Five or six miles."

Two hours. She looked at the sun where it hung low in the sky. It might be dark by then. She didn't think she could walk that far, even though it was downhill. Her muscles were opposed to movement of any kind. But Noah was looking over his shoulder more frequently.

"Why do you keep doing that?" she asked. "It's making me nervous."

"Better to be nervous than caught by surprise."

Maggie had had enough realism. A little fantasy would be genuinely appreciated.

"I'm sure they won't find us," she said. "They can't look everywhere."

"They'll try. They know we've got Alexi. If we escape, this government's days are numbered."

Noah needed to learn that an excess of knowledge detracted from connubial bliss. Of course, she still had to convince him he wanted connubial bliss.

"Walk faster," she said. "I'll keep up."

She did, for another hour. Then her strength failed, and she was certain she couldn't go another step.

"I've got to stop. I'm so tired I can't breathe."

"We're getting close," Noah said. "We have to keep going."

Maggie looked down the valley. She could see a car parked by the roadside.

"Is that police?"

"Yes."

She felt her stomach lurch.

"Bulgarian police. We'll be safe once we reach them." Noah reached out to her. "Take my hand."

"You've been carrying Sasha all day. You don't need me leaning on you."

"I want you to lean on me. I hope it becomes a habit."

Maggie was too tired to figure out what he meant by that statement, but it sounded good. That was enough to hold her until her brain could concentrate on something besides her muscles, her feet and her lungs. She gripped Noah's hand. She was certain he was just as tired as she, but holding him had more to do with emotions than exhaustion. She wanted that bond, and touching him intensified the feeling that they were truly joined.

It took her a while to realize Noah had increased his pace. At first she'd set it down to being so tired. But it wasn't long before she knew for certain he was walking faster.

"It's not that far away," she said. "We'll make it before nightfall."

"I know. It's just that being this close gives me a lot more energy."

Knowing she was close to safety, that the grueling, killing pace was about to end, was sapping her will to keep on. She could hardly summon the power to put one foot in front of the other. Surely they could relax, slow down a little.

Noah looked over his shoulder without slowing his pace. He took a lot longer this time, and his pace increased. Maggie could feel tension, an uncoiling of fear in her belly.

"What do you see?" she asked.

"Nothing."

"Don't lie to me. I'm not a child."

"I don't see anything, but I thought I saw something earlier."

"What?"

"Men."

"What did they look like? What were they doing?"

He hesitated, and she knew it was worse than she thought.

"Tell me. I have a right to know."

"I think they have dogs."

The fatigue fell away from her body, and she lengthened her stride to match Noah's. She had worked in the emergency room when she was a student nurse. She had seen what dogs could do.

"How much farther?" she asked.

"Less than a mile. I'm afraid we're going to have to run."

"Why? Do you see anybody?"

"No, but the police are gathering at the border at the bottom of the mountain."

"Good."

"They have guns."

"Why? They can't be afraid of us."

"The guns aren't for us. They're for whoever is following us."

Maggie wasn't sure she had the strength to make it to the bottom of the mountain. She was certain her heart would burst if she tried to run.

That was before she heard the dog.

She didn't need Noah's shout of *Run!* to convince her to shift from a fast walk to a brisk run. The issue was painfully clear. They had to make it to the border before the dogs reached them.

She didn't look back. She couldn't spare the energy. Her body screamed in rebellion. It took every bit of willpower and courage she had to keep going. Alexi woke and began to cry, whether from a soiled diaper or being jostled as she ran, she didn't know. She knew neither would matter if they didn't reach the border in time.

But her strength was running out. Noah worked out constantly, but she didn't. No matter how hard she struggled, how hard her mind fought, her body simply didn't have any more to give.

"Faster," Noah said.

"I can't."

"Give me the baby."

"It won't make any difference."

"We've got to go faster. They're on horseback."

The crack of pistol fire energized Maggie, but only for a minute. She was utterly and truly exhausted. She couldn't go on.

"Take the baby," she said to Noah. "They don't want me."

"The dogs won't know that," Noah said.

She didn't know where he found the strength to carry both children. Even Atlas couldn't hold up the world forever. She ran beside him, her feet barely touching the ground. They were only a few hundred yards from the border, but the sound of the dogs was much closer now. She had to know if they could make it. She turned, and her blood ran cold.

Even though it couldn't have been more than six men and as many dogs, they seemed to be pouring down the mountain like an unstoppable wave. They were still well behind, but they were moving much faster than she was.

"Their pistols can't reach this far," Noah said. "It's the dogs we have to worry about."

"The Bulgarians can see them. Won't they stop them?"

"The dogs could tear us to ribbons two feet from the border, and the Bulgarians wouldn't do anything."

Maggie realized this was no time to discuss the stupidity of international law, but she meant to bring it up if she lived to get the chance. And right now, that was open to question.

She looked back again. One dog had distanced himself from the pack. Maggie had never liked hound dogs, and she thought this one looked particularly bloodthirsty. His tongue lolled out of an open mouth, revealing a set of very long fangs. Maggie could almost feel them sinking into her calf.

"I'm going to put Sasha down," Noah said. "Take her hand and keep running for the border. Don't look back."

"What are you going to do?"

"Stop that dog."

"You can't—"

"I don't have time to argue. You're supposed to leave stuff like this to me, remember?"

"You never said anything about dogs."

"They're easier to deal with than guns. Keep running. If you're tempted to turn back, think what the dogs would do to those children."

Noah couldn't have said anything more certain to give her the energy she needed to reach the safety of the valley road. But even after she passed through the line of policemen standing on the edge of the road, after she knew she and the children were safe, she felt no sense of relief. Noah was still back there.

Noah wasn't safe.

She turned, and a shriek burst from her throat. The dog had sunk his teeth into Noah's arm. On the mountainside, more dogs raced toward Noah. Farther up, policemen galloped toward him on horseback. Noah was trying to reach the border, dragging the dog behind him as he beat it relentlessly with his free hand, but the dog was large and strong. Noah would never cross the border before the other dogs reached him.

"Do something!" she shouted at the soldiers standing in a line along the road.

One of them shrugged and mumbled something in Bulgarian while the others stood unmoved as they watched the scene unfold before them.

"Take this baby," she said to a soldier as she thrust the crying child into his arms. "And watch Sasha." She snatched a rifle that someone had leaned against a car and ran to Noah.

"Stay back!" he yelled, but she ignored him. Her muscles nearly failed, but she forced herself to run toward the struggling pair. Using the rifle butt, she beat the dog about the head and shoulders as hard as she could. He held on with grim determination as the rest of the pack rapidly drew near. Driven to desperation, Maggie put all her remaining energy into a sharp blow to the dog's head, which caused him to release his hold and howl in pain. Hand in hand, Maggie and Noah sprinted for the border. She could almost feel the breath of the pursuing pack as they fell across the border. Maggie turned to see the soldiers beating back dogs angry at the loss of their prey.

Unable to stand, Maggie sank to the ground. Noah dropped down beside her. She knew she should be looking at his wounds, but she barely had the strength to hold her head up.

"You shouldn't have done that," he said between gasping breaths.

"Wouldn't you have done the same thing for me?"

"Yes, but—"

"Protecting the ones we love isn't an exclusive male province, Noah. Women are allowed."

"I know, but—"

"Shut up and try to be grateful. It'll be a new experience, but I have faith you can do it."

Noah started to laugh slowly and quietly. She wanted to join him, but she didn't have enough energy to smile.

"I love you," he said. "You know that, don't you?"

"I bet it hurts almost as much as having to watch a chick flick."

The Bulgarian police took them to a town where they found a hotel and a doctor to see to Noah and Alexi. Noah talked to Ray on the phone while the doctor stitched up the wounds in his arm. Maggie thought that was carrying this macho thing too far. She'd have to teach Noah to be more of a wimp if she was going to marry him.

After they'd rested, they ate dinner, then gave both children baths and put them to bed.

"I feel like an old married couple," Noah said.

"What I feel is old," Maggie said. "I don't want to think

of what my body will feel like tomorrow. I'll probably never walk again.''

''Then I'll carry you.''

''You won't be able to walk, either.''

''I'm in much better shape than you are.'' He settled on the sofa next to her.

''Don't look at me like that,'' Maggie said. ''I wouldn't care if you were Tom Cruise, Brad Pitt and Mel Gibson all rolled into one, I couldn't make love to you tonight.''

''I hope you won't feel like that for very long.''

''Look, Noah, I think it's time we had a talk.''

''Let me go first?''

She wanted to refuse, to try to convince him he wanted love before he started telling her how he couldn't deal with commitment, that she had misinterpreted his feelings for Sasha and now that they were safe and on their way to America it was best that she go back to being a nurse and not bother him again.

''I've made some mistakes in my life,'' Noah began, ''but you were the biggest of all.''

Well, that took care of that. ''You don't have to say any more,'' she said as she started to get up. ''I can take a hint.''

Noah's arms closed around her. ''You're going to hear everything I have to say. Then if you want to leave, I won't stop you.''

She was glad he didn't say *try*. That would be carrying false modesty too far.

''You were right all those years ago.''

''About what?'' Maggie asked.

''About nearly everything you said.''

''I said a lot of things. Narrow it down a little.''

''You said women shouldn't be the only ones to do the caring, that men had to care, too. Maybe even cry once in a while.''

That let Noah out. She was certain his tear ducts had atrophied at birth.

"I don't think I'd be very good at crying, but I do care about you. I always have. I just didn't want to admit it."

"Because of your mother and aunt?"

"Mostly. Uncle Willis cut himself off, said nothing mattered. It worked for me, too. It worked so well I kept it up through school and everything else. I should have known it wouldn't work with you, but I was afraid. When you're twenty-eight years old and not one single person has ever given a damn whether you lived or died, it's hard to believe that can change."

"But I loved you."

"My mother and aunt were supposed to love me, too. If that was love, I didn't want it. But I know better now, and I do want to be loved. I *need* to be loved just as much as I need to be able to love you."

She could hardly believe her ears. Noah couldn't be saying what she thought he was saying. He'd said the opposite ever since she'd known him.

"I don't know why I lied to myself for so long. Maybe because I was so needy I was afraid not to lie for fear I'd do anything just to have somebody tell me they loved me."

"I can't imagine you doing that."

Noah laughed softly. "I can't imagine that I'm sitting here telling you that I need you to love me. I can't imagine that I want us to get married and adopt Sasha."

"What?"

"Adopt Sasha. I know we haven't talked about it—"

"Whoa, Secretariat. Slow down and let this exhausted nag catch up."

"I'll do all the paperwork. I'm sure it'll be a mess, but I'll take care of everything."

"Back up a couple of sentences. I could have sworn I heard the word *married* in there."

"You did. I want us to get married."

He looked almost shy. Maggie hadn't thought it was possible. This was truly an evening for miracles.

"You mean standing up before a preacher, asking my cantankerous father to give me away, buying a house with the picket fence and me barefoot and pregnant?"

"It does sound like an awful lot when you say it like that, but yes, that's what I mean."

Maggie knew it wasn't polite. She knew it wasn't feminine, but she let out a yell that would have done a hog farmer justice. She probably would have let out a couple more if Noah hadn't clamped his hand over her mouth.

"If you hate it that much—"

"Hate it?" she said, ripping his hand away from her mouth. "I've spent the last few days trying to figure out how to convince you that you wanted to be married, that you wanted to be tied up with me, Sasha and one or two future bundles of joy for the rest of your life. Then you say *please* and walk into my trap with a smile on your face."

"Is it a trap?" Noah asked, but he was smiling.

"Absolutely. Once you're inside, there's no escape."

"What if I don't want to escape?"

"That's all right, too." She turned in the circle of his arms. "If you're very careful, you can kiss me."

"Maybe I don't want to be careful."

"That can wait for later."

He kissed her gently. "It will be like old times."

"It'll be better than old times. We've already been through the rough spots. We know what we want, and we know what we're willing to give up get it."

"I don't feel like I'm giving up anything. I feel free for the first time in my life."

He couldn't have said anything that could make her more certain they had finally grasped the brass ring. Any man who felt taking on a wife and child made him feel free was a treasure beyond price. But then she'd always felt that way about Noah.

"Now about that house with the picket fence. I know most people prefer roses, but what would you think of a nice honeysuckle vine?"

*   *   *   *   *

▼ SILHOUETTE®
SPECIAL EDITION™

AVAILABLE FROM 15TH AUGUST 2003

THE HEART BENEATH Lindsay McKenna
Morgan's Mercenaries

As Lieutenant Wes James and Lieutenant Callie Evans raced to save victims in an earthquake-ravaged city, past pain kept Wes from surrendering his heart. But he ached to make Callie his...

MAC'S BEDSIDE MANNER Marie Ferrarella
Blair Memorial

Dr Harrison MacKenzie wasn't used to women resisting him—but feisty nurse Jolene DeLuca's flashing green eyes told him to keep away. He was captivated...but could he convince her to trust him?

HER BACHELOR CHALLENGE
Cathy Gillen Thacker
The Deveraux Legacy

Businesswoman Bridgett Owens wanted to settle down—but irresistible bachelor Chase Deveraux was not the sort of man she wanted to marry. Until a passionate encounter changed everything...

THE COYOTE'S CRY Jackie Merritt
The Coltons

Falling for off-limits beauty Jenna Elliot was Bram Colton's worst nightmare—and ultimate fantasy. But now that she was sharing his home, he couldn't ignore the intense passion between them...

THE BOSS'S BABY BARGAIN Karen Sandler

Lucas Taylor only married his secretary Allie so that he'd be able to adopt a child—but a night of passion resulted in pregnancy. Could he overcome his past and keep the love he'd always longed for?

HIS ARCH ENEMY'S DAUGHTER Crystal Green
Kane's Crossing

Rebellious Ashlyn Spencer was the daughter of Sam Reno's worst enemy...yet she melted Sam's defences. Could the brooding sheriff forget her family's crimes and think of a future with her?

Maitland Maternity

Where the luckiest babies are born!

For the Sake of a Child
by Stella Bagwell

A marriage on the brink... A little boy in need...
A family in the making?

Drake Logan was a risk-taker, but not when it came
to his wife's life! He has never stopped missing
Hope. But he is sure he is right, that they
shouldn't have children. Even though she is just as
sure he is wrong!

Hope Logan is delighted that
Drake is coming home for his
little nephew's short visit. The
little boy adores him and she is
hoping it might at least give
them a chance to talk about
the baby issue. But talking is
not all they end up doing and
their temporary reunion
could have unexpected
consequences...

4 Books
and a surprise gift!

We would like to take this opportunity to thank you for reading this Silhouette® book by offering you the chance to take FOUR more specially selected titles from the Special Edition™ series absolutely FREE! We're also making this offer to introduce you to the benefits of the Reader Service™—

★ FREE home delivery
★ FREE gifts and competitions
★ FREE monthly Newsletter
★ Books available before they're in the shops
★ Exclusive Reader Service discount

Accepting these FREE books and gift places you under no obligation to buy; you may cancel at any time, even after receiving your free shipment. Simply complete your details below and return the entire page to the address below. **You don't even need a stamp!**

YES! Please send me 4 free Special Edition books and a surprise gift. I understand that unless you hear from me, I will receive 6 superb new titles every month for just £2.90 each, postage and packing free. I am under no obligation to purchase any books and may cancel my subscription at any time. The free books and gift will be mine to keep in any case.

E3ZEF

Ms/Mrs/Miss/Mr ....Initials...
BLOCK CAPITALS PLEASE

Surname...

Address...

....

....Postcode ....

Send this whole page to:
UK: The Reader Service, FREEPOST CN81, Croydon, CR9 3WZ
EIRE: The Reader Service, PO Box 4546, Kilcock, County Kildare (stamp required)